GIRL HELD IN HOME

GIRL HELD IN HOME

NOVEL

Elizabeth Searle

n
RIVERS
e
PRESS
w
MSUM

American Fiction Series

©2011 by Elizabeth Searle
First Edition
Library of Congress Control Number: 2010933711
ISBN: 978-0-89823-258-5
American Fiction Series
Author photo credit to Sarahana Shrestha
Cover and interior design by Amber Power

**FICTION
Searle,
E.**

The publication of *Girl Held in Home* is made possible by the generous support of the McKnight Foundation and other contributors to New Rivers Press.

For academic permission or copyright clearance please contact Frederick T. Courtright at 570-839-7477 or permdude@eclipse.net.

New Rivers Press is a nonprofit literary press associated with Minnesota State University Moorhead.

Alan Davis, Senior Editor
Suzzanne Kelley, Managing Editor
Wayne Gudmundson, Consultant
Allen Sheets, Art Director
Thom Tammaro, Poetry Editor
Kevin Carollo, MVP Poetry Coordinator
Fran Zimmerman, Business Manager

Publishing Interns:
Ryan Christiansen, Katelin Hansen, Jenny Hilleren, Samantha Jones, Tarver Mathison, Jenna Miller, Elizabeth Zirbel

Girl Held in Home Book Team:
Michael Eckroth, Kyle Goethe, Crystal Pound, Sherry Schumaker

Printed in the United States of America

New Rivers Press
c/o MSUM
1104 7th Avenue South
Moorhead, MN 56563
www.newriverspress.com

To My Boys | John & Will

CONTENTS

CHAPTER ONE
POSSIBLE HOSTAGE SITUATION

MAURA

My son and the money were missing.

Not knowing where to start, I burst into barely lit November drizzle and slammed but didn't lock our front door. After all, what if Joezy had simply gone biking? Biking with a thousand bucks? Money meant for 9/11 victims' families. And it was all — my boot heels clicked — *my fault, my fault.* I marched down our rain-glazed brick walk, my heels rat-tatting like shots. And I found myself picturing that strange house on the river. The house my husband and son had taken to calling, since September, our neighborhood's Terrorist Cell.

Home of the boys we all had called, since Halloween, the Terrorist Trick-or-Treaters.

I winced as I slammed my car door, not used to a hangover headache, my first in years. My frozen fingers, still bright with last night's coppery nail polish, fumbled with my keys. Beside me on the seat, my box of bamboo rhythm sticks thwocked. My car lurched down Riverview Road, past the other brick houses, all Sunday silenced.

No one up but us. My husband was still trapped far away in Penn Station, his train delayed due to bomb threats. I switched on my wipers too high, my windshield smearing. Everything in my life spectacularly smearing together, blurring big-time, since September.

Did my good-boy son really steal all the 9/11 Fundraiser money from the Fairwell School PTA? Of course he didn't, I thought at the bottom of the hill, at the same time that I knew: Yes, he did.

And yes, I further sensed, squinting through my wipers across Mystic Avenue. Yes: Joezy's blue bike glinted in the rain in the hydrangea bushes fronting that house. My pulse thumped with the wipers. Joezy's bike leaned in those bushes, half hidden. Half-assedly hidden, like he'd wanted to be found. Good God.

Somehow at 7AM on this chill Sunday morning, my son was visiting the riverfront home where — for these past two fear-ridden fall months — Arabic graffiti regularly appeared and disappeared on the garage doors. Gracefully slashed lettering, unreadable to us.

But that doesn't make the house a terrorist cell, I told myself as sternly as I'd been telling my husband and son all fall. I punched the gas and cut across Mystic, its Sunday morning traffic blessedly light.

I pulled onto the once-luxurious ranch house's ordinary asphalt driveway; I marched up to its ordinary if fadedly painted front door. Shakily, I tried to smooth down my unbrushed rain-frizzed hair.

Then I hammered the new-looking brass knocker, my pulse hammering too. *Rap rap rap.* A demanding policeman beat.

Anything to find Joezy, I thought, pulling my raincoat close over my FAIRWELL SCHOOL: LOVING LEARNING sweatshirt.

Can we please do something else? I found myself thinking as helplessly as I'd done in June in the breast center waiting area, wearing that same sweatshirt, standing because I couldn't stand sitting, bracing for my biopsy. *Can I please be anywhere but here?*

Then shuffling sounds near the door to 22 Mystic Avenue, and it opened a crack. Inside, I faced the oldest tallest boy, the one whom I'd last faced when he was dressed as, he'd told us flatly, a terrorist.

With his head uncovered this morning, with his black hair mussed as if he'd just woken, with old-fashioned dark-rimmed glasses on, he looked younger and less threatening than on Halloween.

He was, I judged as if he were a new student, sixteen or seventeen, his glasses and manly black brows both oversized for his lean light-brown face.

"Excuse me, sorry to disturb you so early but — I see my son's bike in your bushes and he, he's — missing."

"Missing, Missus?" this boy repeated, not impolite, slow-voiced. Unshaven beard bristle shadowed his chin, a beard-to-be.

"Yes, and I — I just have a feeling he may be — here."

At *here*, behind lenses, the boy's sleepy eyes began to light. He licked his lips, swallowed. He straightened so we stood eye to eye.

"He might be with one of the other boys, your brothers? If I could just have a look."

"Here?" This boy still blocked the doorway. "A look in — here?"

I steadied my voice. I tried a brisk nod and a quick tight smile. "Yes. I'm — well — your neighbor from Riverview. Mrs. — Simon."

"Rakeen Jiluwi," this boy announced, pronouncing his grand-sounding name with grown-up poise. He stuck his man-sized hand out the door. I took cautious hold, gave a slight shake, pulled back. His hand felt cool and dry, startlingly strong.

"I believe," Rakeen told me, "I do know where your son may be. Downstairs with One. With, I mean to say, our — servant."

One? I thought dazedly.

He'd said this in a slow voice, as if still sleepy. But his keen dark gaze was fully awake, looking me over. My own mussed hair: my no doubt panicky pale eyes, my hastily pulled on clothes. I found myself wondering if I had my cell phone in my raincoat pocket.

Nevertheless, as Rakeen stepped back, I stepped in.

JOEZY

I had hold of One. I was kissing One, I was all over One when Rakeen and my mom busted into her basement room. I mean, the room where she was being held.

The girl named One.

The girl I was trying to save. Trying to do lots of other things to, too. Our first kisses, my first ever; she was even starting to kiss me back. Soft but chapped lips, big teeth, taste of mango and smoke.

Then the tall Jiluwi boy stood in her doorway, glasses flashing, and head high like he really was son of some Saudi prince.

"Pig-boy," Rakeen Jiluwi pronounced from the doorway, real loud. "Look at your greedy Piggy Boy now — "

I stumbled back, zipping my jeans. One, in her too-small bra and too-big sweatpants, sank to her knees on her mattress on the floor. She bowed her head so her bangs shielded her face. Would he try to hurt her, us? I glared up at Rakeen, braced to—could I?—jump him.

And I froze too. "God, Mom."

My freaking pop-eyed mom had poked her head around the door. She squeezed in the doorway beside Rakeen.

My mom—hair wild, face wild—pushed past Rakeen. She rushed in and grabbed hold of me. God, could she feel my still-half-hard hard-on? Suddenly I was holding my mom as hard as I'd held One.

"What're you *doing* here?" I muttered, wrenching back from her. And what the fuck would Rakeen do? Were we all trapped, maybe, inside Le Ti One's basement room? In the house I'd been watching; the house of the supposedly "royal" Jiluwi family; the house I'd called the Terrorist Cell. But I'd never thought there was a real "cell" there, underground.

"I'm here to take you home," Mom whispered. Then she spun on her heel, like the dancer she used to be. She faced the so-called-prince Jiluwi boy in his Clark Kent glasses.

His bony broad shoulders filled the doorway. He stood planted there like a guard.

"I brought you your mommy, Pig-Boy," he informed me, formal and even freaking polite—except for the Pig part.

Rakeen nodded at me, then at silent Le Ti One. She still knelt, head still bowed. Was she hiding, praying? Or just scared shitless, like me? Beside One on the mattress lay my denim jacket. Bulging in its pocket was the money I'd borrowed. No: stolen.

"What's going on here?" Mom was demanding.

God, had I really stolen that money, kissed this soft-lipped cigarette-breathed girl? Did the Jiluwis, like One claimed, really keep a "military gun" in their safe? I was breathing hard with Mom, the air tasting damp, disinfected. Were Mom and I both going to—like mother, like son—hyperventilate?

"How you two look at me." Rakeen shook his head at Mom, ignoring her question. He straightened his glasses. About to whip them off, morph into Superman. "So easy to scare, so quick to fear my brothers and myself. Just like on Halloween." Rakeen gave Mom a close-lipped smile. "I know you do not want to see me again. But I must make you see what your Pig Boy has been up to, Missus."

MAURA

"God, Mom," my son whispered again, right after that Jiluwi boy called me Missus. "Don't believe anything he says . . ."

Joezy spoke breathlessly, as if the cool commanding Jiluwi boy couldn't understand English. I barely understood it myself, just then.

"You remember Halloween, Mom. What if they won't let us go?"

I gave Joezy a motherly hush frown. By "us," did Joezy mean this half-dressed Asian girl and him or him and me or all three of us? By "them," did he mean, he must mean, the Jiluwis?

The girl on the mattress was buttoning a pink pajama top over her bra. Then she sat, like we'd say in yoga class, lotus style. She gazed up at the oldest Jiluwi boy as if watching him raptly on TV.

Beside me, Joezy stood soldier stiff, his mouth half open so his braces showed, his kinky ginger hair—what Dan called his Irish-Jewish hair—mussed like mine. His face so pale all his freckles stood out. So young I gave his gangly dangling hand a quick squeeze.

Through the room's smeared subterranean window, I heard the light Sunday rumble of traffic picking up on Mystic Avenue.

"We have to go." I straightened as if leading my music and move-ment class. I started to step to the doorway Rakeen blocked.

"No, Missus," he told me, more polite than most of my students.

"No, I can't—we can't—leave?"

He gave the barest of shrugs, like he honestly hadn't decided.

But he was just a boy; we were just strangers, neighbors, misun-derstanding each other, right? My son was just making out with his too-young maid. Right? I drew a shuddery breath of basement mold and Lysol. I heard, from the rec room beyond this small dim cinder-block-walled room, a tock. A ping-pong ball, I realized hopefully.

Tock-tock. The younger Jiluwi brothers? Had they slipped down from upstairs? Was it ordinary after all: this solitary riverfront home guarded by those boys whizzing onto Mystic on suicide skateboards.

"Look," I began again, carefully. "I know my son shouldn't be down here with your, your—with her."

I shot a glance back at the teenage Asian girl in her pajama top. I'd glimpsed her at Whole Foods and hanging clothes in their yard. Up close, she was way too young to be anyone's maid.

The girl hugged her knees, a blurred dragonfly tattoo on her slim forearm. It matched the dragonfly shape imprinted on a strip of raw silk hung above her mattress.

"B-but still, you've gotta let us go," Joezy managed to add.

"Yes, what do you think you're doing—?" was my foolish question.

And I made myself straighten further. Two subtle upward movements: like you've been punched in the stomach, then kicked in the butt, my old dance teacher told me. Just what I told my toughest Youth at Risk kids. I handled them OK, didn't I? I'd handle Rakeen.

I squeezed Joezy's hand again. This time two quick thumb-presses to his palm—our old signal in big crowds, meaning: yes, you've got your mom's hand; yes, you're safe.

And Joezy, who lately shied from my touch, squeezed back.

I steadied my breath, feeling a surge of protective motherly strength. I, high-strung Maura Simon, had to somehow defuse what an absurd news voice in my head called *a possible hostage situation.*

"What do you think, Missus?" the Jiluwi boy asked philosophically. "What am I, what are you doing here?"

He gave these cryptic lines the same regal deadpan delivery that had so unnerved me on Halloween.

Behind him, through the open doorway, the ping-pong ball tock-tocked on. Back and forth; a taut someone's-about-to-miss rhythm.

"I think that you're playing another strange trick-or-treat type game," I told this boy. "But you're going too far now; we aren't playing along this time. So you've got to just step aside, please . . ."

I tugged Joezy's hand; we started stepping forward as one.

"Yes, yes—you cannot—?" the girl was saying softly, springing to her bare feet. She was stepping up fast beside Joezy and me.

And was she — on our side? She stood on tiptoe, petite and poised as if wearing a leotard instead of sliding-down sweatpants. Her jaggedly cut hair half hid her apple-cheeked weak-chinned profile. Just a kid, like Joezy. I had to be the grown-up.

I released Joezy and slipped my hand into my raincoat pocket, groping for my cell phone. God, had I really forgotten it?

"No, Missus, let me see your hand," the Jiluwi boy said, more a request than a command. The ping-pong tock stopped.

I pulled out my blatantly shaky hand. And Joezy rested his own unsteady hand on my shoulder — just like he'd done weeks before, when all this began. Halloween night, 2001.

CHAPTER TWO
AND A DEAD AMERICAN

JOEZY

"Goodness," Mom exclaimed in fake smiley surprise when she swung open our door. Then her shoulders stiffened in freaking real surprise. It was late Halloween night; her curly red-brown hair was springing free from its ponytail. "What are you two supposed to be?"

A tremor in her sing-song made me slip behind Mom's tensed shoulder. I was the man of the house with Dad away on the plane trip Mom had begged him to cancel. To look at least fifteen, I sealed my lips shut over my braces, hidden by plastic vampire teeth.

Mom was holding out her wooden bowl full of homemade popcorn balls and unpopular raisin packets. Lame candy alternatives I'd warned her might get our house toilet-papered.

But even I — only playing a cynical guy back then, before One — felt a jolt in my gut. My lips quivered. Behind Mom, I took them in: two coolly staring dudes. Rakeen (but I didn't know his name then) stood tallest, his head covered in a white (I didn't know this name yet, either) *ghutra*. Only his man-thick brows and narrowed eyes showed. No glasses that night.

His shoulders stuck out like a wire hanger, holding up his draped white robe. In one brown fist, he gripped a metal dog-leash chain.

The leash was clipped to the collar of the Toys"R"Us US Marine uniform that his younger smaller brother, Rasha, wore — its camouflage print splattered with what looked like real dried blood. More blood streaks dripped from Rasha's long-lashed eyes, the red extra bright against his white face-paint.

Rakeen gave Rasha's leash a rough tug. On cue, Rasha stretched his mouth — his teeth all crooked — into a death grimace.

"I can't even guess," Mom managed, still determined to see us all through this awkward moment. Behind the trick-or-treaters, the familiar orange-lit brick houses glowed in neat stair-step order up Riverview Road. Distant kid voices piped in neighboring streets.

"What," Mom prodded gamely, "are you two supposed to be?"

Rakeen stepped forward. Everything silent except for the rumble of traffic on Mystic Avenue.

"A terrorist," Rakeen pronounced, his rr's softened in Arab style. Another tug of the chain leash.

Then Rasha chimed in from his bloody marine uniform, "And a dead American."

Like I said, I didn't know their names then. I knew them as the "Middle-Eastern" (Mom would say) or "A-rab Fucker" (my bro TJ would say) boys on Mystic Avenue. They ran wild around the former rundown house on the river. The house where slanty black must-be-Arab words showed up on the garage door; where United Air boxes littered the curb from mysterious post-midnight deliveries spotted by Riverview Road insomniacs like my dad.

Not to mention what-all TJ and I had spotted close-up from our bikes, on our separate, intersecting patrols.

———————

"And a dead American," Rasha pronounced perfectly, punch line to his and Rakeen's Terrorist Trick-or-Treat routine. But he swallowed hard, no Adam's apple showing in his throat.

The taller calmer Rakeen cracked his close-lipped grin, patting his brother's back.

Mom's shoulders hitched up higher under her oatmeal sweater. Was she going to smack these kids? But my mom never smacked. She faced both of them stiffly, still holding her bowl of healthy treats.

Get the hell outta here, I wanted to say, loud and clear.

Instead I drew a big breath and almost swallowed my fangs. Mom breathed in big too. I pleaded her with brainwaves not to resort to her music teacher voice. Too loud, too clear.

Rakeen flicked his glance at me. Maybe recognizing me from my bike, sizing me up. My lips buckled over my toy teeth. Like I was just an overgrown boy, my mouth stuffed with candy. Mom stood taller. Keep quiet, I thought, resting one hand on her shoulder.

"Do you think that's funny?" Mom asked Rakeen and Rasha.

"No," Rasha answered, his boy-voice factual. Under his blood-stained head bandage, his big-eyed stare fixed on dumbstruck me. He tensed up like he expected a fight. Fuck: from me?

Rakeen shook his ghutraed head, his squinty gaze on Mom. "We are not joking, Missus. You think we are joking?"

Mom drew another breath but didn't or couldn't speak. Rakeen crammed his long-fingered hands into Mom's wood bowl. He scooped out three popcorn balls, leaving the raisin packets.

Rasha reached in next and tilted the bowl Mom gripped, dumping the Sunmaids into his pumpkin-printed bag.

Firmly, Rakeen tugged Rasha's chain. Then they both turned heel, in light-footed unison. Rakeen stumbled on our brick walk.

They ran off into the night, up Riverview Road. Rakeen's ghutra flew out behind him; Rasha's chain clinked. They were not laughing. Mom stepped back fast, bumped me, slammed and locked our door. She let the empty bowl drop to our polished wood floor with a hollow rolling clunk. "Good God, who were they?"

And Mom grabbed me in a hard hug that I found myself returning. Clinging to her slender warmth, surprised how small she felt in my arms since whenever it was we'd hugged this hard.

"Dose kids from dat house," I mumbled through my toy teeth into Mom's shampoo-smelling fallen-down ponytail.

She pulled back from our sudden hug; she met my widened green eyes with hers. Her face looked so white all her freckles looked dark. I reached up and yanked my unmoored vampire teeth: a string of spit like when I used to pull out my retainer. Mom didn't flinch.

"From that *weird* house on the river," I told Mom. "The house Dad and everyone calls a, you know — Terrorist Cell." I stumbled on this part because I knew Mom didn't know, not like I knew. TJ and me. "Listen, lemme go see if they're still on our street —"

I started to step toward the door, half-relieved when Mom took hard hold of my arm. "No, no, Joezy. Those boys could be dangerous. Don't you dare go after them; I need you *here* — "

Because Dad isn't, she didn't need to add. "That house by the river," she was repeating. "Of course; you're right. I'm sure it's nothing really, just some God-awful prank, but . . ." Mom turned as if in a trance. "But let's call your father, see what he says . . ."

She stepped past our crowded bookshelves into our snug kitchen, its smell of roasted salted pumpkin seeds, slightly burnt.

In the living room, between the open shades of the window facing the street, our jack-o-lantern's flame wavered. Mom dialed.

Dad was in Denver. Though he liked to jokingly sing, *Ah found my thrill on Riverview Hill,* Dad made so many consulting trips I'd wondered sometimes where he found his real thrills.

Not that he wasn't Mr. Good-Dad sometimes, but mostly he was away earning the dollars he complained about shelling out for Fairwell. He didn't buy into the school like Mom; he mumbled that Fairwell was a super-PC bubble, shielding me from real life.

This real enough for you? I found myself thinking.

Here Dad had gone and missed a rare shockwave in our quiet brick house, leaving me man of this house. My long arms and legs felt electrified. Mom's urgent voice murmured to long-distance Dad.

But what had I done, facing the Terrorist Trick-or-Treaters, besides almost swallow my Dracula teeth? Besides let my mom talk me out of following them, facing them down like I should've.

I chewed my fingernails, their familiar inky taste. I'd been sketching my latest superhero all afternoon. Vampire-toothed Bat-Boy. In real life, Bat-Boy had freaked when danger came to his door.

"Yes, Dan, I will, we will," Mom was saying, sounding dazed.

I paced the living room, toying with the pumpkin's cap, peering out the candlelit window. Mom was repeating into the phone Dad's instructions about calling the police, even if they were just boys.

Then Mom hung up and re-dialed. I stood still, listening. The police? Wishy washy Mom was calling them right away?

"Frannie," Mom told the kitchen phone. "God, you won't believe what just happened . . . Dan says call the police but somehow I wanted to call you first ... Yeah, maybe because you are the 'toughest mother' I know ..." A throaty chuckle I bet was shared. Those two.

Planted by the window, I rolled my eyes though no one could see me. Mom herself wouldn't see me if I stepped right into the kitchen, not when she was on the phone with Frannie what's-her-face.

Just another Fairwell mom; working with my mom on Fairwell's 9/11 fundraiser — a silent auction, whatever the hell that was.

"'And a dead American,'" Mom was repeating, voice shaky like she might cry or laugh. "No joke. And Dan away and all, just me here with Joezy ... it was probably nothing but good God, I just ..."

She lowered her voice. Like I was a baby who shouldn't overhear. Mom: who'd delayed my braces, feeling so sure her perfect boy's teeth would straighten out. So here I was at fifteen still stuck in braces. And why was Mom gabbing to Frannie longer than to Dad?

Something rustled outside our window. The frosty dried leaves? Footsteps? I leaned close to the window, clutching the pumpkin cap by its stem. My free hand shaking, I lifted our shade.

The pumpkin flickered. And the freaking curtain started smoking. Shit; the curtain hem had somehow dipped into the jack-o-lantern. I snatched it up. As Mom in the kitchen lowered her voice to secret-telling level, I batted the curtain's smoke out against the chill window glass.

Breathing the bitter linen smoke, I paced our living room in patrol mode. I kept peering out the brown-singed curtains. I kept sending brainwaves to TJ to come out on his bike tomorrow.

To meet me in the bushes by the Terrorist Cell.

MAURA

Even when I sniffed something smoky, I found it hard to hang up on Frannie. She was telling me in her reassuringly low and matter-of-fact voice about an incident in her own condo, boys phoning in a bomb threat and police evacuating everyone.

" — and Veronika asking me, 'Mommy, is it a fire?' Veronika

overhearing the word 'bomb' and asking, 'Like chocolate bomb?' My most infamous desert, Maura, which by the way I'll happily concoct for the auction — "

"Mmm," I replied, though still shakily, wanting to lean against the kitchen counter and forget Terrorist Trick-or-Treaters and sink into silent auction-planning mode with Frannie. Wanting to stay on the line with her in a way I hadn't wanted to stay on with earnest tense Dan, who'd taken the trick-or-treaters more seriously, but whose long-distance voice held its too-familiar edge of impatience with me.

" — We'll have to post a 'Sweets Sign-up Sheet' Friday when we put up the banner . . ." I sniffed the air. The faint burnt smell of pumpkin seeds? No: something fresher, smokier. "Hey Frannie, I've gotta go check on Joezy, then call the cops — "

"Sure, but call me if you need to talk, post-police — "

Cutting Frannie short, I hung up and rushed out to Joezy and the shocking smoky curtain. "Joezy, what on earth happened; did those boys come back?"

Not even stopping his shuffly pacing, not even looking up from the floor, Joezy mumbled that it was nothing, the pumpkin; an accident. That he'd gotten distracted looking out the window.

"'Distracted,' yes, guess it's in your genes," I found my shaken self saying. And Joezy merely nodded, well, distractedly.

He didn't catch the dig at his dad that I really shouldn't have made, that Dan really didn't deserve. Of course Dan's distracted half the time, the way he works. So I reminded myself as I stepped closer to Joezy, halting his pacing. I took hold of his shoulders.

"Did you see something out there?" I asked him, eye to eye.

"More like *heard*. Like: footsteps in the leaves or something. Or maybe, maybe nothing . . ." But Joezy kept his pale green eyes (my own wide too-starry eyes) locked with mine. He waited like the kid he still was for his mom to make it better, take some action.

"Your dad is right; we'll call the police," I told him, rallying my firmest mom mode. And Joezy nodded, his boyish freckled face at last relaxing a notch. Much as he too sometimes criticized Dan, we both relied on his steadiness, his firm hand. Even when he was away.

"It was probably nothing," I added to both Joezy and me as I stepped back. "Probably just those poor kids—imagine what they're going through, these days—pulling a gross joke. But just in case . . ."

Joezy nodded as firmly as his father would.

"You go on upstairs," I told him, shooting a glance at our front door. Wondering, if the bell rang again, if I should answer, open that door. Decisively, I switched off our dining room light. With our pumpkin blown out, no lights now welcomed late trick-or-treaters. "We're closed for the night," I told Joezy, who nodded again in shadow. He lifted his latest sketchpad from the table.

He used to show me all his intricate ink sketches eagerly, the moment he'd made them. Now whatever he inked in those pads was secret, like more and more of his increasingly teenage life.

I leaned forward and kissed Joezy on his still-smooth cheek and he, for a change, let me. Then I turned as my son shuffled up the stairs. I made myself pad back into the kitchen and do—as I almost always did—just what Dan advised.

I dialed the Arlington police; I was transferred from a flat-voiced woman to a weary South-Boston-accented man.

"I'm gonna record this call; ya might hear a sound, a mechanical type sound, like a nail gun or something. That's nothing; that's just our recording machine; we got an old-style one. Just keep talking . . ."

I did hear a sound as I told my little story, a startling mechanical clank at unnervingly regular intervals. I jumped a little inside each time it sounded. And I remembered my cold fear back in the humid beginning of summer as I lay on my side on a paper-covered examining table at the breast center, sweating despite the icy air-conditioning and being stripped to my waist.

The biopsy was to sample what they called a lump or mass even though it was too small for my fingers to feel. The mammogram—my tardy first, at age forty-four—had been bad enough, my small soft breasts squeezed between the metal plates in the torture machine surely designed by women-hating men. I'd been too timid to call out as I'd been instructed to do by the deadpan mammogramist, if the pressure became too uncomfortable.

At least the mammogram had been fast. For the excruciatingly drawn-out biopsy, I lay on my side with my hand over my squeezed shut eyes. The radiologist (the lone hairy-fingered male I'd encountered in the breast center, his unexpected unwelcome gender a final nasty surprise) told me he would be taking five samples.

He also informed me, in his detached Dan-like voice, that I would hear a harsh sound from his equipment as he actually took the samples. Some patients experience a startle reflex, he added with barely concealed contempt for such wimps.

"But it's important," he finished flatly, "that you not jump."

Oh God, I know I'm gonna jump, I thought behind my squeezed-shut eyes. I was the jumpy type, the type whose breast was going to be ripped to bloody pulp because I couldn't not startle.

But somehow the paralysis of fear kept my whole curved body rigid as the machine made its nail-gun clank, sucking through its needlelike tube miniscule samples from my anaesthetized breast.

And somehow, despite the jarring mini-nail-gun interruption of the Arlington Police Department's tape player, I managed to keep my voice steady as I described our Terrorist Trick-or-Treaters.

In fact, I was so intent on keeping my voice steady that it wasn't 'til the very end of the call I fully realized I might be getting the boys and their family in big trouble. The policeman asked the exact address on Mystic Avenue where these boys lived.

I hesitated, half wanting to declare my own call a trick-or-treat prank. "I—I'm not sure of the exact address. It—it's on Mystic on the river. And a whole family seems to live there, lots of boys. Not that I've ever seen anything strange going on there or anything—"

"Yes, Ma'am, we are well aware of that house on the river."

Because of the Arabic graffiti on the garage door? Or simply because the family inside the house seemed to be Middle-Eastern?

"Listen, officer, I don't mean to make any trouble for that family there. As I told you, the boys didn't make any threats or anything . . ."

How many times had I scolded Dan and Joezy for "making assumptions" about the house they'd half-seriously dubbed the

Arlington Terrorist Cell. And now here I was not only making assumptions, but also making trouble for this Middle-Eastern family who must be having enough post-9/11 trouble right now.

"Listen sir, I know you do have to look into things, but I want to restate: this might very well just be boys playing a ghastly prank — "

"And it might very well be something more, Ma'am. And we can't be too careful these days, sure you understand. Your report may be passed on to the local FBI office and you may be contacted for further questioning — "

"FBI? Further questioning?" Irrationally, I felt angry at Dan for having suggested this call. Should I have told Dan at all? Should I have taken Frannie's lower-key less-alarmed approach instead?

I mumbled my thanks to the officer; I hung up heavily, exhausted. Listening myself for footsteps outside, inside. The house held the particular echoey silence of Dan being gone. How I missed listening from our warm bed as he'd make his rounds each night, checking that our front door was locked and windows shut. I started toward the front door myself then jumped — inside and outside — when the piercingly cheerful doorbell sounded.

Good God; were they back? I froze in defensive pose, and heard through the door on the stoop outside boyish giggles. My neighbor's apologetic voice called, "It's only Spider-man, Maura!"

I lurched forward, managed a stiff smile as I swung open the door to the latest young mom from up the hill. Her red-masked son clung to her as if the spider webs enwrapping his arms were sticky and real. He held on like Joezy used to hold on to me. Back when Joezy and Dan and I had tramped around this same neighborhood dressed one year as the Berenstain Bear family: Dan actually growing his first experimental middle-aged beard for that night. "We got cleaned out," I breathed, not wanting to tell this beaming mom about the Terrorist Trick-or-Treaters in front of her clingy son. But telling myself I should tell her tomorrow, tell all the moms.

I shut and double-locked the door. Then I padded back to the kitchen, poured myself a glass of White Zinfandel. My mom's cocktail of choice. She was probably sipping one herself down in Providence. Her drinking had grown heavier since her mastectomy and its awful attendant worries. But after all she'd been through, Dad had confided to me by phone, who could deny her "one pleasure"?

I shuddered in my warm, well-lit kitchen to think of those words. To wonder briefly — for I did share Mom's melodramatic melancholic Irish genes — what was my one pleasure, top pleasure, these days?

Frannie, I found myself thinking, pouring more. Just the way she talked to me, listened to me, looked at me. "In wine there is truth," Dan always quoted. But not truths I could tell him.

I sipped slowly, thinking back to July, when in my post-biopsy high — freed by my "benign" lab result from my mom's fate, at least for the immediate future — I decided to do something I'd always wanted to.

I attended an Oberlin College alumni picnic gathering on the Charles River. Dan was out of town, as per usual, but I'd been touched and flattered in a way I hadn't felt in years that he'd phoned several times that afternoon, asking who I might meet from the old days. He'd been wondering like I'd been wondering, though neither of us said so, if I might see Carolyn Zander from Peas Place Co-Op. My almost-girlfriend there, before Dan swept me away.

Carolyn didn't show up, though I knew from alumni directories she lived in the Boston area. But that was where I met Frannie. She'd been several years ahead of me at Oberlin. She stopped tossing her Frisbee when she spotted me. She crossed the grass and told me I wouldn't remember her, but that she remembered me from my dancing at Oberlin. Fat and shy, was all she'd say of her Oberlin College self. She stood before me, stocky and tan and engagingly attentive. Her stylishly chopped black hair stood on end in the humidity; her grey eyes shone, clear and bright, not heat-dazed like everyone else's. And she was fixing on me, like no one had in ages.

She'd just started her own camera business in Lexington and was doing freelance photography and looking for a progressive open-minded private school for her adopted Bosnian daughter Veronika.

Gleeful, ponytailed Veronika frolicked on the grass between and around us as we spoke, spinning with her Frisbee, hugging her mom's solid muscular legs. I recommended Fairwell. Frannie nodded avidly, scribbled down the info. But after I'd tottered away from the picnic, the encounter already fading, I didn't expect to see her again.

I rinsed my Halloween wine glass, resisting a second. I set the glass in the drainer, recalling my surprise at the first PTA meeting in September when Frannie strode up to me, gripped my hand in both of hers, thanked me for steering her and Veronika to Fairwell.

"I'm so glad you listened to me," I'd gasped back, and added jokingly, "No one ever listens to me!"

Frannie had smiled gently like she knew that wasn't all a joke.

Was she joking herself when she flirted with me, playing up her role as, in her words, Fairwell's token single gay mom? Still, even if it wasn't serious, it was nice to be noticed. So I was thinking when, almost as jarringly as the doorbell, the phone buzzed.

I picked up the kitchen line expecting Dan checking up on me. But it was Frannie and that voice of hers, low as a cello.

"Just checking up on you; you must be kind of freaked out by that whole trick-or-treating thing. They didn't come back, did they?"

"No, no, we're fine. I did call the cops, like Dan said to, and, and . . ." I hesitated, then confided to Frannie how guilty I'd felt afterwards. "I mean, they're only boys. And it must be rough on them, being Middle-Eastern or whatever they are, here and now . . ."

"Yeah, I know what you mean. But you can't take any chances, not alone in the house with your own kid. I know that . . ."

"Something else we've got in common," I found myself saying, then — flustered, sensing Frannie was about to say something more, something I wasn't ready to hear — I cut the call short, pleading sleepiness. But I was suddenly wide awake as I re-checked the front door lock, drew the singed shade shut over our front window.

I climbed the stairs slowly, self-consciously, feeling in both good and bad ways that I was being watched.

JOEZY

TJ and me, we started biking by that house on the river on the same freaking freaked-out day. The hushed afternoon of September 11th.

My mom broke into my rainbow-painted ninth-grade classroom at Fairwell School at 10AM that day. Her hair unbrushed and her voice fake-calm. She whisked me home, where Dad waited. Dad in daylight: his face when he hugged me as sobered as Mom's.

We sat 'round the TV, Dad muttering about the damn Palestinians and scratching his curly beard.

All that long morning, Mom softly protested Dad's loud angry comments: Dad drunk not from beer, but from the nonstop TV (usually on only for the one lousy hour I was allowed). All of us drunk, that day, from the planes flying over and over into the buildings that seemed — the weirdest part to me — not to explode but to disintegrate. Zap. Gone.

Mom kept smoothing my wild hair like I was her boy again. Not that I minded, that day.

"Yeah," I egged on my madder and madder dad, when he mumbled something about nukes. "They can't do this to us."

Mom and Dad merely nodded. The two of them at least distracted by the same thing for once; glued to some new news update. I slipped into the day, the sunny silent sky.

No planes flying: only one neighbor, Mr. Spivac, out on our street, mowing his lawn.

"Couldn't watch anymore," he called sheepishly to my bike.

I whizzed down Riverview Road to usually busy Mystic Avenue. They can't do this to us, I chanted as I rode up and down near-empty Mystic, pumping hard with forbidden un-fucking-Fairwell thoughts.

Not that I knew who "they" were; not that I had anything clear in mind as I biked back and forth by the rundown house on the river.

A used-to-be-fancy ranch house on Mystic Avenue, facing Mystic River. Its overgrown yard was deserted like almost every other yard that day. Where was the maybe-Arab family, its boys?

I pedaled way faster than my norm, imagining my home in flames: Dad off on a trip and me rescuing Mom and then me attacking back. Machine-gunning those scary-brave skateboarding boys who'd made me afraid to bike near this house, 'til this day.

And who was that zooming toward me?

"Whoa," I called out. I almost rammed the only other biker on Mystic. His bike wobbled but TJ stayed tall in its seat. His t-shirt proclaimed IT MUST SUCK TO BE YOU.

I straightened in my seat, squaring my narrower shoulders. I shut my lips over my braces, bike to bike with a cool Arlington High dude. His skin was thick with acne; he was showing his full face to me like showing his battle scars. We shot each other soldierly nods.

Then we pedaled off equally fast.

Both of us thinking (I'd find out later) the same things. But it was me the girl in the basement noticed, maybe, from her belowground window. The girl named Le Ti One.

—————

At Fairwell, the rest of September, our teachers got teary-eyed talking about different gods and different cultures and not hating. Gentle Mr. Hamal, our Saudi-born computer tutor, visited each class, telling us in a voice almost too soft to hear about real Muslims.

What about the freaking unreal ones? my new 9/11 self thought. Not that I was any expert on any religion. Me: son of a lapsed-Catholic Irish mom and a just-Hanukkah Jewish dad.

Me: all-American everything-and-nothing kind of guy.

After school, almost every day, I kept up my patrols on the sidewalk in front of that house. Don't bike down to Mystic, the mothers of Riverview Road used to warn us kids. At fifteen, though, I was old enough to brave the Mystic Avenue traffic and troll by the fancy houses on the river. Fancy, anyhow, compared to ours.

But from One's bare basement room — that room I will never stop seeing inside my head — the so-called middleclass houses of Riverview Road must have looked pretty good.

Like I looked to One, at first, maybe. A nice boy, everyone always said, despite my shaggy hair. When I sketched cartoons of me and my six fellow ninth graders — gentle cartoons, since we'd been taught never to make fun of each other — I always drew myself hidden by Scooby-Doo mop-top hair.

"A lurker," Dad told me jokingly. "Like me."

One early October day, I parked my bike behind the riverfront house's hydrangea bushes. And I saw the house's garage door rise.

The yard filled with three women in head shawls who draped damp patterned cloths on the yard's bushes to dry.

Following the women came four black-haired boys. The tallest one wore glasses that bounced as he skateboarded. The women retreated inside in serene single file. The boys swooped up and down the driveway like I'd often seen them do from a distance, pre-9/11.

Hairpin-spinning onto Mystic on battered bikes and what Mom called, as we'd drive by, "suicide skateboards."

Me, I fled. I veered around the soaring spinning boys. I pedaled all the way up Riverview Road to its peak. Panting, I turned and gazed out toward the distant ghostly buildings of Boston.

I imagined I was somehow guarding those buildings, sitting tall in my bike seat. The way I did with TJ beside me.

Joe, I told TJ, instead of Josiah, the day we exchanged names.

That was the late-October day Arab-style graffiti had appeared, sloppily painted, on the house's garage door. Slashed there by the skateboarding boys? Or by sneaky neighborhood white boys, like us?

TJ and I had both stopped our bikes behind the ragged hydrangeas to contemplate it. The freaking unreadable message.

TJ gave me a mumbled account of the two oldest "fucking A-rab boys" at Arlington High. How they hung together and rarely spoke except to claim that their dad (the old guy we'd glimpsed being loaded in and out of Symmes Medical Center vans in a wheelchair) was a "Saudi prince."

I volunteered that my dad called this house Arlington's own

Terrorist Cell. TJ replied that his dad called it way worse. We agreed that the midnight deliveries my dad had spotted must be bombs.

Then TJ spat hard into the bushes. I didn't dare spit; scared I'd do it wrong. Was this football-fit but acne-scarred Arlington High guy somehow joining forces with me?

Me: who'd never even been allowed to play guns.

Me: a Fairwell School boy from a small cozy class of ninth-graders, as familiar to each other as fucking brothers and sisters. Me: a boy who before 9/11 used to "find my thrill" biking by Arlington High to steal glimpses of the unfamiliar giggling girls and daunting jocks bigger than TJ. They crowded the playground there, jostling each other. Fights always brewing.

I'd never learned to fight at Fairwell. I'd learned not to fight. Something I hoped TJ never found out.

He eyed me from his bike like he sometimes did, like he didn't quite trust me. He was way stronger than me. But he had that bad acne and — by luck — I didn't. Then again, his face had the fuzzy traces of bristles that my milky boy-skin still couldn't quite produce. I put on my best close-mouthed tough boy face.

"See ya, Joe," TJ muttered as he biked off. My fellow soldier. The two of us different, sure. But connected by our shared sense that this house needed watching.

So the day after Halloween, after school, I biked down to Mystic Avenue and waited behind the blossomless hydrangeas for TJ. I was bursting to tell him about Halloween night, how it practically proved what we'd suspected all along about the house.

When I heard the whoosh of his mountain bike tires, I fought my wide braces-revealing smile. The bushes rustled; TJ halted beside me, breathing hard, slipping off his black skull-and-bones helmet.

"Whassup, Joe," he mumbled into the bared branches.

"Lots is up," I told TJ, breathing his sweat even in the chill November air, he rode his bike so hard. Like he'd been as eager to see me as I was to see him.

Before I could say why, the Terrorist Cell garage door whined open. The Arab lettering on the outside folded neatly up and away.

The women came out in their usual head shawls. The most bosomy one dragged at her sides two single-bed mattresses. These she dumped in the knee-high grass.

The women stood around the mattresses, wielding brooms.

"Whoa-ho," TJ muttered like they might attack us. He snorted.

The women beat the mattresses. I shifted, feeling a hard-on stir inside my zipped jeans, against my bike seat. Not that these old-as-Mom women in their shapeless robes were sexy to me. Not that I had any control over my hard-ons.

I tried to snort like TJ but it came out a cough. I watched the women gripping those brooms with their strong-looking hands. My hard-on felt like a broom handle. Finally they finished, my hard-on beginning to deflate as mysteriously as it had swelled up.

God, would I ever be able to control it, use it like a real man? The women trooped inside companionably. The garage door stayed half open, half the black Arab-like lettering on display.

I leaned toward TJ, who was picking one of his zits. "Know what those A-rab boys dressed up as last night?"

"Huh? You seen 'em, last night?" TJ lowered his hand.

I gave a chin-jerk nod. TJ's blond eyebrows rose when I described in whisper the boys in their ghutra and bloodstained bandage get-ups.

"'And a dead American,'" TJ repeated in whispered disgust. Then he spat into the bushes. A few dried leaves shivered. "What they want us to be." TJ shook his spiked head. "Dead and all . . ."

He jerked his head toward the other side of Mystic, the upwardly climbing rows of homes on Riverview Road. TJ lived in the more crowded East Arlington. Still, he didn't seem to see me as weak, spoiled.

"Dead to the world," I echoed. Like we were the only ones who weren't, who knew what was really going on.

"We'll all be dead for real, 'less someone does something." TJ turned toward the half open garage. "C'mon."

Before I could think, TJ and I were ducking our heads. We crept together around the bushes, the only barrier to the yard.

"C'mon," TJ commanded again over his shoulder, like I'd be the one to wimp out. So maybe he did see me as weak?

We scurried down the driveway. It was TJ who hesitated, standing in his hydrangea-bush hunch beside the garage.

So I went first. I bent double, ducked under the door. The garage floor was white concrete, stained with oil like any garage.

I scrambled to my feet, panting, alone in the dim empty two-car garage. Was TJ coming at all? I wondered in a mix of pride and panic.

I went first, I imagined saying to my dad. Though I couldn't tell him — or could I? Wasn't this the sort of thing he'd been waiting to hear from me? Some exploit, some adventure, some proof I was no mama's boy?

I stepped blindly forward, blinking in the dimness. As my eyes adjusted, I saw (mentally I took notes like a real spy) piled boxes labeled INSULIN. Metal devices that looked medical. And the infamous plastic US Air delivery bins piled in one corner, neatly.

A regular door leading inside stood ajar, a gleaming tile floor visible. A kitchen? I inched back toward the garage door, not sure if I was going to duck out and flee or drag TJ in with me.

TJ's harsh whisper halted my edging step.

"Dude, dude — something's happening out here," he stage-whispered through the low garage door opening. "They're on the fucking roof!"

"Fuck!" I whispered back. On the roof? Like snipers with rifles?

I dropped to my knees on cold, oil-sticky concrete. I peered under the garage door to see boys swooping down from above.

Rough thumps and gasps and laughter. Their sneakered feet bounced on the freshly beaten mattresses. So they'd jumped down from the single-story roof? To catch us?

"Hey, yo, Pig! You offa here Pig — " A boy shouted, sounding startled. Gracelessly, TJ scrambled into view.

He booked up the sloping driveway, lunging toward the bushes where our bikes were parked. Ditching me.

The skinny boys bounced off the mattresses, racing after TJ.

"Pig, Pig! You offa here — "

Outta here, did they mean? How would I get outta here? I bent lower, still kneeling, when a light hand touched my shoulder.

I jerked upright, wobbling on my knees.

"No hurt, no hurt," the girl begged me, holding up small but womanly hands. She wouldn't hurt me or I shouldn't hurt her?

Standing on my knees, I met her stare, she was so short, girl-sized but with real breasts poking out under her blank t-shirt. Was she maybe fifteen? Sixteen? Her round face was slashed by bright watchful eyes. Her black bangs cut at a jagged angle. Kinda cool, those bangs. Her mouth peachy pale and soft-looking. Her lips half open, showing big front teeth like mine. Kinda cute, to me, this girl.

Not Arab but Asian — but why? What was she doing here?

She jerked out one thin arm. Bravely, like a shy girl, she shoved a folded note into my hand. With her head bowed so her angled bangs hid one eye, she whispered one word. So soft I wasn't sure.

"Please?"

Then a commanding woman's voice called from the kitchen, "One? One?"

The girl spun around, her ponytail bouncing. I wanted to grab that shiny ponytail, pull her back and look at her some more. Try to tell if she was a girl or a woman, brash or super-shy, or both all at once. But she slipped across the garage, shut the door behind her.

She left me sealed in doubled dark.

Too dark now to read the words on her note, except to see that they were sloppy-block-printed in English.

Outside the garage, the boys were jabbering in English too. Like ordinary boys, high after the thrill of chasing off TJ.

"A-gain! Gonna go a-gain," A soft-voiced boy called. And, sounding like any boy anywhere, "Race you — "

Their sneakered feet thumped across the driveway; my heart thudded. Then they were veering as one and thundering on around the house. To climb some drainpipe up to the roof, jump again?

I stuffed the girl's note in my jeans pocket. I wriggled out under the door into an empty yard, empty mattresses knocked askew on the grass. Awaiting those boys diving like paratroopers from above.

I ran. I charged through the high dry grass, fought hydrangea branches for my handlebars. Letting my helmet swing from those bars, I mounted the bike and backed out fast. I could've veered right toward Arlington Center, East Arlington, where TJ might have been waiting along the way for me.

Instead I veered left, toward the Whole Foods Market a mile up Mystic, its parking lot where I could read her note all alone.

Where TJ couldn't see that note, or my shaking hands.

MY NAME LE TI ONE
I AM VIETNAM OF BIRTH
I AM CALLED ONE
MY FAMILY OF HIGH ESTEEM BUT FALL INTO NEED
I AM OF WORK TO THE PRINCE AND FAMILY
BUT NOT OF PAY
MONEY NOTHING HERE AND I HAVE FALL IN NEED
ALL KINDNESS MUCH I PAY BACK.

I did not tell Mom or Dad or the FBI or even TJ.

I knew I should — but it was me this girl had given her note to. This shy girl, scared girl. Cute girl who might be a woman. I wanted, somehow, to be the one to help her. This One. (Maybe in Vietnam first names come last?) Yes: *One*. Yes: I'd find out her facts then I'd figure out what I should do for her. *Me*. Me alone. I pedaled back home from the Whole Foods lot, tall in my bike seat.

Holding in my jeans pocket the first big secret of my life.

A real secret, not some superhero rescue cartoon I'd sketch then crumple, never satisfied with the heroes I invented. Bat Boy with his fangs; Mockingbird Man with his feathered arms or Otter Boy, slinky and impervious to cold. What Mom called me: her Otter Boy swimming the chill offseason waters of Walden Pond with her.

Why was I thinking of Walden Pond, of Mom in her swimsuit that showed the full lengths of her legs, her butt too when she swam hard, and I always worried about other kids staring at that, about me staring too. About the popsicle hard-ons I got under Walden Pond waters sometimes, swimming with Mom and watching distant girls onshore and wondering how I'd ever find a girl who was, well, mine. A very un-Fairwell-type thought. But that's how I was freaking thinking when I chugged back up Riverview Road on my bike, when I rolled into our driveway. I parked my bike in our single-car garage, as dark in that November dusk as hers.

And I double-checked in my pocket for One's folded note.

CHAPTER THREE
YOUR SECRET

MAURA

Oh Frannie, I thought as I peeled my morning mango three days after Halloween, *When did you become the one I talk to in my head?*

Ever since that first PTA meeting, I told myself as mango peels spiraled down to the sink. Frannie had surprised me then by showing up as a new parent and by being the one to agree with me about what charity we should benefit with this year's Fairwell Silent Auction. Shakily, my old stage fright reviving, I'd explained to the group at that September 5th meeting about the Songs for Shelters program I'd been teaching in all summer, visiting area shelters and helping the kids compose and perform their own rap songs.

Most of the PTA'ers had taken my husband's line, nodding sympathetically but questioning how vital this service was for those kids. "Shouldn't we be delivering them fresh food instead?" demanded River Sienna-Ross's mom. "But maybe," new parent Frannie spoke up, "they need soul food — need their own words and music — too."

Of course, everything changed within a week. At our emergency mid-September meeting, we all agreed that the auction must raise funds for victims of 9/11. Even Frannie — as argumentative in life as I was only inside my head — had agreed to that.

"*— following new leads on Bin Laden's whereabouts . . .*"

Down the hall in the TV room, I heard Dan panting away on his Stairmaster above the newscaster's grim voice. Our old one-hour-of-TV-a-day rule had gone out the window this fall, at least for Dan.

He disappeared into hours of Stairmaster-CNN news like

my dad used to disappear behind his evening paper. Like I used
to disappear behind my laptop for emails brainstorming about
the Songs for Shelter benefit that I was no longer choreograph-
ing. Not to mention the half-time teaching job I'd been slotted
for beginning in 2002 that now was "on hold." The fall show
we'd been planning for the shelter kids had been indefinitely
postponed. With so many 9/11 fundraisers going at once, the
project director decided, we wouldn't stand a chance, not this
fall. Likewise, the charitable grant that would have funded my
2002 teaching gig had suddenly, this October, dried up.

"— *investigating yet another Anthrax threat . . .*"

Was it the constant flow of hysterical terrorist news that had
Joezy so jittery lately? I scrubbed a fry pan soaking from last
night's latkes. Joezy's favorite, but he had eaten them silently. How
I missed the way he used to confide in me. What was up with
Joezy? Dan and I had both been wondering last night in bed. Too
sleepy to talk. Or to do — I'd told Dan, making my voice sound
sleepier than I was — anything else. After Dan had started sullenly
snoring, I'd lain awake.

It was Dan I should be talking to now, debriefing about Joezy
before Dan had to drive to work. I plugged in my blender.

"You dry-clean my suit, Babe?" Dan called breathlessly above a
commercial. His best suit for his much-postponed New York trip.

"It'll be ready today," I called back. "All set for next week. And
I'm having them take in the waist on the pants — "

With all his extra Stairmaster hours, plus the jogging Dan had
resumed these last few weeks — burning off extra energy, he'd
explained to me, his face flushed and sweaty like in college after
his track meets — Dan had lost some weight.

"Yeah, thanks," Dan managed to call out from the den.

"No problem," I called back. But I lifted my knife with an inner
surge of worry. *Not just my usual worries, not this trip,* I confided to
Frannie in my head as I'd never really done in life.

How I wished I could confide in Frannie, in someone, about what
I'd heard from another wife in Dan's firm, a catty woman who was
a high-power lawyer herself, who tended to intimidate me at firm

parties. She'd phoned me in early October, after Dan's first post-9/11 trip to Philly. All the planes had been delayed and Dan and her husband had wound up spending an extra night there.

"I heard the two of them went out for a little partying, if you know what I mean," the catty wife had told me slowly by phone, sounding like she might be drunk herself. "Working off all that fear of flying . . ."

"No," I'd said nervously, cutting her short. "No, I don't know what you mean." But I'd hung up spooked. Was it possible that my steady reliable Dan had, in a night of post-9/11 craziness, crossed the line? Was this woman implying the men had—what? Picked up airport prostitutes? Cut loose like death-defying sailors on leave?

Something I never would've believed before, not for my Dan. But 9/11 had blasted many distractions and inhibitions from my own mind. I'd found myself thinking—if not acting—more boldly.

Fantasizing (but not seriously, I told myself) about Frannie.

I raised the peeled mango above the open blender and sliced, letting each chunk fall with a juicy plop. One of my many everyday extravagances. Mangos, expensive but fresh at Whole Foods year round. Mango smoothies: one taste Joezy and I still shared.

A remnant of the days when Joezy would hang about at my side in the kitchen, tasting and loving whatever I cooked him. I used to think of those early Joezy days with a pang of longing, but not lately. Or anyway, less of a pang. Thanks to Frannie; maybe the first person since Joezy to gaze at me with such, well, fascination.

I sliced down to the pit, my grip on the knife both sticky and slippery. Unwillingly, as I gazed into the pulpy mass of fruit, I remembered reading about stunned New Yorkers fleeing the crash on 9/11 finding themselves pelted from the skies by human body parts.

"—*additional forces to invade Afghanistan, officials report . . .*"

Dan thumped out of the TV room, his late-for-work thumps. He was rummaging in the hallway closet for his coat, still listening.

"—*rumors that Bin Laden is hiding in the Tora Bora mountains . . .*"

Bin Laden; the Tora Boras, the spreading war. That's what I

ought to be focused on. Like everyone. I ought to be weighing
in on the PTA email controversy about the possible inappropri-
ateness of a cash-bar at the auction. Yet my mind kept dwelling
instead on the sexy little secrets (the African drumming CD Frannie gave me; our hug after our last late auction meeting) that I
hadn't savored in years. Maybe I was savoring them—and exag-
gerating them—now because I feared my days might be num-
bered? Not that I believed another terrorist attack would really
come. Not that I believed, either, Frannie really had feelings for
me. She was simply playing at being flirtatious. And I was playing
too, right?

I poured milk into the blender, remembering an offhand
remark of Frannie's about my peaches-and-cream-and-freckles
complexion. So what if she wasn't serious? It still felt good, and
harmless—so far.

I heard Dan's steady steps in the hall. So I flipped the blender
switch to drown him out. I half-smiled, secretly giddy like I hadn't
felt since Peas Place Veggie Co-Op at Oberlin College in the '80s.
Back when fat Frannie, unknown to me, had watched me dance.

Back then it had seemed (the blender churned its golden mass)
such an urgent question whether I'd love back the male or the
female co-op mates who loved or at least lusted after me.

Dan, the quiet curly-haired boy from Boston, always watched
me from the background too, back then. "A lurker," he'd called
himself though there was nothing sinister about Dan Simon.

"Gotta go," Dan muttered in my ear, his familiar warm weight
and black-coffee breath right behind me.

I switched off the blender and turned, my ponytail undone, my
face foolishly flushed. From hot thoughts, a premature hot flash?

Dan's bearded face and dark distracted eyes; the same as ever.
Lightly, he patted my ass. Maybe I should have let him do more,
last night. "Careful out there," I ventured. "And did you ask about
your schedule? You do think you'll be able to make it next Saturday . . . ?"

"Saturday?" Dan asked, pulling me toward him. I rested my
head against his firm tweedy shoulder. "Not for that shelter

sing-a-long thing? I thought you'd all wisely decided not to do that this fall . . ."

"We decided to postpone it," I answered, trying not to sound miffed by his dismissive tone toward the Songs for Shelters project: the most satisfying, if lowest paying, gig I'd had in years. "But no, Saturday is the auction." I pushed back from Dan, sounding sharper than I'd intended. He gave his impatient black-coffee sigh.

"Right, right; well I told you it depends on the trains . . ." He was backing away. "Depends on whether I get out of NYC alive . . ."

"Don't joke about that; don't tempt the gods," I chided him. This would be his first trip to his firm's New York offices since 9/11.

Dan gave me his absentminded grin. "Speaking of 'the gods,'" he surprised me by saying. "There's something I'd like to talk to you about when I get back . . . about Joezy. I've been talking to Mark Goldstein about his synagogue; I wanna look into whether it's too late or not for Joezy to be, you know, Bar Mitzvah'd . . ."

"Really?" My eyes widened. Dan had attended synagogue only sporadically over the years; he'd always told Joezy that he was lucky to be let off the Bar Mitzvah hook Dan's parents had hung him from. They'd never forgiven Dan for choosing Oberlin over Brandeis, choosing Irish lapsed-Catholic me over a Jewish girl. "Where's this coming from, Dan? Is it — I mean — since September — ?"

But Dan was looking down and shaking his head like the inarticulate curly-haired boy I'd first met. "We'll talk later . . ."

We were always saying that to each other, but never following through. We used to have our best talks post-sex, but lately there hadn't been all that much sex. Which was mostly my doing. Me: who tended to halt Dan's advances, like last night.

"I want to talk now," I told Dan's retreating tweed back.

"No time. I'll call ya, Babe," Dan answered in his usual distracted manner. How could he drop such a bomb then rush out? I turned back to the blender; the front door shut. I halfway wanted to run after him, at least give my Dan the Man a real goodbye. Tell him that maybe he was right; maybe Joezy needed more guidance than we alone could give him. Tell him that something was up with Joezy.

But when would I have a chance to discuss Joezy or anything else with Dan? After all, I reminded myself at the distant slam of Dan's car door, in a couple days Dan would head off bravely to Manhattan. Dan working his long hours to keep Joezy in Fairwell and mango smoothies. To keep me and Joezy safe, in these terrible times. I should be more grateful, I knew as I got down two glasses.

I poured the thick creamy mix, mesmerized by its gold sheen in the kitchen window light, the weak November sun. God, it was nearly 8 a.m. already and my son still in bed. "Josiah — " I hollered.

I had to get Joezy to Fairwell by 8:30 a.m., had to meet Frannie by the flagpole. Together we would hang the big silent auction banner, the cartoon dollar signs painted over by Frannie and me for this year's somber post-9/11 look.

In previous, more frivolous years, Fairwell's Silent Auction had been my favorite of my many PTA activities. The party was a chance to dress up, show off my still-trim figure, offer, as my auction donation, free yoga lessons, and argue politics with someone besides Dan.

But this year everything was, of course, more serious. And was something serious actually developing between Frannie and me? I filled the second tall glass, foamy liquid overflowing. I finger-scooped a spilled glob. As I licked it, my son shuffled in the kitchen, dragging his feet, looking as dazed and sleep-deprived as I felt.

He lifted his smoothie from the counter and gulped it, his newly prominent Adam's apple bobbing.

"Talk to me," I told Joezy on motherly impulse. He lowered his half-drained glass, eye-to-eye with me. I still couldn't get used to him being so tall. His greenish brown eyes looked dense, teeming today.

"Is it — a girl?"

Joezy snorted at my question, licking his mango-sticky lips. But his gaze turned evasive. "A girl? At, like, good ol' Fairwell? C'mon, Mom." He rolled his eyes, took another gulp of smoothie. "Y'mean one of the three girls I've known since kindergarten?"

"OK, OK; maybe not them . . . but someone? Some girl?"

Joezy shrugged, one shouldered. His jumpy gaze shifted to the counter. I turned too, unsteadily lifted my own cool glass. God, I was the one acting like a lovesick high school kid.

"Y'know, Mom," Joezy mumbled in his glass, maybe reading my mind like always. "You're the one who's all — all hot and bothered lately . . ."

"Hot and bothered?" I shot back, for the second time that morning more sharply than I'd intended.

Another tense one-sided shrug from Joezy. "About the silent auction thingy or — whatever."

Joezy's sullen knowing "whatever" hovered between us.

"Look," I said briskly, sipping. "I just wanted you to know that you can tell me if, if it is a girl . . ."

Joezy didn't nod, keeping his pale-lashed eyes low. He was chewing his lower lip, his braces glinting. For a second I thought he'd blurt out whatever it was, the way he used to rush into my arms when I'd pick him up at Fairwell and instantly tell me everything, how he wanted to marry seven-year-old Alison Jester.

He looked up, his gaze even more intensely distracted than Dan's. "Yo Mom; we gotta go."

Joezy handed me his half drained glass so I held both glasses between us. They weighed down my hands, too much milky sweetness.

"OK then," I told my son, eye-to-eye. "It'll be your secret."

In the car, the tank-like Volvo Dan had insisted on because of its safety record, I listened to NPR's grave British reporter file an Afghanistan report fuzzed by real gunfire. Beside me on the seat, my cardboard box of maracas and rhythm sticks rattled.

Joezy sat slumped in the backseat, deep in his own thoughts. I lurched off Riverview Road into our 8AM traffic jam. In the rearview, I caught my son turning his head toward the Terrorist Trick-or-Treaters' house on the river. I glanced too: the garage door decked with what looked like fresh Arabic graffiti. Saying who knew what.

"Those boys, that house," I began awkwardly, twisting down the knob on NPR. "You haven't been worrying about that, them . . . ?"

Joezy snapped his head back around. God, he looked like a young Dan with his mop of hair and bone-pale face. But my own pale-green panicky stare. Or maybe I was projecting the panic.

"Jeez, Mom, I told you. I'm not scared of those freaking nuts . . ."

"How do you know they're nuts?"

"Duh, Mom; I dunno; maybe 'cause they came to our door dressed as a terrorist and a dead — "

"OK, OK — " I twisted back up NPR, its jaunty deeply familiar end theme. "You don't need to remind me . . ."

As NPR shifted to an interlude of jazz, Joezy's knee behind me began jiggling, so hard it jolted my seat-back.

"Oh honey, are those boys in that house bothering you?"

"No boys are bothering me!"

I halted at the Massachusetts Avenue intersection so suddenly my maracas clacked, letting Joezy's whine pass without an "I don't like your tone."

His knee kept jiggling to the beat of Miles Davis's horn. Joezy had inherited my sense of rhythm. Boldly, I shot forward into the intersection. I gained the other side just ahead of oncoming traffic, pumping the gas. Had Joezy inherited something else from me? Something in the hyper-defensive way he'd said boys. Could it be that Joezy was brooding over some boy? Was this his new secret?

Now that's one whopper of a projection, I imagined Frannie scoffing. Not that I'd really bring up such an outlandish theory about my son to Frannie. Not that I'd ever discussed anything all that personal with the real Frannie.

Only the PTA, Songs for Shelters, and politics. A kick to me to quarrel with someone even further left wing than me — a relief from Dan's and my testy exchanges over his increasingly, at first almost jokingly, right-leaning views. Especially now, since September, when Dan seemed to have taken a hard right turn along with all the flag-flying cars surrounding me. And what was up with him and this sudden Bar Mitzvah plan? Was he transforming into the strict Jewish parents he'd rebelled against ever since college?

ROAD WORK AHEAD; SEEK ALTERNATE ROUTE. I steered through the maze of seemingly permanent construction crews on Pleasant Street. Our car bumped, my box of instruments clip-clopping.

Joezy muttered, a peace offering: "Same old un-Pleasant Street."

I answered with a laugh. "Yep, they'll never be done fixing Pleasure — um, Pleasant — Street . . ."

The words mixed themselves up as if I was buzzed on my nightly wine. *Christ, I could use a White Zinfandel right about now.*

"Pleasure Street, Mom?" Joezy halted his knee.

"Oh c'mon; give your old mom a break . . ."

I turned off Pleasant, picturing what we students had nicknamed the pleasure palace. Peas Place Veggie Co-Op at Oberlin College; a pea-green Victorian house. Those heady dance major days when co-op mates of both genders would watch me as I wafted through the communal kitchen in my sweaty practice leotard. Tired yet wired from my exhilarating practice routines; always so much better than my stiffer more self-conscious performances.

Practicing, testing. That's what I felt I was doing in the co-op TV room, aka fuck room, late nights, after cheap wine and pricey pot and homework by blue TV light. Carolyn: the butch dirty-blonde women's studies major. Karl: the white-blond socialist.

And Dan Simon: the one who watched my whole slow-motion melodrama from the sidelines, at first.

Was it Carolyn or Karl who'd dubbed me "Mara"? I'd taken that up as my new name, freshman year. Maura, the straight-A Catholic school girl, had become Mara, the daring maybe-bi dance major.

"Yo, Mom? We're here; we're over the rainbow . . ."

"Oops — " I screeched our brakes, maracas rattling wildly, our car sailing by the Fairwell School rainbow-arched entrance sign.

I pulled into a sharp risky U-turn. Then I slowed the Volvo sheepishly as we bumped onto the lot. This morning, I didn't line our car up with the others waiting to drop at the door.

"Whatcha doing?" Joezy behind me whined as I angled into a parking space. NPR's news theme piped up again; I shut it off.

"I'm going in today, remember? The auction's next weekend and we need to get the banner up." I jolted the Volvo into park. I twisted round to face Joezy as he noisily gathered his backpack. "What? You don't want to walk in together?"

Joezy already had the back door open. "C'mon Mom, get a life."

He slammed the door; I watched him through the windshield hurrying toward the school, dragging his bulging half-zipped backpack. A young man bursting with his own secrets.

"OK," I muttered to myself above the tick of the Volvo's dying engine. "I will."

——————

SHHH: SILENT AUCTION, SAT NOV 10
THIS YEAR: HELP VICTIMS OF 9/11

The green flyer fluttered in the brisk November breeze, taped to the glass entry doors of Fairwell. A red flag to me, heading toward the building from my car. So Frannie was already here, early as ever, taping up those flyers we'd printed together.

I straightened my posture, shook back my blowing hair. Felt my foolish heart pump. Was that Frannie standing behind the glass door, watching me approach the school as if transfixed?

I raised one hand in mock salute, Frannie's and my shared joke as co-chairs of this year's auction committee. Behind the glass, Frannie snapped her own salute: crisp, convincing. Like she really believed she and I were about to wage some battle, make some daring stand.

"At ease, Officer Max." I burst through the glass doors into the welcome steamy warmth of the school. Frannie had stepped back to let me in, widely smiling. She was, she'd told me, a "morning person."

Her clean-scrubbed face looked ruddy with cold; her black hair stylishly bristled, freshly chopped. The white shock in front seemed more dramatic than ever. Her sharp clear eyes met mine, her gaze the opposite of distracted, of Dan's.

"That's Commander Max to you." Frannie shoved a handful of
green flyers into my hands. Ever obedient, at least with commanding Frannie, I handed flyers to two moms bustling past.

Frannie dug through her red valise. "I got stunning proofs of
you," she told me in the low husky voice I liked. The moms and
kids trooped off down the school's rainbow-painted central corridor.

"Proofs of me?" I asked. I envied Frannie's valise, with its
embossed black stamp of her own MAX CAMERAS.

"Here, see?" Brusquely, Frannie handed me a shiny sheaf of
photos, taken weeks before in the last golden days of October, at
Walden Pond. "My proofs . . ."

Proof that you do have a crush on me, I thought as she displayed the
glowing gold-lit photos. I nodded, trying not to show in my face how
pleased I was. I hadn't looked so good in a photo in years.

I'd never been a real knockout, simply full-haired and slim. My
face too bony and freckled for beauty. The unique thing I did have
was, as my mother put it, "lovely coloring." *A fleeting gift*, I'd often
thought in my early forties, plucking my scattered grey hairs.

In Frannie's fanned-out photos, my hair shone with its natural
reds and golds in Walden Pond sun. My skin looked luminously
white; my lines and freckles all but invisible. Airbrushed out? Or
was it just that abundant late afternoon sun?

Luscious light, Frannie had crowed as she'd posed me in my
smooth black leotard on the rough pinkish granite rocks. Nomi-
nally, the photos were for my own mini-display at the auction
advertising my donation of free yoga lessons. But really, Frannie had told me, it was a treat — after the "endless weddings"
she'd done all summer as she established herself in the freelance
scene — to photograph me.

"See?" Frannie bent close to me in the hallway, her fresh-scented
hair brushing my cheek. Frannie smelled of fall air, like she'd just
come from a long morning walk. "This one, this one I actually
want to put up for bidding; as 'Art' . . ."

"Art? This, me?" I frowned down at the photo.

Me as middle-aged wood nymph; me lounging on the giant
rocks in October sun, impish and slim in my leotard. My loose

reddish hair half hid my face; only one of my green eyes peered
at the camera.

"C'mon, Frannie. It's a fun shot, but who'd want to buy me?"

"Think you know who," Frannie answered near my ear. The
husky whisper I heard so often inside my head. A mellow voice for
otherwise brisk Frannie. She was as decisive as I was indecisive, we'd
decided as co-chairs. And I was as diplomatic as she was brash.

Suddenly Frannie was snatching all the photos back like they were
X-rated. The glass doors opened again, a whoosh of chill air.

"I wanted to put it out, framed, on the sample table," Frannie
informed me, still low-voiced. River Sienna-Ross's mommy hurried
by, dragging River, greeting us in her nasal grating voice. "But yesterday," Frannie went on, "Someone stole Heather Neely's quilt . . ."

"No! Stole it?" I faced Frannie as she zipped her snappy red
valise. "That beautiful handmade quilt? One of our best dona-
tions. Oh someone must've just misunderstood the rules, thought
the samples were free or something. No one would 'steal' at — "

"This perfect PC school?" Frannie slung her zipped valise over
her shoulder. "Honey, you've been at Fairwell too long. The quilt
was damn well stolen. These things do happen, my dear — " Here
Frannie gave me her arresting grey gaze. "Even at Fairwell . . ."

All sorts of stuff can happen here at Fairwell, Frannie's level
gaze seemed to say. Something stirred below my stomach.

Sasha Schiller's stay-at-home dad in his scruffy goatee and
hand-knit scarf trooped in with chattering Sasha. I smiled and
called out a reminder of the auction.

Then Frannie and I slipped into the empty art room and unfolded
the silent auction banner from the crammed storage closet.

Together, at the end of our last meeting, we'd stayed late to
paint over the banner's glittery electric-green dollar signs, making
the background for this post-9/11 auction a solid somber dark
green. Both our hands had been stained green.

"Mommy, Mommy — " a voice piped up. "One-last, one-last — "

Veronika, her ponytail flying like a pony mane, bounced into
the art room, illicitly. She wore her usual electric-purple turtleneck
and worn pink Oshkosh overalls. Frannie dropped her end of the

banner, opened her arms. With one of her strong-legged leaps, Veronika sailed up into Frannie's strong-armed embrace.

One last hug. Veronika still wanted one each morning, like Joezy used to want back in his sweet clingy momma's boy days.

"Be brave, Ronnie," Frannie told her girl. Veronika was already bouncing backward from the hug, spinning and speeding off.

"Love those 'one-last' hugs," I murmured. I was still holding up half the banner, remembering not Joezy long ago but Frannie in the deserted dark Fairwell parking lot after our last meeting, last week.

Did Frannie remember too that warm awkwardly long green-stained hug we'd shared? Was she remembering it now, as we edged out of the Art Room? Frannie and I backed down the brick steps into the same gravel parking lot, sunlit now and crowded with cars.

Was Frannie recalling how I'd pulled away from her extended goodbye hug too abruptly, with too tense a laugh?

Frannie led the way to the flagpole, holding the front edge of the banner, leading us past the rows of bumpers, first her own VW Bug and fading RALPH NADER bumper sticker. We shuffle-stepped along.

Battered AL GORE and GREENPEACE and FRIENDS DON'T LET FRIENDS VOTE REPUBLICAN bumper stickers lined our way; some cars also sported month-old American flag decals. A toy-sized American flag — too ragged to be respect-ful — fluttered from one antenna.

"Halt," Frannie in front commanded. We'd reached the school sign, the flagpole towering above us. Only the previous week had Fairwell stopped flying its US flag at half-mast.

I admired Frannie's strong hands as she and I roped the two ends of the banner to the scroll metal legs of the Fairwell School sign. The sky above the sign's rainbow arch was severely blue; the air felt bracingly cold. Our breaths showed and mingled when Frannie strode over to my side of the sign. She tightened all my knots.

" — learned a good knot from my big brothers; always wanted to follow them to Cub Scouts but Mom wouldn't let me." Frannie tugged the frayed rope ends into neat square knots. "Now

Veronika couldn't care less about knots. Can you believe Ronnie's still enthralled by that damn Britney-style Barbie I never should've given in and gotten her . . ."

I made sounds of sympathy, wanting to pat Frannie's solid shoulder but fearing she might misunderstand (Or would it be a misunderstanding, the way my heart was thumping?).

We headed back to the school slowly, elbows brushing. I found myself confiding to Frannie — Frannie listening as always more intently than anyone else listened, lately — how I missed the old uncomplicated closeness between me and Joezy. How he and I used to be inseparable like her and Veronika. Which, I didn't add, had made Dan's frequent consulting-trip absences so much easier.

"And, you know," I slowed further as we reached the brick steps to the school's less-busy side entrance, "for years I loved that, really, I — lived on it. Joezy's mother-love."

I said this last with a laugh, but Frannie didn't flash her usual grin. She stopped at the side entrance. She asked, locking me in her no-nonsense grey-eyed gaze: "So what do you live on now?"

In unspoken agreement, we sat on those cold brick steps.

"Oh, well, it's not that drastic, it's just . . . now that Joezy doesn't so much need me every second anymore . . . I feel I'm just at — loose ends." I raised then lowered my hands. "I've been trying to jumpstart my teaching. But my dance and drumming gig for '02 just got cancelled due to 'temporary lack of funds.' I was going to teach it at the new arts center that's being launched out in Concord. But now all the grant money around is drying up — and no wonder. Who can give anything these days except 9/11 money and blood?"

"Same problem with that other gig?" Frannie asked like she really cared. "The — what did you call it — Songs for Shelters?"

I couldn't help smiling. Only Frannie would actually recall the name of that all-but-defunct dream of mine.

"Exactly the same problem. Same charity-dollar drain. Yeah, see, I'd been so energized by that Songs for Shelters project, been hoping I could help them wrangle more funding. So maybe it could be more than just a part-time summer project. I mean the kids, even the toughest ones, they love it once they realize we really will let them create their own songs, no matter how rowdy — or anyhow I've fought for this, letting them use their own words, uncensored . . ."

"I'd be with you on that fight." Frannie patted my denim knee.

"I know you would," I went on eagerly. "I mean, you'd love how the kids — we do it mainly with grade-schoolers — how they love our typewriters, the old-fashioned clack-clack; how they sit on our laps and talk all at once, once they start talking. How even at the shelter where none of the plugs worked and we couldn't use our electric keyboard, they loved making songs just with the rhythm sticks . . ."

"I know some women who write arts-project grants in Cambridge. I could introduce you . . ."

"That'd be great. Not that anyone can control the money situation right now," I added. But I couldn't stop the hopeful wing beats in my chest. "The Songs thing. It's hard to give up. I haven't felt so excited about a project in years, not since college . . ."

"All the more reason to push it . . ." Frannie patted my knee again, companionably. "Christ, putting up that banner reminds me of my old days at our alma mater. All my old grand causes, ERA rallies — as a kid, I supported the goddamn glorious ERA . . ."

"And glorious Gloria Steinem?" I chimed in. "My girlhood goddess."

"You too? I had a crush on Gloria in grade school; those great aviator glasses!"

Frannie and I laughed, one big cloud of our laughed breaths.

Then I found myself confiding in a rush about my own days at Oberlin. How going to Oberlin — the college with the peace sign in its O, Frannie reminded me — had been my big act of rebellion against my stubbornly old-fashioned Irish Catholic mom and dad. Born-again Reagan Democrats. How gratifyingly shocked they'd been when I'd majored in dance, roomed in the college's vegetarian co-op.

"God, I was just thinking about those days this morning. How I went by a different name back then —"

"Oh yeah?" Frannie squeezed my knee. "Do tell."

Frannie sounded flatteringly interested. So I let myself say it with throaty drama: the sexy name I hadn't spoken in years. "Mara."

"Mmm," Frannie mumbled, "I like that. It suits you, Mara."

Suits the me that you see, I thought, giving a shy chuckle.

"I've been wondering, Mara . . ." Frannie looked down on her own hand on my knee. I stared at that short-nailed all-weather hand too.

I heard a car entering the gravel side lot. Noticing us?

"I've been wondering," Frannie, usually so sure of herself, repeated, "if we could ever — see each other. I mean, outside of this school stuff, the kids. See each other, you know, alone sometime . . . ?"

"See each other?" I managed, my pulse suddenly hammering again in my throat.

Frannie slid her hand from my knee. She rested both her hands on her own squarish knees. Someone was crunching across the lot.

I made myself raise my eyes, meeting Frannie's waiting stare. In the winter sun, her grey eyes shone like opals.

"Listen," Frannie whispered low and slow as the footsteps neared, "If you ever do want to meet, really meet, just the two of us, Mara . . ."

I pulled myself up. "I'm late for, for my class —" I mumbled, though the class I taught at the arts center wasn't 'til much later.

I hurried off past the Fairwell librarian — watchful behind her red sequined glasses — into the blowsy blue. I fumbled in my jacket pocket for my car keys; I slammed myself back into my Volvo.

The sealed windows shut out the crisp fall air. My unstoppable heart hammered. Breathing heavily, feeling trapped in my square shut-up car, I clicked on the engine, pressed the buttons to roll open the window a crack.

I gulped the fresh fall air, jerking the car into gear. A real and dizzying possibility hit me as I backed out. I could crack open, with Frannie, my whole life.

Instead of driving home to prepare for my little Arlington Arts Center class, my sole pay-job, I drove out to Walden Pond and parked. In swimming weather, there were two beaches: the roped-off one with lifeguards and then the wilder more distant shore without.

Trampling dried fallen leaves and brush, I set off for the unguarded unoccupied beach where Frannie had snapped my photo.

In summer both beaches would be teeming. Today the weekday morning dog-walkers were scattered. Someone had planted a forlorn row of American flags along the border of the guarded beach. The plastic flags fluttered halfheartedly in the breeze. I looked behind my shoulder at them, registering the gesture. Yet more red, white, and blue — everywhere these days. I turned away.

I walked a quarter way around the vast still pond on the same twisted rocky path I'd walked with Frannie weeks ago when all the gold leaves were at their peak. Most of those leaves had dropped now, trampled by my boots.

I ducked beneath low-hanging branches, picturing Carolyn back at Oberlin pushing me on the old wood swing hanging from the low-branched oak outside our co-op. I'd confided in her how much I liked Dan Simon's bristly unshaven kisses.

"You can swing both ways, honey," Carolyn had answered, her dirty-blonde hair alight. "Only one way might just take you — further."

Carolyn Zander was the first woman I'd felt real attraction for and Frannie the first who'd made me feel that, and more. I kept walking the pond's edge, my head down. I was so intent on my own stomping feet, I didn't hear Frannie behind me 'til she called out.

"Mara? Hey Mara, wait up — "

I turned. Frannie jogged up the path toward me. Her footfalls thudded, her breaths even. Her face took on high-color in the sun; her black hair crackled with light.

"Did you follow me?" I asked when she caught up to me.

"Guess you could say that," she admitted, not breathless. She halted her run matter-of-factly. "But don't freak out again — " Frannie held up her hands as if to defend herself from weak flustered me. "I'm not a stalker, sweetie. I just wanted to finish our conversation, OK?"

I nodded then ducked my head again like I had somewhere to go. And I kept tramping toward the unguarded deserted stretch of beach.

Frannie fell in step beside me. She offered me a green apple from her backpack. "Look, I get it that I came on too strong back there at the school, caught you off guard . . ."

"No, no," I told Frannie, biting the sweet tart apple, keeping my eyes on my feet. "It — you — listen, I'd seen it coming. I mean, I've enjoyed talking with you so much, arguing with you. I think I've been, I don't know, sending you 'signals' or whatever. See," I found myself adding, crunching my apple, "it's not the first time I've been — you know — attracted to a woman . . ."

We reached the beach, a short rocky stretch of sand mixed with dirt. As we walked up and down that uneven beach, I told Frannie what I'd never even told Dan, not the whole story.

How in the pleasure palace fuck-room I'd made out with Carolyn, who'd kissed me more tenderly than my freshman-year jock-boyfriend Karl. But how the night Carolyn and I finally got naked, I'd felt overwhelmed. Like I somehow didn't know what to do with all her bounteous womanly flesh. Or with my own shocking throbbing desire. Or my reluctance to stroll out of the shadowy fuck-room onto campus as an official lesbian couple, joined at the hip with pushy avid-eyed Carolyn.

Would that quash my chances with a number of guys I had my eye on, including Dan Simon? I'd been scared, confused, and not ready. So I'd pushed Carolyn away, avoided her further advances. But she'd lingered in my mind, unlike Karl. She'd stayed friendly.

"Just don't marry him," Carolyn had warned me in my sophomore year when I began dating Dan Simon. "Married equals 'marred,'" Carolyn decreed as we kneaded bread in the co-op kitchen.

"An' I don't want my Mara marred," she'd finished, touching my cheek, leaving a smear of whole-wheat flour.

"So you think she was right?" Frannie asked me bluntly as I finished my tale. "Hah — I've shot enough damn weddings to know what she means by 'marred.' You think being married all these years, never acting on other attractions, women or men or whatever . . ." Her hand brushed mine. "You think that has 'marred' you, Mara?"

"Oh — 'marred.' That kind of talk's what my mom would call 'melodramatic' . . ." I tossed my apple core into the pond.

"Look Mara, not to be melodramatic, but . . ." Frannie tossed her apple in too, its ripples intersecting mine. Then she faced me. I felt my hair, like hers, vibrate with sunlight. Light yet not heat.

Frannie's hands felt chilled as she took hold of my hands, her fingers still sticky from apple juice. "I'm scaring you, huh? Or maybe you're scaring you? Honey, I don't wanna do that . . ."

She squeezed my cold hands, not quite warming them.

"No — you don't scare me — " I told close-up Frannie in a rush. "I mean you do, but it's not you — you're right that it's me scaring me."

Frannie nodded, her face so close her pupil-filled eyes took up my sight. Her apple breath smelled sweetish, tempting.

"Hey, that's OK," she was telling me in her lowest most husky voice, soothing as a cello. "I know it's a big decision for you, Mara. I don't want to make trouble for you. But y'know sometimes if you're not sure you'll like something, you can just take — a taste — "

I pressed into it, her. Her thin parted lips felt startlingly soft. I sunk against that softness, our tart green-apple tongues mingling, my eyes shutting. Our kiss stretched out, Frannie's tongue not thrusting like Dan's but swimming with mine, lazily.

She was the one to pull back, cut short our kiss.

"I won't push you," she told me, eye-to-eye. "I want you to think about whether you really could give this, give us, a chance . . ."

Can't we just go on kissing? I wanted to say.

But she was the one, this time, to turn heel, walk away from me. Her stride looked easy, unhurried, as she tramped across the dirty gritty Walden Pond sand, back onto the beaten dirt path.

I breathed in to call after her. But I held that breath. I hugged myself in the November wind off the water, the sun bright but its heat faint. I was savoring the green-apple taste of Frannie's kiss.

At the same time I asked myself: was I suffering from some form of post-9/11 hysteria? Post-9/11 plus, in my case, post-biopsy? Hadn't that been when the changes started in me, the restlessness with my safe and narrow life? When I'd impulsively gone to that Oberlin alumni picnic in July. And now wasn't I just like those people in the newspaper articles lately? All the sudden weddings and impulsive idealistic career changes folks had been diving into since the crash. Most of them, the stories implied, risky choices.

But it had been too long since I'd taken any real risk. I hugged myself harder, my hand brushing through layers of cloth under the curve of my left breast, my almost invisible biopsy scar. For whatever combination of reasons, for the first time in years, I felt my old self stirring again. My bolder dancer self, coming back to life.

I whispered the name in the chill breezy air, absurdly happy just to say it aloud. Not Frannie's name but my own.

Mara.

CHAPTER FOUR
YOU HURT

JOEZY ⁄

I wore the same jeans Friday to Fairwell, carrying One's note against my butt. I didn't touch it all day 'til I settled onto the big oval rag-rug for our final circle. Small class size and extra teacher attention and emphasis on arts were Mom's mantra about Fairwell.

Friday meant art circle. We were supposed to be weaving baskets for Harvest Fest: what our school celebrated instead of Halloween, just like Solstice instead of Christmas.

I bent over my lap-sized sketchbook. But I wasn't creating my "artworks" for any freaking Harvest Fest. I gripped my best Mont Blanc pen hard, cross-hatching One's super-shiny super-girl hair.

One lay prone on my page, her graceful girl-sized body curled up, maybe tied-up. My pen scratch-scratched as I sketched in rope — no, chain? Binding her arms, her legs.

"Hey, whatcha doing?" Joo Lee breathed beside me in his trademark undetectable whisper. I gave my one-shouldered shrug.

In all our circles, me and quiet chunky Ryan and Joo Lee sat side-by-side like we did at recess, gathered 'round Joo's Game Boy.

Across from us, Alison J. sat hunched over her basket so her hanging-down almost-un-bra'd breasts filled her U2 t-shirt. Her sleepy out-late head kept nodding off over her scraggly basket.

"Who's that?" Joo persisted in whisper, eyeing my One.

"She's the One," I mumbled back cryptically, half-hiding my page. But only half, cause I was proud of that cartoon, what it captured. The girl-curve of One's cheeks; the woman-curve of her breasts. The jagged black sweep of her hair.

From across the craft circle, Alison J. actually glanced at me. Alison Jester: Alison Jet-Star in the R-rated cartoons I drew in my room late at night. I dared, over my sketchpad, to stare back. Alison smoothed her already smooth butterscotch hair.

I pictured One, her hair. Long and shiny as Alison's, but cut with angled bangs. But black. Jet-Black Jet-Star. That could be One's cartoon name, I decided, bowing again over my tied-up One.

Alison twisted her hair slowly with one finger, reminding us all in pantomime that she was the only one of us getting any. That she and the mohawked ninth-grade rich-boy from snotty BB&N were sneaking off from their shared Arts Alive! Arts Center classes to screw.

Old Alison thought she was still my not-so-secret number one. But maybe Le Ti One could become — soon, for real — my *one*.

"Comin' over?" Joo bent close again, barely making it a question.

Fridays were short days. One truly cool thing about funky Fairwell School with its rooms connected by a school-long painted rainbow: Friday afternoons were set-aside for Teacher Enrichment.

Usually, I'd bike over to Joo's to Game Boy the afternoon away. That's where Mom would assume I was going when I left after lunch.

"Naw, I gotta — see someone."

"Who? 'The one'?" Joo forgot to whisper. He straightened his sliding-down glasses. Too-thick glasses he'd have been teased for at most schools. He folded his skinny but strong violin-player arms, waiting for my answer. Joo always beat me at thumb-wrestling. Even Joo had made-out once, he'd confided to me, on a Youth Orchestra trip. With a red-haired girl who played flute and kissed, Joo said, *super-hard, super-long.* Words I'd jerked off to, some nights.

Joo Lee was the only one I'd shown my Alison Jet-Star cartoons to. He'd have been the logical person for me to tell about One.

"Later, bro," I told him instead in my new TJ mumble.

Then I shut my sketchpad and stood up even before the bell. *It's my turn*, I was thinking, waiting for that damn bell to sound.

My turn to make-out or more. TJ in regular old Arlington High wouldn't be off on Friday afternoon. No way. I turned my back on my way-too-familiar ninth-grade circle. I stuffed my sketchpad in my backpack. The clangy old-fashioned bell sounded, vibrating inside my chest. No, TJ wouldn't be there to act tough, to leave me stranded in a terrorist garage.

He wouldn't be there to horn in on my — One.

I booked my bike down Riverview Road, too fast, heading straight onto Mystic Avenue. I whizzed across a break in the traffic like the super-cool superhero I felt I was fast becoming. *Super-hard, super-long.* Then suddenly I was careening toward boys on skateboards.

"Yo, Pig," one boy hollered. "Where you going?"

I steered away from him, my bike half-tipping.

A horn blared. An SUV nearly clipped my bike. And I glimpsed — in the open garage, holding an armful of clothes — One.

Freeze frame. She stood watching me like she longed to leap onboard my bike and wrap her slim legs around me and escape. Zap; gone! Her black hair undone, blowing around her tensed shoulders. Shit, I was getting hard again.

Super-hard. I veered onto her driveway, pedaling hard, heading straight toward the skateboarder boy hurling himself into my path.

We crashed in midair. He jolted my handlebars.

"Holy shit — " I called as I lost hold and tilted off my bike. The boy was flung backwards into the bushes. I landed on asphalt, on my elbow. I yelped. The boy sprang back up as if made of rubber.

He bounced on his heels, gaping at me. My elbow throbbed. I lay on my side next to my fallen bike, its wheel still spinning.

"RakeenRakeen — " the kid called, like he'd bagged some prey they'd all been after. But he didn't know what to do with it, me.

Boy steps thudded up the driveway. I sat abruptly and snuffled and feared I'd burst into tears, my elbow throbbing *super-hard.*

I swiped at my nose to compose myself as the bigger boys hustled around the bushes.

And I saw, on my palm, blood. Damn; my freaking nose bleed-ing. I raised my face to theirs: four boys. Rakeen from Halloween, the oldest, stepped forward, wearing his grown-up glasses, bending over me. His lean strong-boned face stood out, the most manly.

I heaved myself to my feet. Despite his man-brows and man-gaze, Rakeen was not much taller than me. Blood trickled from my nose. I brushed past Rakeen, stumbling like a wounded bull down their driveway. Heading right toward her.

One had dropped her pile of patterned clothes. All but one. She stepped toward me holding out that crumpled gold and red glittery-threaded cloth, her mouth half open so her big front teeth showed.

"You her, you her," she cried, scolding the boys following behind me. *You hurt*, I thought she was saying. She stopped before me.

She gripped my elbow, her girl-hand strong.

You hurt him. Or maybe, addressed to me: *You are hurt.*

Either way, she sounded pissed, babysitter-mad at everyone's bad manners. Maybe, no matter how young her round face looked, she was a sitter or nanny or something to these wild boys.

The boys, anyhow, had shut up, following us in abashed silence.

She led me into the wide-open garage and seated me on a splintery wood crate marked TANGERINES. She smelled like cigarettes, fresh smoke. The crate creaked, plywood popping.

"I'b OK — " I managed through my blood-choked nose.

"Shh, shh," she soothed like a professional — what? What were they not paying her to be? She shook back her unevenly cut bangs; she sat beside me so her thigh pressed mine.

No girl my age had sat so close to me, not even in Circle.

"Let me," she told me matter-of-factly.

Then she squeezed my nose hard. She bent me forward so the cloth muffled my mouth. So those boys could sneak up behind me?

Dead American, dead American.

Would they chop off my head the way the Afghans were threatening on TV to chop off some US hostage's head?

I bolted upright, bumping her arm. I locked gazes with her, my breath caught. Her bangs hid one eye. She studied me with a one-eyed intensity that made me hold my caught breath.

No girl had ever looked at me that way. Like I was somehow — but how? — hugely important to her, just then.

The boys backed up, maybe ready to shut the garage, lock me in. I had to wrench my head around, force my eyes off One.

"Don't touch that door," I blurted to the dead American boy and his younger skinnier lookalike. "My mom'll call the police, the F-B-I!"

At "FBI," One stood clutching the bloody cloth, looking purely afraid. Looking at me like I could either wreck her or rescue her.

The dead American piped up: "Our father, he is a Saudi Prince! Your FBI, you cannot touch him! He, he —"

Rakeen shot this eager-eyed clear-voiced kid a look like: Shut up.

Turning unsteadily, I stumbled toward the still-open door. Rakeen muttered as I passed, "Let him go cry to his mommy . . ."

I swiped at thickening blood from my nose, angry at my own teary eyes. I stalked into the garage doorway.

She, One, was the one to follow, on light feet. In the doorway she halted like she didn't dare step further. Rakeen was admonishing the younger boys, mixing in Arab-sounding words.

"Help," One breathed to me, the word a smoky mini-cloud in the chill air. She shot an anxious glance toward Rakeen, who shook his head at his brother's low-voiced arguments, his back to us.

"No moany," she added under her breath. *Moany?*

"I'll help you," I dared whisper, silent Joo-style, just as Rakeen stopped talking. "I'll come back — next Friday . . ."

"Sank —" One reached out with her cold-fingered hands. Her cigarette breath held, like mine.

Just for a second, One clasped my hand.

Man, One. What that did to me: your touch.

"Hey — what is going on?" Rakeen demanded over the heady hammering of my heart. "You get inside of here, One."

Rakeen strode toward us, his bony shoulders squared and his princely head held high. "You leave her be, Pig-Boy —"

Behind his Clark Kent glasses, Rakeen's gaze moved from her to my dumbstruck face. Was he about to erupt into Superman? I backed out of the garage. My braces showing, my lips slack.

"What is Pig asking you, One? To get dirty for his dirty dollars?"

She turned with brisk dignity. She shook her head firmly at Rakeen. A babysitter shake.

Then, her face hidden again by those cool jagged bangs, she brushed past Rakeen, past his watching brothers, into the house.

I spun around. I hurtled up the driveway, amazed not to be chased. Maybe Rakeen was somehow scared of me too, of what I might know? What One might tell me? I fumbled in the bushes for my bike. I knew what she'd meant by *moany*. "Money."

No money.

My bike seat rubbed my crotch as I pedaled faster than ever across Mystic Avenue, snuffling blood. "To get dirty for his dirty dollars?" Rakeen had asked so strangely.

Like One was — God, what was she? Why was she so afraid?

Back up Riverview Road I pedaled to my house. To my bedroom where I re-read One's note. Her plea for help; for my help. Me: her rescuer-to-be. I pictured One leaping on my bike, pressing up behind me, clutching me. I pictured me speeding us down Mystic, me pulling to the side of the road, behind more bushes.

I'd first kiss her: gently, so her big teeth and my braces wouldn't bump. Then I'd kiss harder, 'til my cock got harder. *Super-hard, super-long.* I couldn't stop myself, my overloaded mind, my over-due body. Lying on my bed, picturing her strong girl hands doing a hand-job on me, her soft girl lips doing a blow-job, I jerked off.

Harder than I'd ever been before.

⸺

I didn't tell the FBI. I didn't tell Mom though she asked me, Saturday morning as she made me blueberry pancakes, what was on my mind. Though she looked kinda hurt, saying as I wolfed down the pancakes that I never confided in her anymore. I halfway wanted to blurt it all out to Mom as I carried my sticky syrupy plate to the sink. But I ran hot water hard, rinsed the plate squeaky clean.

I kinda did tell TJ. But only part of it, and not by choice.

He was out biking on Sunday afternoon with a pack of other boys. His gaze barely flashed on me as we passed on Mystic Avenue, but he slowed and let the others speed on ahead. I biked

by him with a nervous nod and he fell in pace beside my bike, his
voice fake-casual.

"So what-all happened, Joe, that day?"

You mean the day you ran out on me? I didn't say.

"You mean the day in the garage?" I asked back, my voice
bumping with my bike.

"Um, yeah." For once it was TJ who sounded tense, uncool.

"I — " I slowed my bike, gliding under overhanging trees, turning to TJ's unsmiling profile. My old desire to impress him flared
up, and I found myself saying: "I met this girl in there, a little older
than us — not part of that family, but some kind of babysitter or
something. Anyway, she, this girl — she told me she needs, like,
help . . ."

"Needs help, huh?" TJ side glanced at me, his voice edgy. "Some
older girl? That what you so worked up about? What: you think if
you give her help she's gonna — give you some?"

He gave those words a mocking sing-song. Like he himself was
getting some. Like everyone was getting some except me.

"No — shit no." I gripped my handlebars. Hearing TJ say it out
loud made it way too real, what I'd been secretly thinking.

"OK, OK — don't get your freakin' panties in a knot," TJ muttered, easing ahead of me. Sounding smug in his usual jock way.

"Y'mean like *you* got yours in a knot when you left me there
alone and ran off scared?" I blurted out to TJ's broad strong back.

"Fuck you," TJ answered, speeding up without bothering to
look back. He stared straight ahead in his skull-and-bone helmet,
his muscular neck stiffened. Maybe TJ, with his mask of acne, was
used to being taunted. But hadn't he just taunted me first?

"Hey, TJ — ?" I called out behind him, braking my bike. He
pedaled on and I stayed stopped on my toes 'til he was out of sight.

Because I was the one. That's what I reminded myself when I
finally pedaled on, alone. I was the one Le Ti One chose. She was
right, I felt sure just then, to trust her note to me. Me alone.

The only other person I told, or came close to telling, was Alison.

I waylaid her on the overcast Fairwell playground on Monday.
I shuffled over and leaned beside her under the bare branches of

what had been, in our grade school days, our climbing tree. Like I've said, we were like freaking brothers and sisters at that school.

"Hey Alison," I began, low-voiced enough that she halted her hand. She'd been reaching into her suede jacket for her cell phone.

"What's up, Joezy?" She glanced at me with maybe actual interest, her butterscotch hair shimmery even without sun. Alison always called me Joezy and Joo Jooey. Like we were two of a kind: a pair of nerdy boys, worthless and harmless.

"Something," I shrugged, bigger-shouldered in my denim jacket. "Something's up. See, well . . ." I took a breath, knowing recess was about to end. "There's this girl, really almost a woman, who I — like."

"Older, huh?" unflappable Alison asked without a blink of her blue-mascaraed lashes. Interest flickered in her zoned-out blue-green eyes. I could practically see myself growing in those eyes.

I heaved another shrug. "A little, I think."

"Perfect, Joezy." Alison leaned close so her chill silky hair brushed my cheek. She lowered her voice like I'd blurted out everything I felt for One. Like it was clear what I was after with One. "Yeah. Lose it to someone a little older, someone you trust . . ."

I was the one to pull back, to blink. My lips stiffened over my braces. I managed a brusque nod before turning to hide my hot face.

Our harsh old-timey school bell was ringing, thank God.

And someone who trusts you, I added to myself. I plodded back toward the school with the rest of the class. *Someone who has to trust you*, I corrected myself uneasily, ducking in the big doors. *Someone who has no one else.*

In study hall, I drew a whole multi-framed cartoon saga about her. One: embedded inside one of my trademark pen and ink maze extravaganzas. One chained up in a gothic garage; long-haired One crouched on her knees before shaggy-haired me.

You will do as I say, I imagined that blackly-inked me saying. All low-voiced and knowing, like Alison Jester.

"Ooh," the real Alison breathed over my shoulder. She'd stopped by my desk, bending close so I could smell the faint famous clove cigarettes on her breath. "You going Goth or something, Joezy?"

"Or something," I answered Alison in a cool deadpan tone I

couldn't have carried off a week before. I didn't even cover it up, my Goth-maze slave-girl cartoon. The best fucking One I'd done.

All day Tuesday and Wednesday, I filled my sketchpads and my head with dramatic black-and-white images. Me carrying One out of that house; the two of us whizzing off together on my bike.

At the same time, with the thinking part of my brain, I was convincing myself I needed to talk to Le Ti One, really talk. What was the set-up in that house? Why did she work there yet have no money? I'd get her whole story, all the facts. Then I truly would find One help. She would be, naturally, grateful to me for life. MUCH, she had promised in block-print. ALL KINDNESS MUCH I PAY BACK.

Of course, I knew she didn't mean "pay back" in the ways I was way wrong to imagine. It wouldn't be like that. It would be like: me helping her out and her falling in love with me, her hero. Maybe everyone, maybe even Dad, would admire me afterwards.

Wednesday before dinner, I damn near told Dad.

He was still home, his New York trip postponed again. He was in his new post-9/11 Good Dad mode. We were playing self-conscious football catch on our cool fast-darkening lawn.

As we tossed the ball, as Dad asked me what I'd been up to, I found myself saying I'd been thinking about those Halloween kids, the ones Mom and I called Terrorist Trick-or-Treaters.

"You worried about them?" Dad tossed me the ball too gently. "Scared they really are terrorists, son?"

Dad's "son" came out stagey. I shrugged, annoyed. I tossed the football back extra hard, while Dad was smoothing his beard. He scrambled to catch it. Then he looked, really looked, at me. His dark eyes lighting up with something. Concern, suspicion.

"Are you scared of them," he asked me, "those folks in that house?"

Dad hurled the ball. When it smacked my palm, I pictured One's breast filling my cupped hand, fitting like it was meant to be.

"Nope," I lied as I threw the ball back.

CHAPTER FIVE
BUT I'M NOT LIKE THAT

MAURA

On our way to Whole Foods on Wednesday evening, Joezy and I spotted the FBI guy. A dark-suited man seated in an ordinary old-fashioned Ford Sedan, parked on Riverview Road, facing Mystic Avenue. Facing the home of those Terrorist Trick-or-Treaters I had reported (should I have done that at all?) to the Arlington police. And now, had those police, as they'd threatened (no, promised), contacted the actual FBI?

"I'm tellin' you, Mom," Joezy insisted as I made a self-consciously slow turn onto Mystic Avenue in the gathering post-dinner dark, "that same exact guy in that same freaking old-fogey car was sitting there after school—and he was still there when Dad and I were out playing catch. I swear; it's gotta be the freaking feds."

"Good God," I muttered, hunching over the wheel as we sped past the house itself, "Surely they wouldn't send federal agents out here just from my one little phone call? I heard those boys pulled that same Terrorist-and-dead-American stunt on the Lindsays down the hill . . . but I'm not sure that Mary did call the police; with those boys of hers running wild—really, they're as crazy with their bikes on this hill as the Terrorist-boys are with their skateboards—Mary might've meant to call the cops too but just plain forgot . . ."

"So what if it was your call? C'mon Mom, this isn't all about you . . ." Joezy nudged me with his elbow, his teasing tone for once mild, companionable. What's more, while he usually chose to sprawl out in the cluttered back seat with his sketchbooks and headphones, as if I were his chauffeur, this evening he'd chosen to sit beside me.

Somehow he had looked a little spooked after playing ball with Dan on the lawn. He'd barely eaten his spinach lasagna. And he'd spontaneously offered to come with me to Whole Foods.

Then he'd moved my music and movement box to the backseat himself and settled beside me up front.

"I can't believe your dad—craving matzo bread and chocolate sauce," I offered, companionable too. "Guess we're really going to 'do up' Hanukkah this year. And y'know, Joezy . . ."

"Yeah, I know, I know," Joezy whined, jiggling his knee furiously. Chill November night air whistled through the passenger-side window. With one finger, Joezy was opening then closing it, just a crack.

"You do know," I made myself go on in mom mode, "You could've been a little more open to Dad's Bar Mitzvah idea. He really does want to look into it and you really could get a lot out of it . . ."

Joezy pressed the window button shut abruptly. "I told Dad I'd think it over and all. It's just kinda—weird. Him going all Jewish-Dad on us, after all these years of him telling me how lucky I am not to be going to Hebrew lessons and wearing the little beanie and all that crap—Dad's word; Dad's word!—His parents pushed him into . . ."

Joezy's knee was jiggling so fast I wanted to reach over and stop it, still it. But then I'd risk him never sitting beside me again.

"What's up with Dad? I mean, I know everyone in, like, the whole US is freaking out and all lately—but what's up with both you guys?"

I steered carefully through the last intersection, glad Joezy in the dark car couldn't see my face heat up. But he did sense it, the extra tension in me. And in Dan too. *Well, I think your dad might've cheated on me, on us,* I couldn't of course say to Joezy. But I couldn't stop the words in my head as I hesitated, flipping my turn signal on sooner than needed, letting its tick fill our pause. *I think after 9/11 your dad maybe fell off the fidelity wagon and now he's guilty; he's been sensing me pulling away and he's been right.*

"Look Joezy, I can't speak for your dad—but you said it yourself.

Everyone's freaking out these days, in their own ways. I know I'm — on edge. You too — isn't that so? I mean ever since Halloween, I've felt just — something. Something is up with you . . ."

"Maybe," Joezy mumbled, and he stopped jiggling his knee like he might even tell me. I slowed the car hopefully, held my breath.

But Joezy reached for the radio dial, snapped on NPR: a faint news voice reporting from Afghanistan, US bombs whistling like the icy wind outside in the background. I pulled into the Whole Foods lot, sighing, hesitating to push Joezy. Because he might push me back? Might demand to know my own secret distraction, these days?

A foolish selfish thought, I scolded myself as Joezy and I trudged toward the warm greenly-lit supermarket. And it was surely equally foolish to imagine that Dan wanting to play catch with Joezy before dinner or wanting chocolate-dipped matzo bread as a treat was some sign that he was overcompensating, was guilty. I had no proof. Wasn't I projecting all that onto him? Me, who'd kissed Frannie?

Joezy and I stepped in under the giant hanging globe labeled WHOLE KIDS on one side and on the other, WHOLE PEOPLE.

"I always worry that damn globe'll fall and crush us."

"Yeah," Joezy agreed flatly. "'Whole People' to 'Crushed People.'"

I grinned and pushed our cart extra fast past the shiny stacked apples — Gala apples, organic Granny Smith, conventional Granny Smith — recalling the tart green-apple taste of Frannie's kiss. Since then, I hadn't answered (but hadn't deleted) Frannie's email asking me over for coffee at her apartment near school. The message itself was innocuous — as if Dan (fat chance) might check my e-mails.

"Oh Joezy." I halted our cart and drew a deep breath of freshly sprayed fruits. Determined to put aside bad thoughts, buy my family some good healthy foods. Reassure my son like a good mom. "Everything is so crazy these days, honey, but it'll all settle down . . ."

Joezy gave his one-shouldered twitch of a shrug. Then — and who could blame him? — he turned away from me and my falsely soothing words. He shuffled off to the tall glass Fruit-of-the-Week juicer sampling machine, bubbling today with something scarlet.

My face felt hot again as I watched Joezy go — a premature hot flash? Or just more burning embarrassment that I'd let down my son? I'd let the moment of connection in the car, the moment when he might really have confided in me, pass. No matter how much good food I bought, how could I call myself, lately, a good mother?

I rolled past the alarmingly named hydroponic tomatoes toward mounds of organic Vermont-grown grapes. I needed a giant-size bunch to bring as snacks for the final silent auction committee meeting on Friday. The next time I'd see Frannie, unless she showed up at the auction item set-up tomorrow afternoon?

She'd told me she might have to work that Thursday afternoon, might not be there. But would she? I reached for a bulging bag of green grapes. That's when I caught sight of them — or, first, of the woman's headscarf. She swept past me and the grapes in floor-length robe-like attire, her hair covered by a patterned scarf. Behind her, pushing her cart, was her tall Terrorist Trick-or-Treater son.

"Yook, MuhMuh — " a piercingly clear kid-voice commanded. Not my own son but a sturdy bulldog-faced three- or four-year-old, perched in his cart, banging his cowboy-booted heels against its metal. The kid scowled and pointed at the robed woman and her son, looking like he wished he had a toy gun to aim at them. His mild-faced mom held a finger to her lips, looking like she wished she could clap her hand over the kid's mouth. "Yook! Yook a' dat Yady — "

Other shoppers too had noticed. A graying professorial guy made a point of smiling and nodding, a gesture the robed woman ignored. Imperiously indifferent, she led her son through the fresh-daily produce with her own gaze downcast. But the tall boy — wearing old-fashioned dark-rimmed glasses — kept his head high. As he pushed the cart, he darted his gaze around like a bodyguard's. And I could feel around me a collective intake of breath, a collective attempt to repress unspoken thoughts.

I was still standing by the grapes when the robed lady unexpectedly turned heel. She led her stoic son into a U-turn around a huge bin of dusty yams, heading back toward the fruit, toward me.

One tight-lipped older woman steered her cart of grain-free cat food pointedly away, out of their path. A mustached man plainly glowered as he tracked the pair. He stood before the white asparagus folding his muscular arms as if defending America itself.

But I'm not like that, I wanted to call out to this woman, this neighbor. She swept past me again, this time close enough that I caught a whiff of expensively sweet body oils. I glimpsed a strong-boned profile, a mole above a mouth lipsticked into a regal near-sneer. But her gaze was still downcast, fixed on a list neatly folded in her hand. It was the boy, that tallest Trick-or-Treater. He was the one who looked, as he pushed his mother's cart past, straight at me.

Behind his glasses, his eyes fixed on my face briefly but keenly. As if to say: *I know you. I know what you did.*

I'm sorry, I found myself wanting to bleat as he passed. *Sorry about the FBI agent in the sedan, watching your house. Sorry about all us skittish middle-class Whole Food shoppers, watching you now.*

But I said nothing, my face stiffened like a face in a police lineup. The boy plodded on, following his mother toward gaily displayed tangerines. A girl emerged from the aisles, her arms loaded with several packages of pita bread from the Whole Foods bakery.

The girl was slim and young and Asian, her black hair cut in slanted bangs. She halted before the robed mother, holding out the bread as if for approval. The woman nodded her scarved head. The young girl gave her own nod, slower, like a bow.

She pivoted on her heel and deftly slipped around the mother to that tall boy who had stopped the family cart. He helped her load the bread in. They were a team, these three. Maybe they were shopping as quickly as possible; maybe anxious to get back to their riverfront house, away from all our subtle and not-so-subtle stares.

Turning away determinedly, wondering who that teenage girl was and how she fit in with that family, I grabbed the big bag of green grapes. I started to swing the bulbous plastic bag into my cart.

But the strained bag was too full and only half sealed; its mouth slit open midair. Half the fat grapes spilled out, one clump plopping on my feet. Individual grapes bounced and rolled.

"Sorry, sorry," I blurted out, to no one. And I saw the black-haired boy start to turn his head, to look my way again. But I bent away from his gaze as if ducking an attacker.

I crouched down to gather the grapes, flushed and flustered. Why wasn't Joezy stepping back over from the juicer to help me? Had he seen — he must have seen — that family too? Was he hiding behind the bubbling juicer, ignoring his bumbling mother?

Surely I was overreacting yet again. That trick-or-treating boy couldn't know it was me — surely it hadn't only been me — who'd called the police. Of course that teenage boy was not singling me out, not waiting for me to rise now so he could — what?

Don't be ridiculous, I told myself. Then I pulled myself up, balancing my half-filled grape bag. Setting the bag in my cart, I glanced over toward the tangerines. I saw the robed mother pointing now toward mangos and bananas. The Asian girl scurried off in that direction, the same corner as the red-bubbling juicer.

But my son — I peered over at the juicer, its table littered by empty paper sample cups — my son was nowhere in sight.

JOEZY

She likes mangos, like me. Cool.

Cool, Cool, Cool, I thought when I first spotted One. I was standing by the Fruit-of-the-Week juicer. Was it really her? I gulped down my teeny paper cup of cranberry-or-raspberry-whatever, cool on my tongue. Taking in, from my corner, One's shiny-dark hair.

One's graceful, kinda-shy walk. Her for sure.

Then — after my way-un-cool mom dropped all her grapes, all freaked out by seeing Rakeen — I ducked behind the juicer. One passed by so close I saw her freaking tongue. A pink flash.

Because, see, when One passed the juicer, she glanced at that juice, those little cups, like she wanted to stop and try some. But then Queen Mother — across the aisle in her flowy robe-dress — made a motion with her hand like: hurry up. Like: no way.

That's when One licked her chapped lips — one tongue-flash — and kept going. So I imagined One's tongue, cool against my tongue.

So I crumpled my empty paper cup. I grabbed another full dentist-office-size cup. I ducked low, crept from behind the juicer, ducked behind more green leafy bins so my un-cool mom wouldn't see. Wouldn't call out in her embarrassing-loud teacher voice, calling me away from supposed danger, away from One.

One walking so graceful-quick, her small but round butt moving so nice inside her sweatpants. No underpants lines showing, like her smooth cool butt inside those sweats was naked.

Then she slowed again, looked kinda longing-like at the mangos. Cool, I thought from behind the bananas, clutching my mini-cup. A nice cool slice of mango; that's what One must be craving. But I bet Queen Bitch Mom won't let her buy any.

Mmm, I was practically saying behind those green-yellow bananas. And I was watching One touch a mango. Just this light little touch. Stroking super-smooth mango skin.

Man, those mangos looked swollen. Like the bananas, like my cock, its stiffness hidden — I hoped — 'cause I was crouching.

"One — ," Queen Bitch Mom called, sharp and too-loud. Just that one word, but it was clear she meant: Move it. Now.

One startled from her mini mango-trance. She nodded over her shoulder, like yeah yeah; I hear you already. And when she looked over her shoulder like that, I got a good view of her breast curves under her zipped jacket. Was it possible she wasn't wearing a bra? No bra, no panties. Just One's super-cool super-smooth skin?

I made my move. Willing my cock to unstiffen, I inched around the bin just as One passed by the conventional bananas. She was stepping around that bin too, toward the far side where the organic bananas resided, maybe just to be out of Queen Bitch Mom's sight.

So I slipped around after her. One paused and lifted a conventional banana bunch, kinda slow and dreamy, like she didn't want to head back to the robed mom. One looked around her at everything but me — at the high ceilings, the real-looking wood pillars with fakey-vines growing up them, the giant WHOLE KIDS/ WHOLE PEOPLE globe. She stared like everything was brand new to her.

Like she didn't — of course she didn't — get out much.

As she hugged the banana bunch to her chest, I stepped right in front of her. I held out my cup of juice. Bright red; a liquid jewel.

"Want some?" I asked Le Ti One in a you-know-who-I-am whisper.

One blinked at me, her chapped-lipped mouth half opening so those big teeth showed. She shook back her slanted fallen bangs. Her black eyes sparked; she knew me, all right.

And she startled me by shoving her banana bunch at me. She snatched that juice, cat-fast. Suddenly I was holding all those bananas and she was lifting that cup to her lips, maybe politely dying of thirst. She gulped the cranberry juice down fast, like someone might take it from her. And someone might, any second. I held my breath, clutching One's damn bananas.

The banana tips stuck out at One. Below the banana-bunch, inside my jeans, my hidden hard-on stuck out too, at her.

"I will help you," I whispered to One as she swallowed. She sucked down the last of the juice; she licked the red remains from her soft-looking chapped lips. She patted her lips with her fingertips, looked at the faint red stain. Then at me. My nose.

"You—you nose—" She touched her own nose. "—OK?"

"My nose? After bleeding? My nose is great, yeah; it's great . . ."

And One nodded, facing me with her drained cup in her hand. I was facing her with the crazy bouquet of bananas I held between us.

One stared into my face—not just my nose but my whole freaking face—like no one ever stared. I sealed my lips over my braces. She took in my pale freckled face like it was, I was, special. Like I'd materialized here as Superman, ready to sweep her away.

"I'll come by the house," I told her, low-voiced in case the frizzy-haired shopper behind One was somehow listening. "I will; I'll—I'll come and see you Friday—"

One nodded at me super-hard, repeating, "Yes-yes. Fly-day."

Fly Day. That killed me. Like I really was Superman. Like One and me really would fly away together, Friday.

"Yeah, Fly-day. I'll be there." Clumsily, I shoved the bananas back into One's arms. I took hold of her drained crumpled cup, the paper cup her lips had touched, sucked.

I crumpled it harder and slipped that cup into my denim jacket pocket. One was still staring up at me. I liked how she was so much shorter than me. I could lift her, carry her away right now.

Away from that freaking embarrassing bitchy mom ordering her around; away from my freaking embarrassing mom crawling around on the floor after spilled grapes.

One giggled like she saw all that too, inside her head. Like she heard every freaking thing I was thinking, inside mine. So I smiled my metal-mouth smile because I couldn't not smile back, her smile was so toothy and beamy. All for me, One's smile.

"One — One — ?" the Queen-Bitch called, closer now.

One gave me her half-nod half-bow, her bangs hiding her eyes. And she fled with her bananas, me watching her go. Her quick steps; her shiny ponytail flickering in the overhead lights then gone.

Then I did something I can't explain. Heading back toward my mom, I grabbed a smooth-skinned mango from the organic mango pile. I slipped it like a miniature football under my denim jacket. I held that mango lightly under my arm.

I kept it in place, hidden by my jacket, as I followed Mom through the store. I shook my head no when she asked me if I'd seen "that family." I wanted it to be a secret, like the mango.

Even in the check-out line, I kept the mango hidden in my biggest jacket pocket. And I followed Mom like a shadowy stalker out into the cold damp lot. Mom loaded the car with our bags; I pushed our cart back toward the store, my mango still straining my pocket.

That's when I glimpsed from halfway across the lot the van: the Jiluwi family's van! Sometimes I'd seen them loading the old guy in the wheelchair into that van. I slowed, catching another glimpse of her. One.

Lit by one of the parking lot lights, she was leaning out the open van's side door. In the darkened front seat, the mother sat facing the wheel. Rakeen stepped from behind the van with a bulging Whole Foods bag. He handed the bag to One, who set it beside her.

Then — I froze, peering across that lot — Rakeen more stealthily slipped One a second much smaller bag: a plastic bag from the CVS

Drugstore beside Whole Foods. This bag One quick-slipped into her sweatpants pocket. Hiding it in that pocket like I'd hid the mango.

Drugs? Birth control pills? I stared hard as One ducked her head back into the van, as Rakeen turned to his empty cart. Pushing that cart back toward the store, like me, he spotted me.

My heart bumped. I whipped my head sideways and rattled my own cart toward the store. Hearing Rakeen's cart rattle in close behind me. Christ; was he chasing me? I U-turned my cart, ready to bolt back toward my mom's car.

And my rattling cart collided, bumper-car style, with his. We both halted, confronting each other beside the dark otherwise deserted shopping cart stand. Rakeen glared at me through his shiny Clark Kent glasses.

"What do you think that you are doing?" he demanded of me.

I stared back at him across our two empty carts, that damn mango hidden in my jacket. Had this all-seeing boy seen me steal it?

"You stay far away from her, from One. You are hearing me?"

So maybe he'd seen her talking to me in the store.

"What — " I managed to ask back, TJ tough. "She your girlfriend?"

"No, and it is not of your business," Rakeen snapped, clanking my cart with his. Bumping me; actually losing his cool. "Nothing of my, my family — it is not of your business — you are hearing this?"

Another metal-on-metal clank, my cart handle ramming me, making me stagger back a step. But I steadied myself and managed a TJ-style shrug. I turned away from glaring Rakeen. I felt him still watching me, like I was his freaking rival or something. Was I?

What the hell was going on between him and One? I felt a kind of power as he stood there watching, as I shuffled back across the lot with my stolen mango in my pocket. Her mango.

I'd give it to her on Friday, along with as much money as I could muster. I vowed this to myself as I sat safely strapped beside Mom in our Volvo, heading home. Mom drove silently, seeming distracted too. Mom's wipers pulsed, scraping ice pellets. *I stole it for you,* I told One in my mind. I never stole anything before. I never did anything like this before. I never felt anything like this before.

CHAPTER SIX
WHAT'S IT WORTH?

MAURA

"What's it worth?" Frannie demanded. "What do you think?"

I blinked up at her, laying down my Sharpie magic marker. I couldn't keep writing suggested first bid tags and ignoring Frannie, not when Frannie had crossed the Fairwell gym to stand in front of me, holding a garishly painted wood mask over her face. Not when Frannie, as she'd loudly mentioned, had rearranged her work schedule so she could sort auction items. So she could see me.

And here Frannie stood before me, lowering the tacky mask, grinning.

"Not much," I murmured more coolly than I meant. Maybe this mask was a joke of Frannie's I wasn't getting. Maybe I ought to laugh, laugh it all off, including her Walden Pond kiss? Had any of it been truly serious?

"Not much for this wanna-be-warrior? You don't like the trying-to-be-tribal motif?" Frannie set the mask onto the table between us with a hollow wood clunk. "It's done by Judy Rothman's artsy-fartsy aunt. No artist of color ever touched this wood."

"And why should they? C'mon now, Frannie. This is like you saying I shouldn't be teaching white kids to dance to African drumming—"

"I never said that, exactly. You oughta come over sometime for coffee, so we can hash it all out . . ." Frannie tried to meet my eyes.

Twice now, Frannie had e-mailed me suggesting we meet for coffee. At her place, while both our kids were at school. But I hadn't answered—or really I hadn't sent any of the answers I'd composed then deleted. Some saying a tentative yes, some an emphatic no.

"Ten bucks," I blurted out to the blank-eyed mask.

"Sold," Frannie told me lightly. "To the sexy redhead mom," she added in that low husky voice I felt I could listen to forever.

"It's just not my kind of — face." I straightened the bid tags I'd just printed, annoyed at my own flustered timidity. "I like a face I can look in the eye," I added, rallying a grin.

Frannie flashed her own playful grin, her opal eyes aglow. "Me too, Mara."

Then we were pricing first bids side by side, our elbows brushing. There was no mistaking the pulse in my throat. And no mistaking, really, that kiss Frannie had given me; and the looks she gave me now. Wasn't that, in fact, worth a lot: someone who studied me with such unabashed interest, who hung on my small talk?

Other mothers bustled around us; at the next table, River Sienna-Ross's mom held forth in favor of a vegan lunch option and against the proposed cash-only pay-bar at the auction. Beside me, Frannie rolled her eyes. Only for me. I couldn't help half-smiling back.

Low-voiced, Frannie asked me about the African drumming concert I'd organized at Fairwell last year, before she was here. I told her how Joezy — back when he and I still did creative projects together, back before he started hiding his cartoons from me — had painted the drums with intricate maze designs. How I'd used those same drums last summer for the rap songs the shelter kids wrote.

"I'll tell you one song kids of all colors sang with equal gusto," I added to Frannie, half wanting to start a quarrel. "The big song they all wrote together: 'If I Be Rich.' All about having a house with six cars and six garages and extra beds so they could have sleepovers . . ."

"'If I Be Rich'? That's what you had those kids writing?" Frannie asked me disapprovingly as she stacked my bid tags.

"I thought you said you'd be with me on letting them write what they want?" I seized the stack of Sharpie-scented tags from her.

We argued our way across the gym. It felt good to argue good-naturedly, the way Dan and I used to. Lately, since September, we'd avoided talking politics, except for the hot-button late-night-news issue of legal rights for terrorism suspects. Maybe I halfway agreed with Dan, who had brushed aside the very notion with a dismissive hand wave. Agreed, but still resented his brusque gesture.

"I saw Dan's name signed up to haul big items," Frannie mentioned when we reached the archway. She glanced behind her as if expecting an attack. "Is he hiding out here somewhere?"

She'd never met him. I kept my own voice low, even.

"Well, he was off to Providence today. Then tomorrow, supposedly, he'll finally go to New York for this big meeting that keeps getting postponed. His first time in the city since — the crash. But he's hoping, we're both hoping, he'll be back by Saturday . . ."

"He's away an awful lot, isn't he?" Frannie set her tags on the main table. I looked down at mine, the top tag still blank.

"Not really," I lied. "But he does work hard, works long hours. He, Dan — he works his butt off for Joezy and me."

This part was true. I stated it with conviction.

"And he gives you — a good life," Frannie added, even-toned. I nodded, marking my top tag, my Sharpie squeaking as I pressed too hard. "And that's — ," Frannie pushed on, "And that's all? And that's why you won't meet for coffee?"

"And that's a hell of a lot to give," I snapped, my marker skidding again. "And yes, Dan is why I won't meet you for coffee."

"So what's it worth?" a slurry voice demanded. Sheila Jester — recently single mom of femme fatale Alison — swept toward us from across the gym, wielding that damn mask. Sheila's new boob-job bounced under her FAIRWELL: LOVING LEARNING t-shirt.

She halted with a final breast-bounce at our table. "Have you two artistes conferred and determined the worth of this rare artifact?"

Sheila sounded slurrily drunk — though surely she wasn't on a Thursday afternoon. Rumor had it her new lover was a college kid; maybe she was drunk on love, on all she was learning of loving.

"We're going with a suggested bid of ten bucks," I announced, uneasy with the way Sheila was looking from Frannie to me. I edged away from Frannie, stepped out from behind the main table.

I stood before frankly staring Sheila with her surprised-looking maybe face-lifted face. No lines in sight. The old Sheila, only not.

"Y'know, Sheila, Dan felt so bad that he couldn't come today; consulting trip, and all. Think I'll go out and haul some 'big items,' in Dan's name . . ." I turned heel on both Sheila and Frannie.

What's it worth, what's it worth? The words pulsed inside me as if I was the one who was Thursday-afternoon tipsy. *A good life, a good life.* I strode through the school's front hall into the half-emptied after-hours parking lot. *If I be rich, if I be rich.*

Joezy was shooting desultory baskets down in the playground.

I gave him a wave he didn't see. Then I approached the open U-Haul that some less-busy Fairwell dad had rented for delivery of our auction's bulkiest items. From its trailer, I lifted a heavy antique mirror. I carried it carefully inside the school, my tensed face wavering, magically aged by the thick yellowed glass.

Not so remarkable a face; a fortyish wife-and-mom face, bonier than ever, darkly freckled and lightly lined. I set down the mirror with care. Who but Frannie saw me, these days, as special?

I straightened, pushed back my springy hair, my pride. Lately I'd sensed my hair losing some of its dense curl, its rich reddish brown. I'd been ashamed of how panicky it made me feel.

So who was I to think free-living Sheila Jester shallow? To push away a strong successful independent woman like Frannie?

"Hey now, Mara." Frannie materialized at my side. I'd known — I'd liked knowing — she'd be back beside me soon. She lowered her voice again, the way I liked it. "Listen, I didn't mean any criticism of, of Dan. I've never even met the guy. I'm just so — curious, Mara, about — " She touched my arm lightly. "You."

"But why?" I burst out, shaking my head in mock-exasperation.

Frannie shrugged, then told me straightforwardly, in that voice pitched only for me: "I like the way you — move."

I flushed; I couldn't stifle a pleased close-lipped smile. "Well, I like the way you — talk," I told Frannie, my voice as low as hers.

"Not that I ever agree with what you say . . ." I averted my eyes from her steady sparkly gaze. Was anyone watching us now?

"Well those are all good reasons, don't ya think, Mara?"

"Maybe 'good' isn't the word," I managed, clumsily shifting the subject. "Y'know how Oberlin College graduates are supposed to 'do good,' not 'do well'? Well, Dan's 'done well' for an Obie. It's up to me to do good, to try to. Not that I have in any way that — matters."

"And you want to 'matter,' don't you Mara?" Frannie asked so intently that I had to look up. Yes, I thought as I nodded.

"I want to matter, sure. To — someone." I whispered those words softly, but Frannie nodded hard. Listening to me like no one else did.

"You sure matter to me, Mara."

"You've got to stop calling me that —" I mumbled, trying to rally a joking tone. "God, if you keep it up, I'll come to the auction with big hair and Vogue with you onstage and scare all the kids . . ."

"You promise that, Material Girl?" Frannie slung her arm around my shoulders, gave me a warm hard squeeze. "Say you will," she whispered to me. "You'll dance with me in front of everyone . . ."

"I — don't think Fairwell's ready for that." I gave an uneasy smile. "I mean come on, Frannie, you act like I'm not married or 'marred' or whatever you call it . . ." I felt her warm solid body stiffen up.

"You're right." Abruptly, Frannie released her hold on me, stepping back. "You're seriously right and I'm seriously late. I've gotta get back to the shop." She announced this last in a flatter voice.

"The shop?" I asked, suddenly not wanting her to leave.

"My shop." For the first time, Frannie sounded a bit impatient with me. "I changed my schedule all around so I could — well, talk to you in person. But I'm feeling like it's not worth losing a whole afternoon. See, I work for a living, remember?"

With that, with her confident take-it-or-leave-it stride, Frannie headed toward the exit, leaving me reeling by the ornately framed mirror. I hugged myself, steadying myself after the harshness of her words, the warmth and strength of her touch.

How natural it had felt, to lean against her for that moment. But what had Frannie just said, implied? That she worked for a living and that despite my part-time teaching I did something different for mine?

I turned on my heel, almost bumped into perpetually startled-looking Sheila Jester. How close had she been standing? Had she overheard our whole exchange? Her new face was unreadable.

"Listen Sheila, I've got to—make a call." And I stalked away, burst out the school's front doors, back into the cold afternoon.

Frannie's distinctive lime-green VW was just putt-putting out of the lot. I ducked and headed for my rectangular tank of a Volvo, moving fast as if I was being chased. She liked the way I moved. But she hated—what? Where was I going? I slipped my hand in my wool skirt pocket and fished out my cell, speed-dialed Dan.

I got his machine. "Hope Providence is OK, Dan the Man. Stay safe on that train. We'll try that chocolate-dipped matzo this weekend, OK? And let me know soon as you know about Saturday, OK?"

I clicked off, shoved the phone back in my pocket. I climbed into my car's front seat, slammed the door and just sat there, trying to catch my breath. Wishing I had a paper bag to breathe into. Fearing I might, as I hadn't done in years, hyperventilate. One of the reasons I'd quit dancing: because I'd get light-headed and breathless onstage, in performance. One time I almost fainted. I stopped mid-dance-step, swaying. And Dan bounded from his front-row seat onto the stage; he led me, gently, off.

I slumped forward in my driver's seat to get my head low, as Dan had advised me in the stage wings. I rested my head in my arms, hunched over the steering wheel, hoping that the dad hauling big items into the school wouldn't notice me.

Sure, I guess I can handle it, young earnest Dan had told me, somewhat shakily, when I'd confessed to him a half-truth about Carolyn. Telling him I'd kissed her once, but not that we'd made out repeatedly, not that we'd stripped down and almost gone all the way. "Long as you stay on the straight and narrow from now on . . . ," Dan had told me, pulling me close. I had nodded; it had sounded easy at the time. I had pulled away from him and smiled. Flipping back my extravagantly permed mass of hair; feeling I was pulling off a successful impersonation of the bold free spirit I wanted to be.

Later, I'd fret over breaking up; I'd worry that smart, steady, history-major track-star Dan the Man wasn't the one for me. And Dan would worry I'd go back to *that girl*. Any girl. He'd skulk around rehearsal halls when my graceful dreadlocked friend Corrie and I choreographed our shows. He attended every one of Corrie's and my troupe's dance concerts. From his stage side seat, Dan led every standing ovation we ever received.

Then after graduation Dan became my excuse to turn down Corrie's offer to move to New York with her and live for six months in the hotel where Sid killed Nancy and try to make a go of our troupe.

Once Dan and I were ensconced in Boston in our studio apartment near BU — living together, to the dismay of both our obligingly disapproving old-fashioned parents; Dan studying for his MBA and me for my Music Education Masters — Dan came to view my lesbian co-op experiment like he viewed my dancing: something wild I'd tried out in college and outgrown.

"You were just experimenting," he'd said to me more than once. "And that's OK. That's what I liked about you, how you jumped up onstage and gave it your all; how you were such an — adventurer."

As for Dan, he seemed satisfied to have acted out his own modest rebellion against his parents simply by having gone to Oberlin instead of Brandeis. By having married Bohemian Irish-Catholic me.

After grad school, Dan clipped his kinky Dylan-esque mass of hair, bought himself a HIPPIE WITH A HAIRCUT t-shirt and a closetful of tweedy suits. He supported hard-nosed Clinton while I longed for soulful Cuomo. He started hinting that I should stop babying Joezy. He listened with sometimes barely disguised impatience to my defensive, sometimes rambling, spaced-out-mommy replies.

And sometimes I felt, maybe unfairly, that the only reminder of Dan's college self was his daily run — which dropped to weekly in recent years — and his prized Bob Dylan collection, including a second never-opened copy of *Dylan Live,* the poster still folded up inside.

Dylan and his psychedelic-colored Jewish-boy afro; like the retro-afro Dan sported at Oberlin.

Dan had tacked the Dylan poster from his original *Dylan Live* album above his boyhood bed in the '70s, longing to be just like Dylan when he grew up. Or just like Dylan 'til he grew out of it.

That second pristine Dylan poster still resided in its plastic-wrapped cardboard album cover in Dan's collection. Just as, somewhere inside the busy successful Dan of today, I imagined his longer-haired more romantic Oberlin College self still lurked.

And still (or was I imagining this, too?) loved me. At least, Dan loved Joezy and me, his family. And he still occasionally lusted after me, my body, despite my own midlife lessening of interest. Or I told Dan it was midlife, premature pre-menopause. Then this past summer, after the mini-trauma of my breast biopsy, I held Dan off for weeks, my greenish half-breast bruise slow to heal.

An excuse, Dan accused me one hot July night. I was using my bruised breast as an excuse to avoid sex. True, I realized guiltily even as I protested that it wasn't.

This was shortly after that Oberlin Alumni picnic where I'd met Frannie. Then came 9/11 and everything went upside down and Dan's trip to Philly and that strange phone call from the other wife who thought Dan and her husband had — well, she never said exactly what she thought the men had gotten into while stranded in Philly. And I'd never called her back. Half afraid to hear it put in words; that Dan might actually have cheated on me. And half caught up in my own — what would it be called, what I had going on with Frannie?

"Hey Mom — Mom!" Joezy called faintly. Was he, even from long distance, reading my mind? I startled from my daze, raising my head, squinting through the windshield. How long had I been in this car?

Joezy ran up to the driver's door, his Nike sneakers thumping. He gripped a FAIRWELL-stamped basketball under his arm. He was panting in his zipped denim jacket, looking red-faced with cold. He glared at me through the sealed Volvo window.

"What're you doing in there?" he called accusingly through the glass. "What—were you gonna drive off and leave me here?"

I shook my head at his angry anxious reddened face.

"No, no, of course not!" I fumbled to open the driver's door; I gazed up at my son, trying to hide how far away I'd been. "No, listen, I just came out here for a second to, to—gather my thoughts . . ."

"*What* thoughts? What's up with you, Mom?" Joezy threw down the basketball, let it bounce wildly off across the lot. He screwed up his face in exaggerated disbelief like Dan did when annoyed by my spacing out. Only more so; Joezy's oversized anger was stiffening his whole tall body. I should be asking him that, I knew. What was up with him? He climbed in the back seat, flinging himself onto it.

"Well if we're gonna go early, let's go," Joezy commanded.

"Don't you want to play more ball?"

"No way; there's just a bunch of twitty sixth graders over there . . ."

"Well, I really was just resting out here. I wasn't going anywhere, believe me. But if you're ready to leave now . . ." I groped in my purse for my keys, suddenly needing to get away from Fairwell too. Needing to get back to my home, mine and Dan's.

Resentfully, as I gripped my keys, I recalled Frannie confiding to me when she'd taken my photo that her longest-term relationship had lasted four years. So what did she know about the work that went into a long-term marriage like Dan's and mine? Plus part-time teaching and full-time raising Joezy. Not that I'd done a great job on any of that, lately. Not that I wasn't damn lucky not to be a single mom like Frannie. Especially since my teaching prospects for next year had dried up and I hadn't found new ones. And Joezy was clearly preoccupied by I had no idea what. God, would I actually have driven off in a naval-gazing daze without my boy today?

"What's up with you, Joezy?" I asked as I revved our engine. "I really want to know. Something going on—at school?"

"Nothing is going on at school," Joezy muttered behind me, sounding as if this at least was true.

"So something — else?" I probed clumsily, steering backwards.

"Just forget it. Forget me. That's what you almost did do, right?"

"Oh c'mon Mister Melodrama," I teased, using Dan's not-so-joking nickname for Joezy. "I'd never forget you — you know that."

Joezy allowed me one neutral grunt. He was still, despite his recent surliness, my boy. And I never can forget him, I reminded myself as I pulled out of the Fairwell lot. Never can forget how much trouble in a marriage can cost a kid. Look at Alison Jester. She'd been a sweet grade-school girl; after the divorce, both Sheila and Alison went — if Fairwell gossip was to be believed — wild.

I pressed the gas as if to outrace my own relentless thoughts. Joezy had always been so close to me. He still was, really. If I dared to go wild myself, who knew what Joezy might do.

CHAPTER SEVEN
ONE

JOEZY

I stole the money for One—filched, I told myself—from freaking Maid Pro. The Maid Pros cleaned our house every other week. Friday afternoons, when I was usually over at Joo's.

Mom always left the maids a big guilty-conscience thirty-buck tip. I'd thought of stealing it before: when I spent my birthday checks too fast on too many art supplies, when I begged Dad to reconsider about allowance. I actually did have my first-ever job lined up, but my paper route wasn't scheduled to start 'til mid-November.

So Friday afternoon, one week after my nosebleed, I told my spacier-than-ever mom I was heading for Joo's. She was heading out too, for some auction meeting or whatever.

Mom was dressed up subtle-like, like me. Not in fancy clothes, but in her best everyday. I mean, along with a new black skirt and her favorite old orange-brown sweater, she was wearing what I knew to be her favorite scarf, the one I'd given her last Christmas/Hanukkah. Dark green with orangey flecks.

"I still say it's crazy to auction me off," she was telling our phone in secret-pleased tones of disapproval. "Who'd pay that much for a photo of me? Even a photo done by you . . ."

Jeez. I shook my head. Not that Mom saw. She was pacing circles with the kitchen phone cradled under her chin. Her new friend Frannie Who's-it was a wedding-type photographer, big deal.

Using Mom as a model; maybe reminding Mom of those black-and-white college photos of her in her long-red-hair black-leotard dance troupe days? Photos I'd picture sometimes when I beat off, back when I was just a horny boy with no place real to go.

These past two days, I'd slip my — soon to be One's — mango out of my sock drawer. Not ripe yet, this taut green mango. I'd hold it and stroke its super-smooth skin and picture handing it, like I was about to do, to One. Then my cock would grow taut too.

I stomped upstairs to change my t-shirt to solid black. I slipped the mango into my biggest jacket pocket. I stalled, last to leave. Mom left first in her fluttery scarf, holding her Whole Foods grapes, giving me a backwards wave. I slipped the Maid Pro envelope in the smaller pocket of my denim jacket. My heart thudded double-time. My mango pocket strained.

I pedaled off into sunlit cold. I'd avoided biking past One's house the last few days. See, I didn't want to cross paths again with TJ. I'd been smart to tell One that I'd come Friday, while TJ was still stuck in school. I didn't want TJ's dirty mind taking over my story.

Story of how I'd (this part was still fuzzy) rescue Le Ti One.

Since Whole Foods, I had filled my sketchpads and my head with badass black-and-white images. Me punching out Rakeen and carrying One out of his house, me and One feeding each other drippy golden slices of mango, me and One whizzing off on my bike. But with the thinking part of my brain, I was convincing myself I first needed to talk to One, really talk. Get her whole story, all the facts.

Then I'd somehow find her help. Make her happy and safe and grateful to me for life. I'd be a hero for real, at least to her. This girl or woman who only I knew about. Who was my secret, my One.

Was she Rakeen's secret too? Was that why he'd acted so crazy-jealous at Whole Foods? Was she — like homeless teenage girls I'd seen on CNN — a sex slave in that house? Rakeen's sex slave?

I hid my bike in the bushes. And I heard boy voices — damn, shouldn't they be in school? I peeked through the branches. Rasha and the skinnier younger Jiluwi were goofing around by the garage door on their skateboards. Rasha doing wheelies. The littler brother snapping photos of him with a yellow cardboard camera like you buy at Walgreens.

Then a voice — Rakeen? — called them into the house. Should I beat it, because the boys were there? But weren't they always there?

Feeling watched by every shaded window in her house, I stepped toward the Terrorist Cell's closed garage. And I glimpsed One's head inside there. A faint rapping: her fist on the garage door window. So she'd remembered I was coming today. She'd watched for me.

I squinted into the garage window. Her hand pointed me around to the back of the house. Then — emphatically — her hand pointed up.

I scurried around the side of the house; I faced a tall wood fence. Had One signaled me to scale it? Could I scale it? I climbed into the low branches of a nearby tree, my mango pocket sagging. Stretching, I grabbed at the splintery fence top. I heaved myself over, dangled, fell onto the ground. The tall grass. A back yard, on the other side.

I pulled myself up, patting my mango. Glad I hadn't landed on it.

The tall fence enclosed a smallish overgrown yard. The fence blocked what would have been a direct view of the Mystic River. An odd fence because there was no gate, no opening.

I ducked down, pushing apart dry knee-high grass, even taller than the grass out front. An American GI in 'Nam, trudging through a rice field after the Vietnamese girl he will — what?

Rescue, I reminded my bowed-over tensed-up self.

And I heard a door open. An inset basement door, half belowground. One stood in the brightly lit doorway, motioning me closer.

I scrambled to her, down overgrown concrete steps. Past a giant coffee can with Arabic lettering, filled by sand and cigarette butts. One held open that lowest level door for me. I stepped inside like she was my doorman, squinting in fluorescent bright light.

A freaking rec room? In the Terrorist Cell?

Or, anyhow: a carpeted basement half filled with a ping-pong table and carelessly stacked skateboards, boy bikes. One fished a cigarette and matches from her sweatpants pocket. She stayed put in the open doorway, whispering to me: "Mistress Jiluwi hear door — " One nodded at the door she'd just held open. "Must see smoke."

Leaning in that doorway in a practiced way, One lit up. She drew a slow drag, her throat curved. And she blew a big stream of smoke out into chill air. I stood just inside the room.

"So you mean: you're allowed to open the door to — to smoke?"

"Smoke only." One inhaled again, exhaled a bigger cloud. "Mistress hear door. She watch — window, from up . . ."

One rolled her eyes to the ceiling. Companionably, she held out the cigarette. I put it to my own lips, barely inhaled. My throat tickled. I held the smoky cigarette back out to One.

But she was watching a plane: its light tracing a lone line across grey November sky. One watched hard, like she too was waiting for the plane to dip suddenly, dive-bomb toward Boston.

"Did you see — on TV — the, um, planes? Crashing the towers?"

If they only let her outside into her fenced yard to smoke, maybe they never let her watch TV. But One nodded, sucking more smoke, exhaling more slowly. "We watch. Day only. Together . . ."

"You and — the family?"

She nodded again, her black bangs stirring in the breeze. Clearly she could speak and understand — more than write — English. I was here, I reminded myself, to get her story.

"How, how'd you meet this family? The — what did you say? — Jiluwis? Did they, you know, hire you or what — ?"

One shook her head, sending her next smoke stream out sideways through her flexible mouth. "Hospital, Saigon — Mama there. She meet Prince, he sick, meet Mistress Jiluwi . . ."

"Your Mom was sick too?"

"More no." One drew a deep drag. "Mama sick. More no . . ."

"She — died?" I asked awkwardly. One nodded hard.

She blew slow smoke. And she asked me, facing the fenced yard, the hidden water: "What mean, 'Mystic River'?"

"Mystic? It means, y'know, mysterious. Like: of another world . . ."

One nodded again. "I also am. Of — other world . . ."

"Yeah," I breathed, admiring her super-shiny hair, so much finer than mine. Wanting to keep her talking. To keep listening to her soft but certain voice. "So your mom was sick — was dying . . ."

"She find Jiluwi family, Muslim family. She and Madame Jiluwi, they are talk. They say I am work them. They tell Mama they take me — America . . ." One shivered in her sweatshirt in the doorway.

"You — cold?" I asked. She snuffled, shrugged, let out a drag.

"Cold — all ways. Here; land of — cold . . ."

"Land of cold?" I gave a short laugh. A sly close-mouthed smile curved One's chapped lips. "It's supposed to be 'land of the free' . . ."

"Ha," said One shortly, drawing a last drag. She gestured to the top of her open door: a big bolt lock on its outside. "They lock night; Mistress Jiluwi watch day. No me, no free."

One tossed her butt into the jumbo coffee can. Then she heaved shut the basement door, sealing us in the rec room together. From the floor above, I heard the sound of televised explosions. Those boys. And maybe Rakeen too. Playing hooky?

"So you aren't, we aren't — " I glanced up. "Alone?"

One shook her head hard at my dopey question. "No-no," she told me. "All-the-time. They watch. Old man, doctor's now. But boys . . ." She rolled her eyes. "They school-skip. Mistress let. Rakeen bring home. Lunch here and — they stay, today . . ."

And Rakeen, I wanted to ask, what else does he bring home? What was he giving you so secret-like in the Whole Foods lot?

More muffled explosions and screams and sirens.

A Terrorist Cell, TJ and I had decided. With no proof except for the boys' Halloween stunt. Would real terrorists be so stupid, so conspicuous? Was there something way different going on here? *Was* this girl some kind of sex slave? I faced One in the harsh rec room light. She wore a faded blank sweatshirt, but clean, ironed-looking. The outline of her bra showed; her breasts poked out at me.

"Saw you — in at store." She pushed back her bangs. Pink acne dotted her forehead. Her round face looked coarser skinned than in my fantasies. Her angled bangs fell back into place, over one eye.

"Whole Foods, yeah," I filled in. Her visible eye and her clean hair shone. Her mouth looked ready to give me another smile.

So I pulled out my mango. Still green and whole. I held it out to her. And — like magic, like at Whole Foods — her smile split her face. Her big teeth showed, her eyes holding for a second a softer light.

"I — I saw you looking at those mangos at, at the store and . . ."
And I stole this for you, I didn't have the guts to say.

One gave her nod like a bow. She took the fruit, her fingertips brushing my hand. Then, in a carefully polite near-whisper, with a flicker of disappointment in her eyes: "Sank you. That — it?"

She was cradling my mango below her breasts.

"'It'? No-no; no listen, I brought more. Brought — moany."

Accidentally I said the word like her. She nodded gravely. Then she nodded at a shut door behind the ping-pong table. A secret storage room? Where the family kept their anthrax and bombs?

"See-see," she demanded of me, stepping over to that door, cradling my mango now under one arm. She opened the door.

"W-what? See what?" I edged around the ping pong table. Telling myself of course there were no bombs. "This — is where you live?"

One nodded. We stood together at the doorway to a small cinderblock-walled room, a mattress (one of the jumped-upon mattresses) on the floor. Sheets were flung back at the foot of the mattress. Was this where jealous Rakeen had his way with her?

Tacked to the wall above the mattress: a piece of silk printed with a purple dragonfly shape. Clothes were folded in a cardboard box under the room's half-oval half-underground window.

A spider suddenly dangled down from the doorframe, on invisible silk. One made a neat chopping motion, breaking its thread.

"Wish have — lizard," she muttered to the fallen spider. Either dead or playing dead. She gripped her mango again in both hands, gently.

"Lizard?" I asked, not sure I'd heard right.

One giggled. An ordinary girl-sounding giggle. She turned toward me in the doorway. Looking up at me, only inches from me.

"Gec-kos," she told me, smoke-breathed, eyeing me through her bangs. "Mama's apartment, Saigon? Geckos, they — bug-eat."

"And you, you liked them, those geckos? You — ?"

"Play!" She handed me my mango; she wiggled her fingers under her shell-like ears. "Bite — no hurt! — ears. They hang like, like — "

"Earrings?" I guessed. She actually laughed, then hid her buck teeth with her hand. But I liked her teeth, her big toothy smile.

"Yes-yes; earring!" One reached up. She fluttered her fingers under my ears, butterfly-brushing my earlobes.

God, what was happening here? I grinned down at her, close-lipped to hide my braces. I squeezed that smooth-skinned mango between both my hands. "Hey, I could buy you a pet gecko, at Petco," I blurted out, my face all hot.

"You — 'buy me' — ?" One sounded confused, maybe scared. I handed the mango back to her fast, pushed it into her hands.

"I just meant as a present, like the mango. For your — room . . ."

"Room is my," One told me, not laughing now. She edged into the room, set the mango carefully into the cardboard box of clothes.

"Your room. And they, the family — " I still stood by the doorway, scared to step closer. "They make you, um, clean their house?"

"All." One stepped back over to me. "All they make me — work-house. Clean-house. Muslim family, you see?" She folded her arms, facing me so she was blocking my way.

She wanted me to understand this before she'd let me closer: "Muslim. Mama know — Mama right, this — they not-touch not-Muslim girl. Not-Muslim girl not clean, to they. They not-touch . . ."

Touch her? As in have sex with her?

"So the men, the boys," I was somehow saying to One, somehow sounding calm. "They never — touch you."

She nodded hard, like I'd finally gotten the point. But could I believe her claim? Any more than I believed Mr. Hamal at school when he preached to us about how non-violent real Muslims are?

Still, I nodded like I believed that, yeah, Mr. Terrorist Trick-or-Treater never laid a hand on her. One stepped back, making room for me. Cautiously, I took one step forward.

"What most-matter, Mama say. Family not touch. Family give job. Family take me Land of Free." One gave another knowing close-lipped smile. "Mama know not — family not — pay. No pay, no to me . . ."

"To someone else?" I felt in my pocket for my Maid Pro money.

"No pay. No can — tell," she added, confusing me. But she pushed on: "No give visa. Hide my visa. Say I here — not-legal."

"But they can't do that," I told One eagerly, bending closer. "They're the ones who're — not legal. They can't keep a visa from you, if you've got one. I'm pretty sure of that. And I know they can't make you work without pay. They can't hold you here . . ."

"Hold?" She hugged her arms, stiffening like I might grab her.

"Look," I told her, wanting to calm her. "I said I'd help you . . ."

I tugged out the Maid Pro money, held it up to her. One took the bills from me, fingered them. She looked at me through her bangs, disappointment flickering again in her all-black seen-it-all eyes.

"Sank," she murmured. But I felt it was her heart that had sunk.

"S-sorry, maybe you wanted, I mean I know you want — more?"

"More." She nodded hard and inched closer so we stood toe-to-toe. I smelled her fresh smoke. She shook back her bangs and drew a breath like she was gathering courage. Then she nodded again. "Yes-yes. You give more, if, if — you want more?"

If I want more? What was she saying, this girl? This almost-grown-up woman, this maybe-sex-slave facing me in this bedroom?

"No, no, I mean yes," I stammered, starting to stiffen up all over, including in my jeans. Wishing TJ was here with me. No, wishing I was a jock like TJ, a muscleman jock any girl would want.

But — I swallowed, pressing my lips in a manly line over my braces — was it possible One wanted me? Me, not just more moany.

I want moany, I thought. I blurted: "I mean I don't have more. Not with me, right now. First I want to, um, know more. About you, I mean. Are you, like, a h-hostage? Should I, like, call someone for you; call, um — the FBI?"

"No-no —" One blurted back, echoing me. "FBI — send me back . . ."

She's even more scared than me, I thought as she brushed by me. Then, surprising me, she shut her room door.

God, were we locked in? She flicked on the light fast. Like she didn't want me getting any (too late on that) ideas. She shook her head at me, sternly. "No-no FBI! No-no; listen: what want you?"

I shook my head, in over my head. Did she think I was threatening her? "It's OK, look, I won't call the FBI, OK? I don't even know how to call the FBI, OK?" I stepped closer to her again.

With the door shut, I felt the chill of her little room. Without
thinking, I took hold of her arms, thin but hard-muscled under
her sweatshirt.

She didn't pull back. She just lowered her eyes behind her bangs.

"You help? You — pay?" She whispered. Eyes still low, like she
was ashamed of what she was saying, doing.

"Yeah, I — I promise I'll help you," I told One, quiet too. Holding her arms tighter to keep my hands from shaking. "But no,
I'm not, like, giving you — pay. See? Not pay. Just, if you want,
um — " I was suddenly saying, I don't know why, " — play. We
can, y'know — play."

Play? Like with her old lizards? God, had I really said that,
holding this girl's, this woman's arms? One still didn't raise her
eyes. Still ashamed. And I felt she could see or sense, at my zipped
crotch, my hard-on. She gave a brief uncertain laugh like a cough.

"Play," One repeated. "You want?" she repeated too, though I
had meant to be asking her. She raised her eyes, looking as confused as me. Her lips sealed scared-tight.

"You want?" I asked, my voice shakier than hers. But my grip on
her stayed firm, like I knew what I was doing. "I mean, I want to
if you do. I mean — How, how old are you?"

"Eighteen," she answered so fast it must've been a lie.

Might've been something she'd been trained to say. By Rakeen,
if she really was some underage sex slave, made to have make-
believe-legal sex. So I should let go; I should go.

She was looking down again, was snuffling. I snuffled too, my
nose slightly runny in the basement chill. I thought of bending and
kissing One but I hesitated, tasting the metal of my braces. I wanted
to tell her I was fifteen, even though I still wore fucking braces.

"I — " she began again. She drew a big breath like now she'd tell
me what I'd supposedly come for. What was going on here; what I
could do to help her, free her. But she stopped.

"I sank you," she repeated instead in an odd stiff voice, bowing
her head. She slid downward, out of my grasp. She knelt before
me, just like in my drawings. She faced my stirred-up crotch.

Man, my cock jumped at that. So stiff so fast.

She was mumbling straight to my crotch. "Sank you, you help. Want you — we play?"

Her hands: so steady she must have done this before. She was no dumb virgin like me. Maybe she was eighteen. Maybe she did want to play, like me? Did she, could she, like me?

No, I knew I should say. But my head on its own jerked a nod.

Then her quick hands: unzipping my jeans. God, was this real? I held myself stock still, frozen. Should I help her, stop her? I couldn't hear anything but my heavy breaths. Like I might hyperventilate, like I used to.

I was so hard, as her fingers freed me, I moaned.

Moany; she wanted only the moany. She was desperate for moany. I could see that in her tensed-up neck. I was telling myself that inside my head. But my head was just nodding and nodding.

"Yeah," I mumbled. Then I gasped as One roughly tugged my jeans down around my knees. So I was bound at the knees; so I couldn't leave this room.

Tock, tock, tock.

She bent forward. Her hair brushed my balls. Her tongue flicked against my penis. Against me. Lights flashed on inside me; I squeezed shut my eyes. I sucked in my breath to moan again. Tock.

But tock, tock stopped me.

A freaking ping-pong ball? Those boys down from upstairs? Tock tock. Boys playing ping-pong right outside One's door?

One must hear it too, I thought in blurred panic. I blinked. Stop, I started to say. But I looked down to see One's shiny-haired head go lower, closer.

Her cushy-lipped smooth-tongued mouth surrounded me. Me, me. All of me engulfed in hot moist pressure. All of me funneled into the hardness she sucked. "God," I moaned, clenching my teeth.

She sucked me harder. *Super-hard, super-long.* The tocks had stopped; everything stopped. Pleasure and pressure gripped me, my fullness about to burst. The door cracked open.

And her mouth opened, releasing me. Strings of warmed spit. I jolted as she pulled away; I cried out in protest and staggered sideways. Blinking and reeling, still hard.

Rakeen in mad flashing glasses charged into the doorway. He waved a ping-pong paddle in one hand and something yellow in the other.

"What has Pig done to you?" He demanded of One. And he pointed, sweeping his paddle toward me. One gaped at him, at me.

I bumped the mattress, falling. I landed on my bare ass on her mattress. Then I grabbed handfuls of sheet to cover me, my poking-out penis. Dumb American about to be killed.

"Pig-Boy —" Rakeen turned his fury on me. He stepped to the edge of the mattress wielding the ping pong paddle. "You have defiled her, Pig-Boy!" He whacked my face.

Smack against my cheek: a blow that popped my eyes out. So I barely saw, stinging, what else he held. That yellow cardboard mini-camera his brothers had been playing with. Christ, had those kids spotted me? "I warned you, Pig-Boy; I took a photograph — Pig-Boy, I caught a photograph of you and her and — what you do to her —"

Caught, I was thinking in frozen smack-faced fear. *He caught me.* Rakeen stuffed the yellow camera in his jeans pocket. Fast; everything just then happening fast. Behind Rakeen in the doorway, the smallest brother — thank God, the smallest one — hovered.

"Izrin, you will go to get Rasha." Rakeen turned to the scared-looking moon-faced boy. Before he turned back, I pulled myself to my feet. I yanked my pants up.

One still knelt on the floor, regarding Rakeen and me with blank-faced shock. Her body quivered like she might hop up and flee.

"Him?" Rakeen jeered, straight at her. Like he'd warned her too about me; like they'd discussed me. "What is it you have told to him?"

She shook her head, teary-eyed, looking as confused as me. But was she? Was she in on this somehow? "No-thing, no-thing of — Uncle," One murmured. Rakeen gave a curt nod. Uncle? Her uncle?

"She is ours and we never defile her, Pig," Rakeen turned back to lecture me. He waved that paddle at my stinging smacked face. "Pig, I will tell your mommy. I will show her . . ."

He patted his shirt pocket, the small square bulge of his brother's camera. He and I glared at each other, breathing hard.

"Don't," I pleaded with a stupid squeak in my voice.

"You get — for me — much money, Pig," Rakeen told me. Beside him on the floor, One kept staring up at him. Rapt and dumbstruck, his audience. Like she couldn't believe, either, what he was saying so smoothly. Or did she know what he would say? But then why had he asked her so angrily what she'd told me?

"You hear, Pig? You got money, your daddy got it. You bring — a thousand dollars here, by weekend. For me and — One. Then you may have the camera, the film inside. You may have it all." He patted his pocket again, making sure that camera was there. "Or else I — I will show your mother what you are. Such a dirty greedy pig . . ."

I shook my head hard, my stomach churning. My throat tightened like I might throw up. I had to get out of that room.

I bulled past Rakeen, not looking back at One. Taking advantage of the emptied doorway, I lunged into it and charged across the rec room. Rasha came rushing down the basement's carpeted steps. I recognized in one side-glance his skinny body and rounded eyes.

He ogled me, that boy from Halloween. And he gave a warrior cry. He hurtled toward me like he'd be the one to kill me.

But I seized the doorknob. Bastard boy — I felt sure he had spotted me, told Rakeen I was sneaking in the house. He'd given Rakeen that fucking camera. I thrust open the basement door; I ran into the cold day, the tall dead grass, all still there.

God, God, I thought as I ran through the grass to the fence. This time, fueled by fear, I seized the splintery top of the fence on my first leap. I hoisted myself up, scrambled down.

Stumbling, panting, I plunged through the front lawn, up the driveway. Someone shouted behind me.

I mounted my bike, my pants still unzipped. I pedaled faster and wobblier than ever before. *For me and One, me and One.*

Was Rakeen her boyfriend? Her protector, her pimp?

The bike seat rubbed my damp-crotched briefs. I gripped my handlebars, hearing in my mind Mom's voice. The question she used to call to me whenever I came out of the bathroom, 'til I told her I was too old for her to ask that.

"All clean?" she'd singsong to her boy. "Are you all clean?"

———

Man, I was scared. I'd never been so scared, never been hit hard like Rakeen hit me with the damn paddle. Who knew what else he might do? This boy with the face of a man. This boy who'd dressed up as a terrorist; who hated me like no one had ever hated me.

I'd never, really, been scared at all.

A thousand dollars, I kept repeating to myself as I pedaled up and down Mystic Avenue. How could I get one thousand dollars? How could I get One out of that house? What had Rakeen meant, money for him and One? How could I even consider getting that bully one thousand dollars? Surely he wouldn't share it with One, his hostage.

His sex slave?

Of course I had no proof. Of course she'd denied it; she'd said they never touched her. Even though she did say they held her in that house. And if today had been some set-up, would those brothers have been right out in front of the house goofing around with the camera Rakeen was going to use? No, I sensed when I finally biked back up Riverview Road.

The brothers had spotted me on their own, had told Rakeen; he'd taken their little camera. One hadn't known. Right?

Home in my own clean and emptied house, shivering from my bike ride, I took a long shower, my penis raw and pink. Despite the steamy heat, I couldn't stop my shakes, questions raining down.

If I somehow gave Rakeen the money, would he really give me the freaking cardboard camera, film undeveloped? Was there really a clear incriminating picture of us? How old was One, really? Would Rakeen somehow show that photo to Mom, tell Mom what I'd done?

And what had I done? What would Mom say?

That I'd taken advantage of a poor desperate girl who might be — for weeks I'd known she might be — in real trouble.

I clenched shut my eyes under the stream, guilty tears welling up. Or maybe just scared-little-boy tears. Wouldn't I be in real trouble too, shouldn't I be, because I'd known about One and told nobody? Known and tried to (when I'd told her I wouldn't) buy her?

But the camera, I thought. Just a drugstore camera. If Rakeen had planned it, he'd have used digital. With this cheapo camera, if Rakeen really did give me it, if I destroyed it all, I'd be safe, right?

Safe, at least, from anyone finding out what I'd done. Then maybe I could still do the right thing. Tell the FBI, tell at least Dad?

My face felt sore where the paddle had hit. When I rubbed a steamy circle in the bathroom mirror, a reddish bruise showed. I hid up in my room, paralyzed, listening as Mom arrived home, Dad too. Supposedly, he'd leave early tomorrow, Saturday, for New York.

I felt tentative relief, hearing Dad still here. Maybe I could get advice from him, without him knowing.

When I crept downstairs, Dad was watching CNN in the cramped back room where Mom made us hide our TV. Dad's Stairmaster creaked. I paced our living room, hearing the muffled news voices talking anthrax and Afghanistan. Then Mom's clearer live voice calling into Dad to "turn all that off," to come and eat.

Mom was big on all of us eating together lately. She and Dad were trying, since September, to make me feel safe. *It's not just my measly life,* I reminded myself, bee-lining toward the kitchen. *The whole country's freaking out.*

As he stepped in behind me, Dad told Mom that he'd looked into the train schedules. He'd try to take an early-afternoon train back for Mom's silent auction thingy.

"Really? You'll do that?" Mom asked, giving him a hug before we all sat down. It felt good, to see them hug. She was right; we had to stick together. "Oh Joezy," Mom exclaimed, tipsy-sounding. "What's that on your face? How on earth did you bruise yourself?"

"Just — fell on my bike. No biggy." I shrugged Mom's question off, the three of us crowded round the kitchen table. But I found myself shaking over Mom's vegetarian chili. My fork rattled on my plate and I finally set it down, feeling Mom and Dad both watch.

"Joezy, please talk to us. What's wrong? Have you been in a — fight?" Mom leaned forward, still wearing her orange sweater but not the scarf. Her hair shone, clean and brushed.

At his end of the table, Dad blinked over his beer, maybe startled from his buzz. He wiped his beard. He looked, really looked, at me.

"Yeah. Something wrong, Joezy? You seem like you're all — " Dad gave the next words a rock n' roll sing-song. "*All Shook Up* . . ."

His hopeful joking tone; he didn't like to get too serious, like me. I swallowed my chili, half wanting to blurt it all out.

"I, um. I saw — saw those boys skateboarding round that, that strange house today. Almost ran into one of 'em . . ."

"Is that how you fell off your bike?" Mom asked, half rising in her seat. As if she'd march over and confront those boys.

"No, no, that happened later; I — did it to myself."

"Oh, Joezy. Those boys." Mom sipped her wine. "The way that oldest boy looked at me — I told you, Dan — when Joezy and I were shopping the other night. You haven't spoken to them, have you, Joezy? Tell me: are those boys bothering you?"

She set down her glass, her lips gleaming from the wine.

"Not to worry, Mom." I gulped my milk. "Those boys are just acting as crazy as ever, is all. I mean it must suck to be Arab right around now. Plus — plus I heard that those guys, they go around telling kids at Arlington High that they're some kinda royal family." I turned to Dad. "You think that old wheelchair guy really is a prince?"

Dad swallowed, considered. He wiped his beard with his napkin, slow like he sensed something was up. But he answered in his usual steady way; he was a dad you could count on to know stuff.

"Sure. As I understand it, there are hundreds of so-called 'princes' connected to the Saudi family. Maybe that explains those midnight deliveries of who-the-hell-knows-what that no one believes I see when I'm up late — trucks pulling into that garage with boxes — "

"We do believe you, Dan," Mom cut in. "We sure believe you now, after Halloween. I'm sure those FBI agents — if that's really what they are — are taking note of those deliveries. Taking care of it all . . ."

"Oh sure; it's all A-OK," I muttered, rolling my eyes.

Dad shook his head too but shifted the subject, not piling on Mom. "At any rate, yes, the man could be a prince. Half the country claims to be royalty. No doubt the other half is their so-called servants. Some of 'em working for next to nothing, for life. It's a . . ."

"A different culture," Mom put in beside him, sipping her wine.

"And the sons of bitches miss it," Dad finished boldly. The older he got, Mom said lately, the more Jewish he got. Often from his Stairmaster he'd shout at the TV about Israel. Plus wanting me to consider a late Bar Mitzvah and all. Dad took a gulp of his beer. "The ones who're living here, most of 'em are probably trying their bandit-best to get back. Bush went and flew a bunch of 'em back on our dime. The princely life they lead back there . . . it gives them all this damned — this inborn sense of entitlement."

"But we've got servants, too," I ventured after a chewing pause. That part about servants, working for life. Did that explain One?

Mom cut in, "What, you mean the Maid Pros? Sweetie, we pay — and tip — them very well for the work they do . . ."

"Not lately," I muttered, thinking of the thirty dollars I'd stolen. Thinking: I am royally fucked if that family really is royalty. Thinking: who knows what ties they've got, what ways of crushing me if I don't do what they say. Was it true what the younger brother had claimed, that even the FBI couldn't touch his dad the prince?

"Joezy. Earth to Joezy. What was that? What about 'lately'?" Mom studied me again across the table, her face showing concern and maybe something more. "You OK, Joezy? I mean, not that any of us is really OK these days. You say those boys didn't bother you. But did they? Or are you still thinking of Halloween? Believe me, I was upset by that too. That's why I called the police . . ."

"Arlington's finest," I muttered, wondering as I forced another bite of chili if those same police might soon come after me.

"Now Joezy," Mom told me with a wine-scented sigh. "Don't worry yourself over all that. We tried. We did what we could."

I sure did, I thought. And I pulled myself up, all at once unable to meet Mom's concerned gaze. I stepped over to the fridge, yanked it open. I bent into its welcome chill and gripped the milk carton. I held my glass steady, pictured One bending and kneeling before me.

Yes, I did what I could. I took what I could, I thought as I poured a wobbly white stream. Now would I pay for it?

CHAPTER EIGHT
SILENT AUCTION

MAURA

What you're doing to my life, Frannie, I kept thinking Saturday morning as I baked my pineapple upside-down cake. Turning it upside-down. Or you would if I let you.

Ever since she'd run out on me Thursday at the school, I'd avoided Frannie in person: dropping off Joezy from the car Friday morning, chatting with her pleasantly as ever about auction details on the phone but shying away from Frannie's pointed glances at Friday afternoon's final silent auction meeting, wondering like a high-school girl if she was not interested in me anymore. If she'd grown impatient (and who could blame her?) with my alternate flirting and backing away, never answering her e-mails.

Maybe it was for the best, I'd tried to tell myself as the meeting droned on. But then River's mother was launching her final arguments against the auction cash-bar. She was actually suggesting instead that her husband, as he'd done for Fairwell's Renaissance Faire, make his famous — his notorious — honeyed meade.

Frannie beside me met my eyes the way she'd done in the first PTA meeting of the year, when River's mom first held forth about the vegan lunch option. Frannie and me eyeing each other like we were the only two carnivores in the room.

How good it felt to have someone whose sparkling gaze I could meet, the way Dan and I used to exchange fond fellow-parent glances back when Joezy was younger, when Dan was around more.

At meeting's end, after we'd almost-unanimously approved the cash-bar, Frannie stepped up in front of the whole silent auction committee. She announced that she wanted to present a token of esteem to her silent auction co-chair, to me.

A small wrapped box I accepted with a wide smile and quick hug but did not unwrap 'til I was alone in my Volvo.

Then Saturday morning I'd called in sick, illicitly skipping the big set-up session at the school's gym.

At noon, with my fingertips still sticky from melted brown sugar, I logged on to check my emails, wondering if maybe Dan had sent one, since I'd only been able to reach his voicemail. Had he actually reached New York? What was it like there?

This was what I was wondering when I found my one and only new message. From FrannieX@yahoo.com.

mara — hope you r feeling better; hope you aren't just staying away this AM to avoid me; hope most of all to see you tonight; don't worry; i won't push; but don't u think we need to talk, mara? hope that necklace didn't freak you out; i just saw it & thought of you. seems like i can't stop thinking of you — f.

I re-read the message, then deleted it. And didn't answer. I tried Dan's cell again, left a message asking him to please call, to let us know he was OK, to let me know if he could catch the early train back, be there tonight. You have to be, I added in what I meant as a light tone. But after I hung up I realized it would seem demanding, selfish. Wasn't I, too often? There he was at Ground Zero and all I could think about was this silent auction and that woman named Frannie.

I made myself clean up my pineapple-syrup-scented bowls and pans (the kind of mess I'd usually leave stacked in the sink). I washed and carefully blow-dried my hair. Joezy had been hiding out in his room sketching and hunching over his computer all morning.

He finally shuffled into the kitchen as if in shock, opened the fridge and gulped orange juice right from the carton.

"You're helping me out tonight, remember?" I turned, my hair clean and springy. I was chopping up nuts for my topping.

"Aw Mom, do I have to? For your auction thingy?" Joezy turned his shaggy head to face me. His shifty gaze seemed every bit as distracted as his dad's during our hasty pre-dawn goodbye.

"Someone's got to help me tonight," I answered, waving my mini nut-chopping knife, suddenly irrationally mad at Dan. "Your dad hasn't even called yet about the trains from New York . . ."

"Oh yeah? Anything on the news?" Joezy was the one to pad down the hall and turn on CNN as I hadn't even thought to do, to check for terrorist attacks in New York.

The rest of the afternoon, Joezy sat slumped in the TV room as if hypnotized, watching an extended CNN report on "Our Eyes and Ears: Reporting Suspicious Activity in YOUR Neighborhood."

When I checked on him to offer a snack, he was staring at a group interview with United Air flight attendants, one teary eyed, Joezy's knee jiggling violently. Two flight attendants hugged onscreen and I felt teary myself at the fervent sisterly embrace.

My own hands felt slightly shaky in the master-bedroom as I rifled through my clothes, selecting something that could be both subtly sexy (for Frannie) and suitably somber (for a 9/11 fundraiser).

I settled on a dress Dan had bought me: a close-fitting but modestly cut black knit with a ballerina neckline that showed off my collarbone. Not to mention the gorgeous coppery necklace Frannie had given me at the end of Friday's meeting. Fine strands of copper chain, studded with burnt-orange coral. Just my colors.

But then again, I reminded myself as I pulled on my silky slip, *Dan had picked just the right dress for me.* Years ago, when he still watched me at times he thought I wasn't looking; when he still stayed by my side at parties. When did all that attention stop; no: lessen?

And I had been the one, really, who most often turned away in bed. Especially this past summer. Hadn't he been right, mid-summer, when he'd claimed I'd used my bruised post-biopsy breast as an excuse not to have sex? Or had the biopsy — my first brush with mortality, followed by my first brush with Frannie — re-awakened my old feelings for, well, women? Only it didn't feel like that to me; it felt like my meeting Frannie awakened feelings for — Frannie.

From the bedroom phone, sitting in my slip and twisting the cord, I dialed Dan's cell yet again. My pulse thumped in my throat along with its distant fuzzy rings. God; what if he actually had been unfaithful in his September trip to Philly? What if something was happening now in the distant cursed city of New York?

"This's Dan," his own live voice said. Broken up with cell static but as always reassuringly steady. I wrapped the phone cord round my wedding ring finger, surprised at my surge of wifely relief.

"Oh thank God, you're OK; God, what's it like there?"

"Hi to you, too, Babe. It's—normal and not, y'know? I can smell it in the air, Maura, I swear—in the taxi, through the windows. . . . Something big and burnt and—yeah, yeah, another for me."

"Where are you?" I could make out laughter in the background.

"Some bar near Penn Station; see, the earlier train got delayed and we're waiting for word on the 5PM; but even if I get that—"

More laughter behind him, Dan joining in, maybe drunk already. So far away in that shell-shocked anything-goes city without me.

"You won't be here for tonight. . . ." I said those all-too-familiar words with a new pang of worry over what drunk Dan the Man might get up to later in the evening. But I felt too another secret and surprising surge of relief. So Dan wouldn't be back tonight; so Frannie and I would get to—yes, we did need to—talk.

"—sorry 'bout that Babe; I know you wanted me there. You go and, and have yourself a good time; OK? Party on, you hear?—"

This last brought a peal of cell-fuzzed laughter from his bar comrades. Not strictly male laughter, either, if I was not mistaken. Rowdier laughter than I usually overheard when I'd catch Dan in some other long-distance businessman's bar. But of course they were all stranded at Ground Zero in 2001. What could they do but drink, but party like there's no tomorrow? A long jumbled pause.

God, I thought more clearly than I usually allowed myself to think when Dan was away. Had I been foolish to imagine all these years that Dan with his fondness for too much beer, Dan with his ever-distracted gaze, had played the good husband on all his many trips? Was Philly the first time he'd really crossed the line? Had he?

"Oh, I hear you, Dan the Man. I hear and obey. You stay safe there and, and call later, OK?"

But our connection had gone dead. I sat on the edge of our bed holding the cut-off phone for a long few minutes. Picturing Dan in the New York bar, hollering about politics 'til late. Then with his lopsided drunk Dan grin staggering off to his hotel — alone?

No, I tried telling myself. Maybe he didn't always stagger off alone. Or maybe it had only been in Philly, in the immediate wake of 9/11. If it had happened at all. I needed to confront Dan, talk to him in person. And if he confessed? Did I want him to confess?

I hung up the phone at last. I stood and smoothed our bedspread, thinking of all the furtive sometimes-tender sometimes-brusque love-making we'd snuck in here, with Joezy asleep down the hall. Joezy asleep between us for years, for too long.

All our intimate whispered quarrels in this bed. Some about Joezy, me supposedly spoiling him, Dan being too hard on him. Some about sex; why we couldn't both be in the mood at the same time anymore. Dan when drunk wanting me to go down on him but not him on me. That he'd do, dutifully, only when sober. Playing the good husband, the sensitive Oberlin guy.

But he could be way worse, I reminded myself, wriggling into my sheerest panty-hose. He took care of Joezy and me in the old-fashioned sense, my mom's sense. A good provider; a caring, if often absent, Dad. Wasn't he in fact sensitive compared to the louts my old friends had married, more than half divorced and more miserable than ever now? And yes, wasn't the distance between us my fault too? My fault more? I had pulled back from him too often, in bed.

I thought of Dan holding me close, of his vigorous bristly kisses, of his beard rubbing between my thighs and how sometimes I liked that roughness, sometimes not.

"You can swing both ways," Carolyn had told me so long ago, in the sunny co-op back yard. "Only one way might just take you — further." What if she'd been right about me, what if I was meant to swing both ways, swing the female way, and I never tried?

I caressed my breasts, my biopsy scar. What if I got breast

cancer like poor Mom? What if America was blown up tomorrow? And I never got to really try; to have sex with a woman I may love.

Or I knew she loved me. And I knew I loved that, needed that.

I pulled on my slinky dress, hooked on my delicate necklace. I told Frannie in my mind: *No, Dan couldn't come. He's stuck in New York. So I'm alone, just me and Joezy. Alone — you were right — a lot.*

At 6:30PM. I tottered downstairs on my high heels to find Joezy pacing the living room, still in his sloppy Batman t-shirt and jeans. But at least he was waiting, keyed up. Hoping to catch a glimpse of whoever might be his own secret crush at the auction?

"Hey Mom. Can I man the table up front? Can I take the tickets and raffle tickets and all?" Joezy asked me this in a stagey-sounding casual manner as he reluctantly shrugged into his one suit jacket. "I mean," he added, "I want, like, a real job this year . . ."

"Sure," I agreed absently, and I clicked back to the kitchen. I covered the pineapple upside-down cake pan with aluminum foil. "Glad you reminded me. . . . Oh, and I almost forgot our money bag!"

I dug into the pantry and fished out the clunky zippered money bag we'd used at the last Fairwell bake sale. FAIRWELL written across the bag in Sharpie, by me. As treasurer of the PTA, I was the one to make deposits, this year anyway, in the school bank account.

"Think we're gonna be, um, handling lotsa cash tonight?" Joezy asked this as if he was actually interested, holding the front door for me. In a brown tweedy jacket he and his dad had chosen, with his reddish brown hair brushed for once, he looked older, a young man.

"Hope so," I told my tall son as I stepped out the door.

Maybe all that CNN terrorist talk today had awakened his latent patriotic interests. Or maybe he just wanted to somehow impress whoever it was he'd been brooding about all day.

What a pair we are, I thought, clicking down our darkened brick walk. I shot Joezy a lipsticked grin. Like the old comradely mother-son grins we used to exchange all the time, back when we'd set out for routine errands as if on a shared adventure.

I led the way through the November dusk to my Volvo, swinging the heavy yet empty money bag. "I'll make sure you handle lots of cash tonight, Joezy. We're gonna make a killing."

"But for good," Joezy reminded me, in mumble. "Right Mom?" he asked. I was unlocking the car, maybe only imagining an odd extra edge in his voice. "A killing for a good cause."

———

At Fairwell, in the modestly be-decked gym, we PTA moms ran about in our usual fluster of last-minute crises. Joezy was dispatched to set up our money table. In all the hub-bub, I didn't see Frannie at first. I wondered if she'd actually not come, miffed that I'd ignored her email. I was wondering too if I dared try her cell when Joezy emerged from the art room supply closet. He announced that the credit-card processing thingy was nowhere to be found.

So I printed in Sharpie script an apologetic sign — CASH & CHECK ONLY, PLEASE! — and taped it to the metal cash drawer.

"With twenty-five bucks just to get in, plus the cash bar, you're gonna need a Brinks guard to take you home, Mrs. Treasurer . . ." Sheila Jester told me this with an already-drunk-sounding laugh. I asked Joezy again if he was sure he could handle manning the money table.

He patted the empty zippered moneybag and insisted he'd be fine. He even hung up my coat in the makeshift coat-rack stand the PTA dads had erected by the downstairs bathroom.

"Thanks. I really appreciate you, y'know, being here . . ." I patted my son's surprisingly sturdy shoulder — solid, like his dad's — and I slipped gratefully into the gym, hurrying past the bidding tables to the cash bar, the wine. Still not catching sight of Frannie.

By 8PM, the old-fashioned wood-floored gym was packed with Fairwell parents lined up at the tables of donated items, scribbling their bids. On my third glass, and my second compliment for my necklace, I was feeling comfortable with my dress choice, my black blending in with the blacks and dark knits of the other women.

Yet I felt I was standing out too. More than one Fairwell dad shot me a second glance after taking in Frannie's golden-lit portrait of me in my leotard. It was on display, framed with its own separate bidding card beside my handmade yoga lesson flyer.

But where was Frannie, to see it all?

"I didn't know you had a degree in dance," Sasha Schiller's dad commented as I hoisted my fourth or fifth glass of wine. I smiled up at him, his homely-handsome ex-hippie face, his longish hair swept back to hide his bald spot. Over his shoulder I scanned the gym yet again and finally caught sight of her. Frannie in a black mock-tux, making an entrance in a gaggle of moms, laughing as rowdily as Dan's buddies in that far-away bar. Only she was right across the gym.

" — bid fifty big ones for my daughter for your lesson — think I could come watch, if I win it?"

"All dancers love to be watched." I flashed my widest sienna-lipsticked smile up at Sasha's dad. What was his first name? He was beaming at me; Frannie — I could feel it — was glancing over, keeping watch. I felt my face flush pleasantly with wine, attention.

"Saw Josiah out there, taking money like a pro," Sasha's dad went on, leaning on one leg, clearly just wanting to chat.

"Yes, he's such a sweetie; letting me have a — " I lifted my paper cup in a mini-toast, " — Mom's night out!"

"Dad's too." Sasha's dad touched his cup to mine. And I side-glimpsed Frannie in her dashing tux, with her black and white hair dramatically spiked up, heading closer. My pulse began to pump.

But I hadn't lost my touch. I fixed again on Sasha's dad; I felt Frannie's determined inquiring gaze, Frannie only a few feet away.

"Oh Maura; I'm glad I caught you."

A hand tugged my elbow and I made myself turn from both Frannie and Sasha's dad. I faced, instead, Joyce Lee, Joo's mom. With unusual insistence, Joyce pulled me aside, away from Sasha's dad and Frannie and Frannie's friends and the whole teeming auction party. The usually demure Joyce led me beyond the crowded drink table to a relatively quiet corner of the gym.

"I saw Joezy taking tickets. First time I've seen him in ages, you know. Where's he been lately? I've got to tell you, Joo's felt pretty hurt that Joezy's stopped coming over on Fridays . . ."

"Stopped?" I repeated, blinking, trying to clear my wine-dizzied head. To focus on Joyce's expression of motherly worry. I should be worried too, I knew, sensing as I shook my head that I should be checking on Joezy right now, out at the ticket table. "What do you mean, stopped? He's told me — he's acted like — he's been going over to Joo's just like always, to Game Boy and, and . . ."

Joyce shook her head emphatically, her glossy short-cut black hair swinging in gentle rebuke. Her made-up eyes flashed with concern but also a faint accusatory glint.

Aren't you keeping track of your own son? Joyce's gaze demanded as she told me firmly, "No, no. Not for a while, it seems like. Joo said Joezy has just been claiming he's got stuff to do. Says he has been acting like he's got some big secret going on . . ."

I allowed myself a gulp of wine. "A secret, yes — I've noticed that too, actually. I — thank you, Joyce for telling me. I have noticed he's been distracted lately, but I — I guess I've been so distracted myself . . ."

By what? Joyce with her finely-cocked eyebrow seemed to ask.

"I mean with Dan traveling so much, on airplanes and all . . ."

"Oh." Joyce made a face a sympathy. Maybe reminding herself that this was, after all, a 9/11 fundraiser.

"I'll ask Joezy about it; I'll find out what's going on and, and let you know, I promise . . ." I was backing away, telling myself I really should check on Joezy, relieve him out there at the table.

But the silent auction gavel was sounding. The salt-and-pepper haired caftan-clad Fairwell principal: Leona Zimmer. She gamely whacked the old-fashioned wood podium on the gym's stage with the wood gavel I had bought myself. "Order, order at the auction! Welcome friends and family of Fairwell. Great to see this great turn-out. Let us begin our 2001 Fundraiser with a moment of silence for those who died in September, in New York . . ."

It was during the uneasy rustly moment of silence, everyone stopped in their tracks, that I found Frannie again. My head bowed but my eyes roving round the gym, I located her black tuxedo back; I began, even before the moment had ended, edging her way.

"Yes. And now," Leona's miked voice broke the self-conscious silence with audible relief. She shifted maybe too quickly back to her jocular big-woman voice. "Now, to raise money — this year — for the families of those who died, let the un-silent big-item bidding begin!"

But first, of course, the tipsy assembled parents had to be herded closer to the stage.

"Excuse me, sorry," I murmured, and I made my way through the thicket of moms in dark dresses toward Frannie in her tux. Onstage, Leona was making her way through the usual dutiful round of thanks.

By the time I reached Frannie's side, Leona was asking "a super-big Fairwell hand for our fearless co-chairs, that dynamic duo, our longtime auction diva Maura Simon and new-parent volunteer Frannie Max!"

Suddenly Frannie and I were side-by-side, practically holding hands as we stepped up to the stage. We exchanged giddy sheepish grins, facing two hundred or so clapping parents.

What are we supposed to do now? I wondered, wobbling on my heels, scanning past the smiling middle-aged faces of the crowd. I was trying to glimpse my son through the gym's open archway, alone in the school's front hall. Up to no good out there?

Where in hell had he been disappearing to on Friday afternoons? Was he in fact seeing some girl somewhere? Frannie nudged me as the applause died down. Together, Frannie and I backed up into seats arrayed behind the podium. The volunteer auctioneer — a friend of Frannie's; a tall commanding Hispanic woman — strode onstage.

In a loud dizzyingly quick voice, the auctioneer commenced bidding on the biggest items that Frannie and I had worked hardest to collect. Each one had occasioned a congratulatory phone call or e-mail exchange between us. The weekend at a Boston hotel, the New Mexican pottery made of earth blessed in native tradition, the Museum of Science birthday party, the genuine African safari.

Frannie laughed heartily at the bidding wars. Perched beside her on the uncomfortable cafeteria chairs, I managed a five-wines-to-the-wind smile. My mind kept spinning round the fact that Joezy had been lying to me, that I was considering lying and worse to Dan.

I applauded each reckless bid with Frannie, our elbows bumping. I didn't trust myself to side-glance at Frannie onstage. Anyway, I noted, Frannie's whole onstage attention seemed to be fixed on her showy red-clad friend, the auctioneer.

"And now, for those of you still mucho-hungry for more . . ." The auctioneer turned broadly to wink at Frannie.

"The cakes," Frannie hissed to me, nudging me hard. And I rose automatically. I clicked on my heels to the side of the stage where Frannie's and my freshly baked cakes were displayed. I lifted first Frannie's elaborately frosted chocolate bomb.

Stiffly, overdosing at last on too many eyes on me, I displayed the cake for the crowd. The auctioneer badgered them in her brassy fast-talking stage voice.

"One hundred one hundred one hundred, c'mon this is Frannie's bliss bomb; famous in some circles; chocolate sensation satisfaction, and I mean lip-smackin' satisfaction guaranteed; do I hear one-fifty? Sold for one-fifty to the lady with the biggest appetite for bliss!"

A plump PTA mom bustled up to the edge of the stage. I bent awkwardly in my heels to deliver the cake, everyone clapping. My head buzzed; my breath felt short as I straightened up again.

I should've saved Frannie's cake for last, I realized as I clicked back to my own much plainer pineapple upside-down, famous in no circles. I don't have a circle, I thought as I carried my uncovered cake to the stage's edge. Who would want my lumpy brown and yellow creation? But it tastes good underneath, I felt like coaxing.

I held it up for shy display. The audience'd rather look at you than me, sweetie, Frannie had assured me, deeming me the Vanna White cake displayer. But standing center-stage again, shakily displaying my unremarkable cake, I remembered in a rush the stage-fright that had made me an uncertain performer even in my dance troupe days. I would never really fit in with Frannie the semi-pro photographer and her artsy ballsy friends, would I?

I shot a look behind me. Frannie's auctioneer friend seemed to be sizing me up herself with her darkly appraising glance, seemed to be wondering with her overly expressive stage face: so this hippie-dippie Fairwell mommy is Frannie's latest crush?

"What do I hear bid for the lovely Maura Simon's pineapple upside-down?"

Sasha's dad gallantly called out thirty; a more tired PTA-mom voice chimed in with fifty. I flushed, wishing Dan was there to save me with a husbandly hundred-plus bid.

"Only fifty? For 9/11 victims' families, for one of our last items of the night? People, dig deeper! Fifty going once, going twice . . ."

My smile felt clenched, my lipstick faded which always made my whole face fade too. I scanned the watching faces, wishing I could catch sight of Joezy. I'd been neglecting him these past weeks, so caught up in this silly soon-to-be-finished auction and Frannie's no-doubt fleeting attentions. What had it all been worth?

"Two hundred and fifty!" Frannie behind me boomed to a collective gasp, led by me. My mouth hung open like Joezy's; I clutched my upside-down cake's pan as the audience applauded.

"Two-Five-Oh!" the auctioneer repeated, frankly incredulous, maybe wondering — as I was wondering — why on earth I was worth so much to Frannie. "Going once, going twice: Sold!"

The audience burst into hearty applause, some laughter too. Frannie was striding toward me in her tux as if about to — surely not — grab me and kiss me in front of the whole Fairwell PTA. Frannie stopped beside me and wrapped her arm round my shoulder in a sideways stage hug. I turned to face her, the cake between us.

Stiff-armed, trying to halt any kiss before it began, I shoved the cake-pan toward Frannie. A wet plop: the pan tilted and sugar-glazed pineapple slices tipped onto her, spilling down her front, staining her finely fitted jacket. All the pineapple topping; all over Frannie.

"Oh my God, I'm so sorry," I sputtered as the applause faltered. Clumsily, I righted my pan, my ruined cake.

But Frannie scooped one glop with her finger, licked it and pronounced, as loud and sure as the auctioneer: "Delicious!"

In the little burst of chuckles and applause that followed, Frannie seized my arm. She led me and my tilty pan off the stage, down the steps. I set down the cake pan on a table we passed and grabbed a full martini glass. Stole it, olive and all.

"And they *are* a dynamic duo," the auctioneer declared from onstage as Frannie and I crossed the length of the gym. "Cochairs of tonight's event: Maura Simon and Frannie Max—"

Gamely, the crowd was applauding us yet again, and Frannie was giving them a final jaunty wave, me a mock toast. I downed half my stolen martini. Then Frannie led me out the gym's rear archway into the school's front hall. We were laughing, giggling really, like girls.

But Joezy's face stopped me. He was alone at the ticket-taking table, facing the glass main doors. And he twisted toward us in his seat, his green gaze so startled, maybe guilty.

Did he know Joo's mom had told me he'd been lying? Was he scared I'd find out why he'd been lying, where he'd been going on Fridays? Or maybe he was just upset by—had he seen the cake dump?—the spectacle his mom was making of herself.

"Joezy, are you OK?"

Joezy answered too fast, eying Frannie in her pineappled suit. "Um, sure. Hey, isn't this thing due to end soon? Alison's mom told me to stop selling tickets and even the raffle tickets and all. . . .She also said you've gotta remember all the cash bar money. . . ."

Behind me in the gym, I could hear the principal intoning the raffle winners. Yes, I remembered as if from long ago, pre-martini; yes, we were supposed to end the event by nine.

"Soon, honey. But I—as you can see, I have to help poor Frannie here—" I felt conscious of trying to control my wine-plus-martini slur. Trying not to look guilty to my pale guilty-faced boy. "See, I went and dumped my upside-down cake upside-down all over her. . . ."

Somehow this set Frannie and me giggling again. She's drunk too, I told or warned myself. And I was the one who took her arm, steering her around the corner to the principal's office and the narrow coat-rack-clogged corridor, to the small adults bathroom.

"Whoa, what-all goes on in *here?*" Frannie asked with a nod to the suddenly comical UNISEX/ADULTS ONLY sign. So we entered the single-stall bathroom on another gale of high-schoolish giggles.

I ran water, wet one of the thick brown paper towels they only sell to schools. That damp-paper-towel smell of my own long-ago high school girl's room, of certain tough-sexy girls I'd eye in the mirror as they touched up their tarry mascara.

I balled up the wet towel; I faced Frannie, inches away.

"So where's ol' Dan, this time?" Frannie asked, her usually direct stare off-center. Her breath smelled of rum punch. And I was way past my usual drink limit.

"Ol' Dan's stranded in N-Y-C; he's 'de-layed' there. He was last heard de-laughing his ass off at some bar there. . . ."

Was this really me, trash-talking my husband and swaying on my heels. I dabbed the sticky stained jacket of Frannie. Beneath the satiny fabric, I could feel the firm curve of her breasts. Bigger than mine, I told myself dizzily; smaller than Carolyn's back at the co-op. What was I thinking, doing?

Frannie took the balled-up towel from my hand as if about to scrub the stain herself. Instead she let the paper towel drop.

"De-laughing his ass off, huh?" Frannie asked me as I'd more or less invited her to ask. She lined up her blurred, concerned, turned-on eyes with mine. "Are you saying you — you think he's — having himself too good a time? Out there in the Big Apple, without you. . . .?"

Big apples, I thought as I nodded. Her breasts like big apples. Her heart, beneath those breasts, no doubt beating big like mine.

"Yeah. No." I shook my head, trying to clear it. "I don't know. Maybe . . ." And I was swaying again, light-headed like I used to sometimes get on the dance stage. A dance, yes; that's what this bold Frannie was trying to do with me. Only I didn't know, or I'd forgotten, the steps. I blinked; I stopped my own swaying.

Frannie took hold of my arms as if to hold me still. Her touch both gentle and firm, like Dan's used to be. She gripped my plainly shaky hands.

"What's making you shake, sweetie?"

"Fear," I whispered, finding myself adding, in too-drunk-too-fast-to-stop honesty, "Fear is my ruling emotion . . ."

"God, Mara." A sharp glint flared in Frannie's eyes. Pity plus contempt, I sensed. "Don't say something like that . . ."

Don't be something like that, she meant. Don't be scared suburban-mom Maura. Be bold sexy long-lost Mara. But I'm not, I was thinking mutely. But Frannie was gazing at my face again as if I was. Was Mara, her Mara.

"Man, that necklace. It's perfect on you . . ." Frannie lifted one hand and fingered the light coppery chains at my throat. Her warm fingertips brushing the thinnest skin that stretched over my collarbone. "Whoever picked that out," she pronounced in a low joking tone that was serious too, "really knew what she was doing . . ."

Frannie squeezed my hand, the one she still held, raising her grey blurry-bright eyes again to mine. She's saying, I told my drunk stiff-limbed self, that she really knows what she's doing. In love. And in bed; that she'd really know, in bed.

"I — know you do. Know what you're doing . . ."

And how to *do* me, if I'd let you. How to love me.

That's what I was thinking. But then Frannie leaned toward me, closing in. I pulled back as automatically and gracelessly as I'd done onstage. And I bumped the damp sink; Frannie in her sticky stained jacket straightened up, keeping her cool.

"Well, my tux is shot. I gotta change, but into what?" Frannie turned with a resigned sigh and slipped off her tux jacket. Underneath she was wearing a short-sleeved formal white shirt, stained and ruined too. On her arm, above her elbow, I saw half a tattoo — a blue-green twisty vine. Was there more above the sleeve: some lover's name?

Frannie picked up the paper towel she'd dropped. She kept her back to me. She held her jacket over the sink, scrubbing off the chunky pineapple as she told me, lightly, "Look, I just wanna say that I feel like the two of us . . . we really *could* be a dynamic duo . . ."

Here she glanced up in the mirror to see if I was listening. I nodded dumbly, my face all hot. Oh, I was listening.

"But OK, OK." Frannie bowed her stylishly bristly head, scrubbing the no-doubt-permanent stain. "I get it that you're married, that you're scared. I get it that you want to — you told me this yourself — 'matter' to someone. Well, you damn well matter to me, Mara. But hell, I'll back off, if that's what you really want . . ."

And Frannie tossed the paper towel almost offhandedly in the trash. She slipped back on her wet jacket, her shoulders suddenly broader. And she pushed open the bathroom door.

But it's not, I thought as soon as the door thumped shut. My life without Frannie, without her attention. It's not what I really want.

I stumbled forward in my heels, twisted the doorknob myself. At first it stuck, an old-fashioned door in an old-fashioned school building. I banged on the door with the heel of my hand, twisting the stuck knob hard, feeling trapped. Feeling like my last chance to break out of this cramped yet empty space was fast disappearing.

Then the knob gave, the door burst open, I came stumbling out. I bumped Frannie, who stood with her broad back to me, into the densely packed coat rack. Frannie pitched forward, cushioned by coats. She turned to me grinning, then we both were laughing, trying to muffle our laughs, alone in that coat rack corridor.

Hidden, or that's how it felt.

And it felt good, felt cozy and daring all at once, to be pressed up against Frannie's warm solid body in this secret space, the chatter of the soon-to-end auction sounding far away.

"Hey, I know what you can change into," I whispered. Then I turned, taking her hand. We ploughed past the coats, past the principal's office, into the darkened paint-scented art room.

From inside, we could hear the auction crowd begin to break up. The clean-up committee would be starting their work in the gym.

"Over here — " I crossed the dark classroom to the art supply closet; I pulled out a box of FAIRWELL: LOVING LEARNING t-shirts. "I silkscreened these last year, before you were at the school . . ."

"Back when life was simple, huh?" Frannie stepped up to the wide-open closet, the two of us hidden now by two layers of doors.

"In the closet," I slurred in some lame addled attempt at a joke. And Frannie stepped closer, holding her finger to her lips.

"Not so loud," she told me in her lowest surest voice, that cello voice I felt I could listen to all day, all night.

"OK, let's just be quiet together," I found myself whispering back, under the coat-gathering hubbub out in the hall.

"OK, let's just — " Frannie added like we were two kids, "Look."

And she pulled off her ruined jacket, her unbuttoned pineapple-smelling shirt. She let them drop. I blinked, my eyes adjusting to the dark. Frannie stood before me in a tank-top-style jogging bra, her breasts not fake-round like Sheila Jester's but soft looking, touchable. Her nipples stood up under the cloth.

I leaned toward Frannie, this strong woman who somehow loved weak me. For years I'd known deep inside I wanted a woman. Now, this moment, I felt I knew which woman. Frannie; I mattered to Frannie. I took hold of Frannie, pressing against her breasts, nuzzling into her neck, her rum-and-pineapple scented sweat.

"C'mon now, Mara," Frannie murmured. "You've really gotta, y'know, come over to my house some morning next week . . ."

"I'll come," I whispered back into her dense bristly hair.

"And we'll have," Frannie went. "Breakfast in bed, Mara . . ." Her hand was tracing down my spine, halfway unzipping my dress.

"Yes, yes," I was murmuring back. "Yes, I'll come, I'll come . . ."

"Mom?"

My son's voice, startlingly loud and near.

"*Joezy?*" I pushed away Frannie. I poked my spinning head from behind the open supply closet door. Joezy — taller than ever in his jacket — was stepping up to me across the classroom, away from its open door. How long had he been in this room? I was fumbling to hold up my sliding-down unzipped dress.

"Joezy — we — we were just changing — I mean, Frannie was, because of my upside-down cake — "

And upside-down life, I was thinking. God, I'd said no to a woman years ago when I should've said yes and yes, now, when I should've said no. Should've known my wide-eyed son might see.

"Hey," Frannie managed as she struggled to pull on a clean t-shirt. I was reaching behind myself, zipping my dress. Joezy was standing right in front of us, frankly staring. "Hey guys, I found the credit-card thing. It was right here behind the t-shirt box . . ."

"Really?" I was yanking up my zipper, pinching skin. "Goodness. How could you not see that, Joezy?"

"I see just fine," Joezy answered flatly.

Then in awkward silence we three marched back out into the emptied hall. I pulled on my coat. Frannie said we ought to help with the clean-up; Joezy protested that he wanted to go right home.

"We've got all the money already," Joezy whined, an edge in his voice that made me scared to say no. "Can't we just go?"

"I'll tell Sheila that, that Joezy needed to leave," Frannie told me, a new nervous edge in even her voice. "I'll take care of everything . . ."

Joezy stepped up to the money table and slipped the bulging zippered money bag under his arm, terse and manly in his jacket, his eyes avoiding mine. Frannie shot me a quick what-can-we-do look.

Then Joezy and I hurried out into the cold dark night with our money bag, our heads ducked like two thieves.

In our cold car, NPR came on with the engine. Before I could question Joezy about his Joo lie or he could let me know what-all he'd seen or heard in the art room, an NPR newsman reported a series of bomb threats this evening on New York City trains.

"You think Dad's on one of those trains?" Joezy asked me, his voice suddenly open and boyish again. My boy. "God, Mom, you think these threats-or-whatever are for real?"

"No, no; I'm sure none of it's real," I told Joezy over the newscasters' voice, hoping in my muddled mind that he'd know I meant Frannie and I weren't real either.

We drove home listening to the news on various stations. I clutched the steering wheel, driving fast yet with super-concentration because

I knew really I was too drunk to be behind the wheel. Too drunk to process all that was happening this overcrowded night.

I just wanted to get my son home, to make sure my husband was safe. Yes, that was all I wanted, all I should want.

We arrived to a garbled message from Dan on our kitchen phone machine. We both listened to it, side by side.

"calling from Penn Station . . . wouldn't believe . . . got here then our train was cancelled again . . . damn bomb threats, they say . . . stuck here 'til the train's cleared to go . . . sleeping on the wait-area chairs, all kinds of folks wandering by . . . just want to get home to you two . . ."

Dan's usually unflappable voice sounded shaken. I tried his cell after we'd listened to the message; Joezy stood closer beside me as the phone started to ring. Then it was halted by a mechanical voice saying the system was down in this calling area; please try again. Joezy stalked to the den and switched on CNN; we saw nothing on the crawl about actual bomb attacks on New York trains.

"I'll keep trying his cell," I assured Joezy. He was watching the TV screen: stock footage of Osama Bin Laden in his tent.

"Yeah right," Joezy answered me in his new edgy voice. Leaving the TV on, he brushed past me and Dan's Stairmaster. He thumped up our real stairs to his room, thumped shut his door.

I shut off CNN and followed, kicking off my heels, suddenly exhausted. I trudged up the stairs, picturing Dan trying to sleep in a wait-area chair in Penn Station. I wondered if I'd locked the front door like Dan always did each night. I wondered if Joezy had carried that damn packed moneybag in from the car. Yes, he had, I felt sure. I brushed my teeth, trying to rinse the lingering martini taste away.

Yes, I had seen that bulging bag resting on our kitchen counter as we'd listened to Dan's message. I'd count our take tomorrow.

I heard, as I stepped from the bathroom, Joezy's bedsprings squeak. Really, I should talk to him, tell him what Joo's mother had told me, ask him what he'd been doing these past few Fridays.

And if he asked me what I'd been doing with Frannie in the art room? Well, wasn't it better that he asked me now, when he and I were alone? I stepped up to his closed bedroom door, barefoot in my nylons and black dress. So sleepy my knock came out soft.

No answer; not even bedsprings. Stubborn silence. Or maybe he really was asleep. Maybe everything would look different, look less alarming, after we'd both had a good night's sleep.

I shuffled off to my bed, to Dan's and my bed. I fell across it horizontally, still in my black dress. I burrowed into my pillow, or was it Dan's pillow? I fell into a deep dreamless wine-fueled sleep.

The kind of sleep I didn't deserve, shouldn't have allowed myself. I woke just before 7AM, sitting up abruptly, pain between my eyes. But I felt sobered, regretful, and ready to do mother duty. Confront my son.

Where was he? I padded out into the hall, the bathroom, past his shut bedroom door. He almost never slept this late. Craving coffee to clear my head, to brace me for confronting Joezy, I slipped down to the kitchen. I set water on the stove, cranked the knob to high, pictured with another stab between my eyes Frannie, half undressed. No wonder Joezy was avoiding me.

Waiting for the water to boil, I turned to the kitchen counter, the zippered money bag. Still zipped, yet not — I blinked — still bulging. Had I imagined that big bulge of money last night?

I was PTA treasurer; I was silent auction co-chair. I'd have to report our total to co-chair Frannie today; I'd have to tell Frannie that I'd been drunk last night, that I hadn't been myself. Or would I tell her (would this be too corny?) that I *had* been myself, last night? That I felt more myself with her than I had for years.

I unzipped the money bag, stuck my nail polished hand inside. I wiggled my fingers in the almost empty space. Something was wrong. I pulled out an envelope of checks and a thin wad of bills, quick-counted a mere two hundred dollars. But there had been hundreds of parents crammed in that gym last night, paying twenty-five bucks a piece for tickets, buying drinks at the cash-bar.

We should have cleared two thousand dollars in cash not two hundred dollars; where the hell was the rest of our money? God, I thought as I slurped down my instant coffee black, too distracted for sugar or milk; God, I've lost the silent auction money. Or maybe, somehow, Joezy had lost it?

Joezy, who I'd found out last night had been lying to me for weeks. Joezy, who I should have confronted last night, no matter how tired or tipsy I was. How drunk; how irresponsible.

"Joezy, Joezy," I called out from the foot of the steps, my hungover headache panging. And I felt, as my voice echoed, suddenly sickeningly aware that I was alone in this 7AM Sunday-morning house. That Joezy had gone — where? Where on Earth?

I stampeded up to his room, thrust open the door without knocking. His bed stood empty, unmade. The new Spiderman and vintage Superman and Escher-maze posters on his walls hung mute. I stupidly scanned his pen-and-ink cluttered desk for a note. None.

Even when he went off on a bike ride, he'd tell me. And he never, normally, left the house this early. But this was no normal day.

I spun on my heel, marched into the master-bedroom, pulled off my funky rumpled dress. Joezy, Joezy. Where on earth had he gone so early, not saying a word? Of course I was passed out on my bed, sleeping off a bender, so who was there to say a word to?

Not taking time for a shower, I pulled on my jeans and my own faded FAIRWELL SCHOOL: LOVING LEARNING t-shirt. I grabbed my raincoat and keys. Was he biking the streets, dealing drugs in Arlington Center with the money he might have stolen, meeting some secret teen sex partner? What on Earth else?

First I had to find him, my missing son.

I raced down the stairs and out the front door into the drizzly barely lit day, not even sure where to start.

CHAPTER NINE

A THOUSAND DOLLARS

JOEZY

Booking downhill past sleeping Sunday houses, I pedaled so hard my bike wobbled way-bad. Outta control, like me. But I had to get down Riverview Road super-fast, so that Mom — I'd heard her bedsprings as I'd slipped out the door, into the garage — didn't somehow see me. So that I could get this money, this freaking stolen money, to One.

To Rakeen and One, I corrected myself. Ha, I thought. I skidded to a stop at the foot of Riverview Road. Wet wind hit my face. Church-bound traffic whipped by. Sparse but fast and deadly as ever.

An Arlington police car yelped its siren once, closing in on me, all lights pulsing. I froze my blank, freaked-out face.

God, how would I get away with it? A thousand dollars in cash swelled my jacket: packed along with a folded drawing of One. All zipped in my pocket like it had been zipped in that money bag.

God, God, I kind of prayed to the pulse of the cop car's lights.

It zoomed past. I stood poised on my bike on my toes, ready to launch out across Mystic Avenue at first chance. And I went over the story I'd been constructing in my mind all night.

Part of it true, like the best lies.

Because I really did leave the money bag unattended right before my mom dumped her pineapple cake all over Frannie, her girlfriend-or-whatever, in front of the whole PTA. Deliberately dumb, I tracked down Alison's mom in the gym and asked her when I could close up. Then I made a big deal of saying in front of her and the other dressed-up made-up skunk-drunk moms:

"Oh my Gosh, I gotta get back there; I shouldn't have left that money bag unwatched."

Then I ran back to the front-hall table; then my mom dumped the cake and disappeared with Frannie who's-it; then when I went looking for Mom, I found her and that Frannie half undressed in the art supply closet. Fucking talking dirty; maybe kissing in there.

Like really kissing, with tongues? Like I — even though One went down on me and all — like I'd never fucking kissed.

But maybe today, I told myself, launching into a wide-open space. Maybe today, somehow, with One? If somehow I made her see Rakeen was — how would I say it — the bad guy? The hostage holder. If somehow I got her outta that house? If, then, I'd be a hero to One?

I pedaled superhero fast across Mystic Avenue, nearly crashing into the bare-branched hydrangeas. I panted, trying to lean my bike so no one could see. God, that freaky lezbo love scene. And Mom too scared to ask me if I saw. But Mom must know I saw — heard too.

Was that really my mom? Whisper-talking, "I'll come, I'll come" and that shit?

I ducked past the bushes onto the frosted crunchy grass of the yard. Was this really me? Only days before I'd been a so-called good boy, hadn't I? Then One sucked me off and Rakeen snapped that supposed photo and suddenly I was stealing a thousand dollars. Screwing over the Fairwell PTA; screwing over my maybe-crazy maybe-lesbian PTA-treasurer mom.

Or maybe it's me who's crazy, I thought. And I peeked into the garage windows. I saw only my own dark shadowy reflection. Of course One wouldn't be watching for me, waiting for me this time.

Though Rakeen was waiting somewhere in that closed-up soundless house. This weekend, he'd told me so clearly. One thousand dollars by this weekend or he'd show my mom that photo. He'd claim I'd defiled One. But it wasn't like that, I wanted to tell him, wanted most of all to tell One.

I wanted just to see One, talk to her. That's the one thing I felt clear about as I ducked lower and crept around the garage to the side of the house. I was panting clouds of breath. I was remembering smoking with One, talking with One in her doorway.

That part had been like a date, hadn't it? Through the kitchen window, I spotted her. One; all alone in the Terrorist Cell kitchen.

Under the shadows of the eves, in the darkened glass of the window, I cupped my hands around my eyes. Yes: black-haired One standing before a sink, her head bowed.

I drew a deep breath and — cold-knuckled — rapped the glass.

Inside, so dim I almost couldn't see, One froze. Then turned her head, fast. I pressed my face to the icy glass. It was only me.

She crept slowly over to the window, looking scared. Of me? When I motioned her to open the window, One did reach out — fast, maybe to quiet me down — and jerk the window open. Just a crack.

Into the small space of air between us, I told her, low-voiced, "Lemme in, OK? I won't — won't hurt you — "

Why had I said that last part? I wondered as One shoved the unscreened kitchen window open. She backed up; I scrambled over the sill. Because she's scared of me. I knew this, wobbling on my feet. One backed away, eyes wide and wary. Yep, scared. Of the boy she'd invited into her bedroom, only a day ago?

One held her jaw rigid, maybe fighting a scream. Her stare vibrated, so bright and black. God, I asked myself, standing there uninvited in that kitchen, *had* I hurt her?

"Th-thanks for — letting me, um, in."

And for sucking me off, a crazed part of me wanted to add. Wanting to remind this paralyzed girl that I was no stranger to her. That I was — how could I make her see it? — here to help her.

I patted the zipped pocket of my denim jacket, making sure the bump of money was still there. The house around this clean empty kitchen felt quiet but not empty. Of course Rakeen and the rest of the family were here, asleep or maybe up and listening.

One raised her finger to her lips, a babysitter frown creasing her round stern face. I nodded to show I got it, I had to shut up. And I took one cautious step toward her. She backed up again, stiff-legged.

One was wearing, this chilly November morning, her usual oversized sweatpants and a faded pink pajama-type top. I glanced around the gleaming kitchen, a last-night trace of something fried and spicy in the air. A normal kitchen, normal table and chairs.

On the marble counter beside the sink there sat a small bowl of what looked like sliced mango. Mango! My mango? A sign, I felt silently sure. Beside the bowl was an open glossy fashion magazine — the kind that is mostly photos; the kind One might've studied for her angled do-it-yourself haircut.

One stood silent before me, hugging her thin arms.

"I brought the money," I whispered, pronouncing that word with care. Just to snap her out of her daze.

And she did blink. She spoke, babysitter brisk. "Shishh — they hear you. Boys in-sleep but . . . moany?"

"The money Rakeen asked for," I reminded her. She nodded, her brightened gaze showing she remembered what he'd demanded.

"For you and for him, he said," I pushed on, and this drew another avid nod from One. Her hair today hung limply, less shiny than before. She pushed her bangs out of her eyes. "Why did he say that, One? Did he mean it — he'd really share the money with you?"

She shrugged hard. She shook her head hard too. "Some-time — " She spoke to the swirly beige tile floor. "Rakeen — he some-time say will help me. But he — not. And I, I — " She shook her lank-haired head.

"Y-You don't know if you can trust him?" I filled in, my whisper eager. Maybe he hadn't slept with her, after all? Rakeen Jiluwi, who'd blackmailed me; who was older than me, better looking. *Were* they having sex? Was that why she kept looking down?

Yet she was biting her lips, not yelling for Rakeen. She was letting me stand here in this kitchen. From somewhere far back in the house, a door thumped. Muffled TV cartoon clamor.

"Well you *can't* trust him," I began, forgetting to whisper.

"Shish," One cut me off, a cat-hiss sound. And she motioned me to follow her. She padded backward toward an open door, keeping her eyes on me. She slipped down carpeted creaky steps into the rec room.

I followed her, blinking in the too-bright light, keeping my hand planted on my pocket, my money bulge. Incredible but true: one thousand dollars in cash, fresh from the hands of Fairwell moms and dads. I'd hidden the credit-card thingy last night and no one had found out.

I'm on a roll, I told myself at the foot of the basement steps.

Then, One turned to face me. She stood planted in front of me again, maybe deciding how far into this room she'd let me go. The same rec room with its ping pong table, its sheets of plywood leaning against the wall, its motionless bikes and skateboards.

One was regarding me now with plain interest, her soft lips pressed over her teeth in a hard determined line.

All because of my *moany*? If she'd sucked me off when I had only thirty bucks, what would this girl do for a thousand? But God, I didn't want that, hadn't wanted it before, either: One doing me for money. That's what I drew breath to tell the tense girl standing before me. Studying me so freaking hard; maybe trying to figure out — I was trying too — what kind of boy I was, really.

"Look, I — I'm sorry." I stumbled over the words. "I mean, sorry if you got in trouble and all, l-last time . . ."

Last time, first time. The one time One and I were together. One nodded at me. She wasn't sure — me neither — she should trust me. Still, she took a small step toward me.

"But I really do want to help you." I made my best earnest American boy face.

"There, under there," she answered, matter-of-fact. Like that was where I could start helping, right here and now.

And she slipped around me, motioned me toward a darkened space underneath the stairs. She ducked into it, bent beside a washer-dryer hidden there — along with something else. I peered in. One sat crouched beside a small metal safe with a combination lock.

She tried the lock, then looked over her shoulder at me. I was bending too, shuffling into the dim detergent-scented space.

"Here, in-side." One patted the metal door of the safe. "This where — may-be — they hide visa. They say it, visa-paper they got from uncle, they say it — not-legal. I — not-know. Sure-for . . ."

I crouched beside One at the safe, our knees softly bumping. I tried the lock too; it held. What did she expect me to do?

"Al-so and," One whispered quickly, maybe on impulse: "A — gun. In there. Mil-i-tary gun, father-prince's gun. In too . . ."

"A real gun?" I repeated stupidly, fingering the ordinary combination lock. The kind of safe they sell in hardware stores. Was I inches away from a live loaded weapon?

"Wow; you think they got any other — w-weapons around?"

"O-ther?" One shook her head. "Just — mil-i-tary sword. In his — Master Jiluwi; Prince's — bed-room . . ."

"No, no — " I grinned as if joking, though I wasn't. "No bombs or anything like that . . . ?"

One rolled her eyes toward the cobwebbed undersides of the steps. "No-no. They no — like that. Like you think, all you — " With that contemptuous "you," she stood, her head ducked.

"But I *don't* think anything — " I stood too, too fast, bumping my head hard on the inside-out stairway. "I mean — " I stumbled out after her into the light, my head smarting, "I don't know anything here, I'm trying to find out — what they are, this family . . ."

One pushed her bangs back from her flashing eyes. "They no that. No bomb. Mama right I — I am here safe. That why Mama before die make deal with family. More safe than — Madame Jiluwi; she say more safe I be, than on streets. Land of cold, I out in cold."

"And you'd rather be trapped down here?" I asked her, picking cobwebs from my hair. In the bright light, her round-cheeked face looked tired, washed out. She shook her head reluctantly, no.

Above us the TV sounds had grown louder. Footsteps thumped.

"Boys — " One nodded to that vibrating ceiling. "They — not-bad. Family — not bad, not so simple you think. Not-bad boys. Rakeen — "

"Rakeen is 'not bad'?" My voice squeaked as I tried to keep it down. "He hit me; he threatened me; he yelled at me for even talking to you at the store. He made me bring him a thousand dollars — "

"You bring?" One cut in, edging toward the shut door of her basement room. Right where I wanted her to be. "You bring — all?"

I nodded, closing my lips over my braces, trying to look as manly as Rakeen. At last I had her attention. I had something right in my pocket that Rakeen couldn't give her — not unless I did give all this money to him. And would I be crazy to do that?

"Look," I told One as she hovered beside her room door, maybe deciding whether to open it again to me. "What Rakeen and his family are doing to you, holding you down here, not letting you leave — it *is* bad; it's even illegal. I mean: not legal. Way not-legal."

One didn't nod, didn't blink, listening. I took a step closer to her, to her door, and she didn't flinch.

"See, I was looking it all up on the net yesterday, on my computer. There've been cases, One, where these rich families held illegals from Mexico, y'know, and they got in big trouble. The families, I mean, got in big trouble — holding those illegals with no pay; they got arrested and all — "

"Ar-rest? Po-lice?" One looked panicky, her big teeth showing, her whisper pleading. "No po-lice; cannot go po-lice!"

"But the families, it's the *families* who get arrested — " I told One, forgetting to whisper, stepping right up to her, to the still-shut door.

"Shish," One hissed, glancing toward the TV sounds above us. She nodded sideways; she opened the door to her room.

I followed her so fast I almost stepped on her heels. One's room. Her mattress on the floor with the sheets drawn up over it this time. Her dragonfly on silk. The room lit today only by drizzly grey light coming through the half-underground window.

This time, shutting the door, One didn't flick on the lights. A sign? I wondered, lightheaded with a feeling of power. I did, really did, have one thousand dollars in cash in my pocket.

"Look," I found myself saying to One, stepping up close to her. "What if we — screw this family. Report 'em to the police . . ."

"No," One snapped, backing away from me. "We can-not. No; the family, it not all wrong. No po-lice; I be — sent back."

"To Vietnam? Y'mean if your visa really isn't legal?"

One began pacing a small square in front of her mattress. A

practiced two-step pacing. "No, can-not; you no know. Other ones, they — they hurt. If I out get — "

"What other ones? Who'd get hurt if you got outta here? Have the Jiluwi's been, like, threatening you, threatening your family?

"Can-not say to you, can-not." One was shaking her head. "Almost all family gone. Only ones left in Vietnam — my mama's brother. Uncle. Many children. They had — house on, house on-to river . . ."

"House on a river?" I cut in, "But that sounds, like, nice . . ."

"Was!" One stopped pacing, throwing up her hands. "We lost. House on-to water — onto legs onto water. Not build way-back, way way-from river like — " She gestured to the walls around her. "House here; like you-all scared river. When here, when river — " She fluttered her fingers. "One thing I — no scared. Here . . ."

A catch in her voice. I stepped closer. "What's up with your uncle? How come you told Rakeen you didn't 'tell' about him?"

"No thing is up in him, in Uncle," she cried, shaking back her limp bangs. I touched just her hunched shoulder, warm through her pajama top. I knew not to ask more questions, yet.

I patted her skin-and-bones shoulder, awkward-like. Then I started to take hold of her other shoulder. One pulled back with a jerk. Her eyes tearless but bright, fierce.

"No, no," she told me, like she'd already said it over and over. "Never I shoulda — I pro-mised Mama, when she die — I not, I never — sell . . ."

She cut herself short, looked down at her thin rigid body.

"I don't want that either," I told One, my voice hitting its whiny pitch again. "I don't want, *didn't* want you selling — you know. To me and all. See, I thought — last time, last week — you wanted — it. Me. W-wanted to, y'know, with, with me . . ."

One raised her hands, fluttered all her fingers derisively. "You want," she told me, "Want be nice-boy. Want not — same time."

"Yeah," I blurted out, thinking she might be halfway joking. "Maybe I did, do, want that. . . . But look — I really do wanna help you, too. That's what I wanted last week, I swear, but then Rakeen busted in like he was gonna arrest me or something . . ."

One barely nodded, studying me coolly, unblinking like Rakeen. Her face in this dim room looked shadowy, older now.

"Look — " I asked flatly. "Just tell me. Were you — are you — like, working with him? With Rakeen? Working together to get this — " I patted my zipped pocket, "money from me?"

One shook her head, looking again as confused as me. "No-no — I try talk him — Rakeen no tell. Not me. I no know — what he . . . to-up."

"Up to," I corrected. And I unzipped my pocket. "'Up to' is right. See, that Rakeen, I've seen him do some crazy things. He might be planning anything. You say yourself you don't know what. But me, I swear — I just wanna make things right for you, with you . . ."

Should I give it all to One? I wondered. Surely she wouldn't have snuck me down here alone if she was somehow working with Rakeen. And I did somehow believe her: her confusion that seemed to match my own. I drew out, first, from between the rubber-banded clumps of money, the ink sketch I'd done. Shakily, I unfolded the thick white paper.

I held it up to One. She took it from my hand, then raised it close to her face. She squinted in dim window light.

"I did this," I told her quietly. "Of — you . . ."

"Me?" One asked, quiet too. "No-no; I no — pretty-like-that . . ."

She raised her eyes to mine. Her vibrating-bright eyes. She was still tensed up, but she was letting me look her full in the face.

"You are to me," I jumped to say, "Pretty like that . . ." Then I took my black and white sketch out of her hands. I rested it in her box of clothes. She was staring frankly at my unzipped pocket.

"Hey," I said, taking hold of her stiff-fingered hands, "How about if, if — we get outta here? If you come — home with me?"

"Home?" she gasped like it was a foreign word. But she still wasn't pulling back. I squeezed her cold hands, testing.

Had I really said what I'd just said? A crazy thing to suggest, I knew. "I mean my house, we could hide you there, figure out what to do," I was telling One like I knew what I was talking about.

Like I wasn't hearing that upstairs TV, picturing those brothers dressed as terrorists, picturing Rakeen smacking me with that paddle. Who knew what he was capable of?

And wasn't that all the more reason to try to — wasn't it what I was trying to do? — rescue this girl.

Daringly, I released her hands. I took hold of her arms again, pulled her toward me. I'd never even hugged her — this girl who had sucked me off. And here I was offering to take her in, to rescue her from the possibly dangerous Rakeen.

So why did she pull back again? Why was she looking at me, so freaking scared-like, like I was the one who was dangerous?

"Home, y'know, to my house," I explained to her and to myself, this crazy idea forming as I spoke. "My mom'll know — what to do — "

Especially if I threaten to tell her secret to my dad, I thought dizzyingly fast. Then maybe she'd agree to keep my secret. Even if Rakeen did bust me, did show her that freaking so-called photo.

"No-no," One was insisting like she was tired of saying that word to me. "No — mamas, they go po-lice — "

"Not if I tell her not to," I told One, feeling so powerful. Feeling the hold I had on Mom, the money that bulged in my jacket pocket.

I was sweating in that jacket in this closed-up room. Boldly, I pulled it off, tossed it onto One's mattress. I didn't want that bulge of money between us. One turned to look at the jacket lying there. That's when I took hold of her arms again.

She snapped her head back around. I breathed her smoky fruity breath as she spoke. "May-be you do, you can — you help me?"

"Yes, yes," I insisted, pulling her close. "I do, I swear. I wanna — "

Help you, I meant to say. But then I was jerking my head forward and squeezing my mouth shut so she wouldn't feel my sharp metal braces. I was mashing my mouth against hers.

Kissing her, though it felt wrong that first time, our mouths not fitting. One jerked her own head back, gasping.

"You, you *want* to — right?" I asked her dumbly.

And her face broke. Her mouth stretched out, like a sudden gash. Then she was crying, tears squeezed from her shut eyes. I still had hold of her arms. Only now it felt like I was holding her up.

"Mama — promise Mama — when Mama die — No sell, no sell — " She was twisting her head back and forth, a silent no-no.

"But it's *not* selling," I told this girl, this girl-woman I was holding. "Look, OK, forget it, forget it — " I was shaking my head hard too, just wanting her to please stop crying.

What had I done to her with my one klutzy kiss? What if Rakeen, if anyone, came in here and found me holding this scared crying girl? Her sobs were like an alarm bell I had to muffle, shut up.

I pushed away from her too fast. She swayed; I waved my hands like a referee in a game gone wild. She stopped sobbing. She wiped her runny nose with the back of her hand.

"Look, I'm sorry I came, OK? I'll go, I'm going, OK?" I bent forward, started to reach with my long arms for my jacket on her mattress. My stolen money. I had to get out of this whole mess I'd made.

"No-no," One burst out, only different than before. And she grabbed hold of me, hard, straightening me up. "No-no- You stay."

I was nodding, yes-yes. That's what her super-bright stare seemed to be telling me. And her softly half-open mouth. I was feeling my hard-on form at my crotch. Yes-yes; yes-yes. I was pulling at One's pajama top, its little buttons coming undone. Then I was bending forward into her, tugging her pajama top off. And she was fucking letting me.

This time we fit. Our lips pressed together, my mouth half opening despite my braces, her mouth opening too.

A moist taste of smoke, tear-salt, my mango.

CHAPTER TEN
YOU AMERICANS

MAURA

Anything to find my son. That's what I was thinking, all I was thinking, when I stepped inside 22 Mystic Avenue behind Rakeen Jiluwi.

Wearing a neat ironed Nike sweatsuit, Rakeen stood in an empty tiled front hall, a living room visible beyond him. Giant patterned pillows arrayed on a lavish rug in front of a big-screen TV. Smaller rugs—prayer rugs?—arranged before the picture window. From some far-off room, cartoons blared, boys laughed.

"So he might be downstairs, with your—what did you say—maid?"

Rakeen gave a brief nod. He turned and led me through the entry hall into a clean if sparsely furnished kitchen. The muffled cartoon noises and boyish laughter seemed reassuring. Wasn't this a normal house, after all? I was always preaching tolerance to Joezy; I shouldn't be making kneejerk assumptions about this family. Hadn't the boys simply been playing a ghastly prank on Halloween?

Once I found Joezy, we'd talk it all out, clear it all up.

I followed Rakeen down carpeted steps into an ordinary brightly lit rec room, complete with a ping-pong table. Rakeen slowed his step as if sneaking up on someone. He crept over to a closed door behind the ping pong table. I followed, making my own boot-steps stealthy too. Anything to find Joezy.

I hovered beside Rakeen at the door; Rakeen hunched as if straining to hear movement inside that room. He did not knock on the door. He simply reached for the knob, turned it fast. He thrust the door open so suddenly that I had to duck out of its way. Rakeen alone stood in the doorway holding the door, glaring into the room.

Over his tensed bony shoulder, I glimpsed my Joezy's mass of curls. *Thank God*, I thought with a surge in my heart, just as Rakeen called my son a Pig-Boy.

"Look," this Rakeen was asking or commanding me. Look what your Pig-Boy son was doing now.

That's when I thrust my head into the doorway, Rakeen's sharp shoulder jabbing me. That's when I saw my stunned-looking son face me with his jeans unzipped, with a half-dressed black-haired girl kneeling behind him on a mattress on the floor. The Asian girl from Whole Foods. And I was breaking in on them just like Joezy the night before had broken in on me and Frannie, half-dressed too.

So my first dizzied thought as I gaped from the doorway was: Now I'm going to pay.

JOEZY

When I was six, I fell off some monkey bars where I'd been hanging upside-down. I banged my head on asphalt, knocking myself out. When I came to, I was gasping for breath, blood streaming unstoppably from my nose. I was clinging to my mom.

Some other mom had phoned an ambulance and it screamed up to the curb of Beaver Brook Park. Two EMT guys tried to strap me onto a stretcher. But I wouldn't let go of my mom.

I held on tight, even though I could barely breathe. So finally the men strapped us onto the stretcher together: me on top of Mom, mini-oxygen tubes taped to my bloody nose. We rode all the way to the hospital like that, me lying on Mom, still clinging to her. Mom beneath me singing the Sesame Street song.

"Come and play; everything's A-OK —"

I started chanting these lame babyish words to myself as Mom gripped me in One's basement room; as I squeezed my mom's shoulder and we faced Rakeen. After telling my mom she couldn't reach into her coat pocket, Rakeen started reaching into his own sweat-jacket pocket.

Reaching so slowly, deliberately, that all I could think was: gun. That military gun One had said the Jiluwi's kept hidden in their safe? *Jump him*, I told my frozen-stiff self.

"Jump them, why didn't they all just jump up and tackle them?" I'd kept asking my dad in the days after 9/11.

A whole planeload of people; they could've overwhelmed the packing-knife-wielding terrorists. "They didn't know the terrorists would really crash the plane," Dad had explained to me, grim-voiced, then he'd added with a note of bitter hope: "And you can bet that won't happen again. Next planeload of people's gonna jump those goddamn goons like nobody's business."

I wasn't on any airplane, though the floor sure felt unsteady under my feet. I was trapped in a secret freaking basement room with my mom and my — whatever One was.

I was the boy, the almost-man, who ought to be saving us all.

But my breath was wheezing again in my throat and Rakeen's hand was hidden inside his pocket. His hand started to draw out his weapon-or-whatever. My own hand released my mom's shoulder.

Both my hands were shaking. Both my hands were jerking up — stiff and stagey, like this was some play — high above my head.

MAURA

A damned camera.

The tall Rakeen boy reached into his sweat jacket pocket, scared my Joezy into surrender pose. Then pulled out a damned card-board camera. Rakeen held this ordinary yellow camera up — not like he was about to snap our stunned-faced photo, but like he was presenting a distasteful object in court, as evidence.

"You see, Missus. You will see. I borrowed this camera from my brother, who spotted your son sneaking 'round our house. I had to see; you have to see. Your Pig-Boy: what he has been up to . . ."

Joezy beside me was lowering his raised hands, sheepishly. He slumped his shoulders and gazed down as if, in fact, his jig was up.

"Yes — " I managed to speak almost as clearly as the Jiluwi boy, who was maintaining a deadpan expression. Through the lenses of his professorial glasses, he levelly met my gaze. "Yes, I do want to know. Please do tell me. What has my son been doing here?"

Rakeen abruptly lowered the camera. He swallowed so his prominent Adam's apple bobbed. That apple and his eyebrows and his black-rimmed glasses were all oversized for his teenage face.

"Wait, this's crazy, Mom," Joezy burst out beside me. He stepped forward so he stood between the Jiluwi boy and me. Joezy's shouders tensed up like he might try — *Please Don't*, I thought — punching that boy out, shoving him aside. Instead, Joezy turned heel and faced me, looking abashed but determined. "I don't know what he's got on that stupid film in that stupid camera — but you gotta believe me, what really happened. I — see, I found One here, found out — "

Joezy shot a hopeful glance to the Asian girl at my side. She had slipped on a pink cotton top, still half unbuttoned. And she met Joezy's stare with a clear mute look of warning.

"I mean, one day I snuck into the garage here and she, she — " Joezy hesitated and went on more carefully. "And I — I wound up finding out that, that — she shouldn't be here. She's being held here. And we've gotta help her, gotta rescue her from here . . ."

"Ha," the Jiluwi boy in the doorway interrupted.

Joezy wrenched his head around to Rakeen. Rakeen addressed him in a coolly contemptuous voice. "Ha, yes, Pig-Boy, you want to help this girl? Rescue this girl? A laugh, that is — when you are the one who *defiles* her, right here in this room. And I have the proof, Pig-Boy — " Rakeen shook the small camera. "Right here."

"Defiled this girl?" I cut in incredulously. Had my fifteen-year-old son slept with the Jiluwi's maid?

No, I felt somehow sure — no, I would have sensed that change in him, sensed it if he'd lost his virginity.

The girl herself was looking down, her bangs half hiding her face. She fingered her buttons as if she didn't know how to work them.

Rakeen waved the cardboard camera once again. "You see, Missus; you have a problem with your greedy Pig-Boy. This girl, this Le Ti One, she is but seventeen. She is, her mother has told us before she dies, an innocent girl. Her mother trusts this girl to us, to a good Muslim family, and we protect her from you Americans, your loose and greedy ways. But your boy, he takes advantage of this girl! He comes to this basement with his money and he forces her — "

"Forces her?" Joezy's boyish voice rose to a defensive squeak. "Mom, you know I didn't, I'd never — "

I looked from my boy to the girl, who fiddled with one button, her face downcast and her receding chin quivery.

"Oh, Joezy," I murmured, stepping up to him. His own long jaw braced as if for a punch. I lowered my voice so I hoped only he could hear. "You can tell me the truth. I — I do want to believe you — "

I started to take hold of his hand.

"*Want* to?" Joezy pulled his hand from mine.

Even in that basement, it hurt me to have Joezy pull away — the son who'd once clung to me so steadfastly. And I sensed, in our tense four-way silence, he would have liked to cling to me again.

But the two of us stood haplessly planted in place as Rakeen shifted his demanding stare to One.

Slowly, obediently, she raised her face.

JOEZY

"I didn't, did I?" I asked One when she finally looked up. Not at me but at him, fucking Rakeen. "C'mon, One. Tell them. I didn't — you know, what he said — f-force you? Make you, you know — ?"

But I couldn't — she wouldn't freaking let me — meet her gaze. She was looking only at Rakeen. Waiting on some cue?

"You see, Missus, she does not answer. And I do have this pic-ture-proof. Against even you-American's laws, it is — to pay a girl only in her teens, pay her and make her — "

"I didn't pay her for *that*," I blurted out. Realizing on the *that* I'd just admitted—what? My breath felt all wheezy, my head all light.

"But you did give her money," Rakeen fired back at me like a freaking lawyer or something.

"Yeah, but—"

"Yes," Rakeen repeated with relish. He fingered his chin, a prickly morning-beard like I'd never yet grown. "Tell me," Rakeen told One. "I perhaps can, at long last, help you. But you must tell. Did this Pig-Boy pay you for—what you did in this room, with him?"

One was staring hard at her bare feet, her lips clenched like she might throw up or something. She'd heave; I'd hyperventilate. My head was buzzing and my stupid breath wheezing. One gave one head-jerk of a nod. But when she raised her brightened eyes again, she looked again as confused as I felt. Tears stung my eyes too.

"I didn't mean to," I told One desperately, stepping forward to stand face to face, both of us about to bawl. I could smell the smoke on her breath, could still taste the smoky mango of her mouth.

My mango; it must've been my mango.

One blinked back her tears. With her round face screwed up in that about-to-cry way, she looked younger than ever, babyish.

How could I have brought that money here, told her I'd bring more money? How could I have thought this hostage girl might somehow want me, not just my fucking money?

"Honest," I told One like some choked-up lying boy. "That's not what I meant to do, not at all—"

"Ha," Rakeen from the doorway cut in, flatly. I didn't look at him and I sure didn't look at my mom, standing dead silent behind me. I kept my eyes on One, on her bangs really, because she lowered her head further as Rakeen talked louder. "That is always the way: you Americans. Yes, for sure, you never 'mean' any wrong—"

"Look, I wanted to, to—like—r-rescue you, save you," I whispered to One. Did her head move in the barest nod, a nod she didn't want Rakeen to see? He was still holding forth from the doorway.

"Oh 'save,' yes, always the way. You Pig-Boy American boys, you want to 'save' always some country not your own, its children and women. Then you march in and you defile them, you rape — "

"*Rape* — ?" Mom burst out behind me. Mom's voice cracked like she might be the one to actually burst into tears. "What are you saying, young man? Are you trying to accuse my son of raping this girl?"

Mom brushed past One and me; she stepped right up to Rakeen. He looked smaller when he shut up; he looked almost like some smart-ass student. And Mom was the teacher who'd been pushed too far, who was finally facing him down.

"What if One said that he did, Missus?" Rakeen asked in his quieter flatter voice, trying this out. He still held that stupid camera. "What if One were to say that he, your son, he raped her?"

Though his voice stayed so flat, Rakeen's face seemed to me tense, unusually uncertain. Like he was gambling big-time and knew he might lose. He didn't look — didn't dare look? — at One.

He kept his eyes on Mom's face. I could only see the back of Mom's head, her unbrushed hair and stiffened shoulders, her body bracing for its next blow. How could I have freaking done this to Mom, to One? But I hadn't raped One, I reminded myself.

I wasn't the one holding One hostage here.

I drew my wheezy breath to say so, say something.

"What if she, if One was to say that, Missus?" Rakeen pushed on, unsteadily like he was improvising. "Unless you pay . . . ?" Rakeen paused, taking in my mom, sizing her up. "A thousand dollars. One thousand — to keep One and me from going to the, the police . . ."

"Po-lice?" One burst out, springing to life. She bolted toward Rakeen, elbowing aside Mom. Then Mom turned to me, her face paler, her freckles and eyes darker.

"No-no," One whispered urgently to Rakeen like: What are you thinking? No-no, like she'd whispered to me. If only I'd listened.

I made myself meet my mom's glassy green stare. What have you done? Mom seemed to ask. What have you done, what can we do?

Rakeen began shaking his head at One; she bounced nervously on her heels. "It will be all right," Rakeen told her like he alone really believed that. "You have not told them — our — whole arrangement?"

At this mysterious question, One shook her head no.

"You will trust to me; you will allow me to handle — *them.*"

"Yes-yes," One whispered, a soft catch in her throat. I couldn't see her face; I didn't want to see the intense way I sensed she was looking at him, Rakeen. And she added, "But-but — no po-lice."

"This Pig-Boy is not going to get away with this," Rakeen lectured her, shooting me a slap of a glance. "Always *they* do get away. But we will not let him get away with, with what he has done to — "

"What about what *you* have done to her?" I found my voice, my words mangled up. I gulped a breath and pushed on, emboldened by the fast-fading smirk on Rakeen's know-it-all face. "I gave One that money 'cause *your* crazy family won't give her any! 'Cause she wants to get outta here! *You* talk about 'against-the-law'; you guys are the ones who're gonna be in the biggest trouble — " I stepped closer, adding meanly to Rakeen, whose face tightened: "Who d'ya think the Arlington Police would believe, my family or *yours?*"

Rakeen lurched forward from the doorway, his glasses flashing. "It is not of your business, Pig-Boy! It is not what you think; my family is not what you think — " He raised that little camera to throw at me.

But One stopped him. She clutched his sweat jacket sleeve like a kid. Then she tugged his sleeve, frowning like a longtime babysitter. "No-no," she told him in low-voiced scold, "No po-lice, no I want — "

"You want out of here?" Rakeen demanded of One. She hesitated.

"My — uncle, his children, many children," she murmured.

Rakeen cut her short, yanking back his arm, his voice low too but still commanding. "Your uncle, he, this deal he made — my mother, she did not understand. All her life she has had maidservants. But your uncle, he did not do the right thing, for you, in this deal — "

"He did for children," One cut in, "Many, his children — "

"For money," Rakeen told her in that lowest voice. And I thought: he sold her? The uncle? Rakeen shot a glance at Mom and me as if he'd forgotten us. He raised his voice. "You, One: you say you want to be in the Land of the Free, want to be like them, the Americans?"

One nodded, but shot her own wary glance at us.

"Then we must, I must end it, this situation that can no longer be. You must not think of your uncle. You must — what Americans, they always — do what is the best for you. For you. You are hearing me?"

One nodded again, harder now, as if trying to convince herself.

"Yes, it is decided, then. Yes, I will help you as I have always said I would try to do. But you must let me handle this, handle *them* . . ."

Rakeen's *them* vibrated with contempt. The air between him and One seemed to vibrate too, with — what? What had Rakeen meant by our whole arrangement? Sex, after all? I clamped my lips over my braces. What girl wouldn't prefer bad boy Prince Rakeen to me?

"Ra-keen — " the deep, distant Madame Jiluwi voice called down from above. A word in must-be-Arabic, then: "The van — "

Her imperious command carried clearly through One's open door. It sounded like Madame Jiluwi must be standing in the open kitchen doorway leading to the basement steps.

Rakeen turned brusquely. He shouted out the door of One's room: "Yes, I hear — I come!"

Then he spun back around, facing the three of us. Behind his Clark Kent glasses, his eyes narrowed. He told One in tense whisper: "I am locking the door to outside, from outside, as it is at night."

One jerked her head in automatic nod. But Mom spoke up.

"Wait a minute now, you can't lock us in here — " she began.

"Yes, Missus, I can," Rakeen told Mom so matter-of-factly she seemed stumped. "And you will please show me what it is in your pocket? What it is you were reaching for, before . . ."

Don't do it Mom, I thought in brainwaves. *Don't give him your cell phone.* If she even had that phone she so often forgot.

Stiffly, Mom pulled both her raincoat pockets inside out, showing they were empty. Was Rakeen going to frisk her or something? I tensed up, ready to stop him. Or to try.

But he glanced at the pockets and met Mom's eyes almost like they were allies. Then he nodded like: yeah, he trusted her.

"Really, you can't *do* this — " Mom repeated but Rakeen gave no sign of even hearing her words. He slipped the camera that he still held into his own pocket. He stepped out the door, shut it quietly.

Leaving me standing between them, scared to look at either of them: Mom or One.

———————————

MAURA

Joezy broke the sealed-up silence that Rakeen left behind. "I swear, I didn't mean for any shit like this to happen . . ."

"I know," I took his hand, gave it a quick stiff squeeze.

Through the room's shut door, we heard another bigger door — the door Rakeen had promised to lock — open then slam shut. Locked in: I felt it.

I stuffed my inside-out raincoat pockets back in place. The girl, One, turned and padded over to her porthole-like window.

Too narrow a window for any of us to squeeze through.

But I stepped up beside the girl, our arms lightly brushing. I peered with her into the raindrop-blurred glass. A Symmes Medical Center van stood parked in the driveway, its giant side door open.

Two women in shawls were laboriously steering a wheelchair toward the van. In the chair, I made out Rakeen's strong-boned hawk-nosed profile on a hunched older man, his balding head held high. Rakeen himself suddenly appeared, striding from the back of the house, brushing leaves off his sweat jacket shoulders.

Halting at the van doors, Rakeen took over the wheelchair. With practiced motions, he maneuvered the chair onto the van's wheelchair lift. Then he bent forward and quickly kissed the sagging jowly cheek of his father. Glancing up, Rakeen gave the van driver a nod. The wheelchair rose, stately and slow in the drizzle.

Then Rakeen helped the two shawl-wrapped women into the back of the van; he heaved the van doors shut. A decent son.

"Were those women — one of them — his mother?" I asked One.

"No-no." One shook her head as the Symmes van trundled away. "Mother-sisters. Madame Jiluwi, she is — " One rolled her eyes toward the ceiling. "Up the stairs, always."

"Do you think she knows we're down here?"

One shrugged, her dragonfly tattoo showing. And I pictured Frannie's tattoo, last night. Only last night a rum-flavored kiss from Frannie had seemed incredible, life-quaking. Now — what was I, what were we, facing? If only Dan wasn't stuck in New York. If only he were back at the house to miss us. What would he do, here?

As if I knew, I turned from One and the window. I hurried back over to the door where Joezy hovered.

"This might be, like, our one chance to get outta here," Joezy mumbled. Reading my thoughts. He took hold of the doorknob.

"No." I reached out and pressed my hand over his, firmly. "If anyone's going to open that door, it'll be me," I told Joezy, finding my old mother voice. Always so much surer sounding than I ever felt. But I turned the knob, pushed the door quietly open.

Just a crack. I leaned into that space, heard clearly — from the top of the stairs — boys giggling. Hearing me right now? I shut the door, fast but soft. I met Joezy's eyes: as plainly afraid as mine.

"OK, OK; so those other boys are just waiting for us to try something. Look, I've gotta know — " I lowered my voice as if One by the window couldn't hear. "You've got to tell me, now, fast — what's really going on here. What you've really done."

JOEZY

Man, I wanted to bust out of that room — even though I knew that those freaking boys were waiting. That freaking Rakeen had locked the door to the fenced-in backyard. That I didn't dare sneak up the stairs with those boys plus Madame Jiluwi lurking. Not to mention Rakeen himself, who'd soon come striding down the basement stairs.

Still, facing any of them felt easier than facing my mom.

I looked at the door, not her. Not at One either. She and Mom both waiting, and Rakeen on his way back to us. If we were somehow going to die down here, then I could at least tell the truth.

But what was true? It was true that I hadn't meant to buy One, but also true that I sort of had. It was true that I'd wanted to save her, but also true that she was in more danger than before, because of me. I drew a big breath; it wheezed.

"I fucked up," I managed to Mom on exhale.

Beside me, Mom didn't flinch at that word like she would have done an hour ago, back in our old life.

"I first came over to *help* One, then she, then we — she, um, you know — " I lowered my voice as far as it would go. "With her mouth."

I paused and the world didn't blow up. Mom and One were both still listening. But I had to say everything fast, right now.

"You gotta believe me, Mom, she really is being held here." I turned to One, her face shadowy. "That part's true, right? They, this family, they won't let you go? And they never pay you?"

One nodded. But then she added, less certainly: "No in moany. No to me . . ."

"To who?" I blurted out. "To your uncle?"

But One was shaking her head no. Mom by the door flicked on the light. One and I blinked from opposite sides of the room.

"Is it also true," Mom asked loudly, like she was talking from the head of a classroom, "that my son *did* 'pay' you — ?

Here, One shifted an uneasy squinting gaze to me.

"She might've, must've — *thought* that's what I meant to do, last week. But just now?" I faced a confused-looking One. "Just now, when we were, um, just before Rakeen came in — ?"

When you were kissing me back, I meant. *When you were letting me taste mango and smoke on your tongue?*

One shook her head — maybe saying, No, that part was real? Or maybe saying, No, only in your dreams? "I — no-know." She still shook her head. "Today, no-know. Other day, you do. You pay."

I nodded too: one hard OK-I-did nod.

My mother actually asked, her voice still teacher-sized, "Besides saying he paid you, Rakeen claimed that my son — my son 'forced' you, 'made' you — ?"

"*I* make me." One looked down fast, done with both of us. She studied her bare feet again. "For dollars; for me be — free. For me, One, me-sell. What I want, you son know. Be free . . ."

At this last, One looked pointedly at my limp denim jacket lying on her mattress, its overfilled pocket.

"Well hell, maybe we can get you free," I blurted out. "Maybe we *can* help each other," I blathered on in Fairwell-speak.

I stepped toward One so I stood on one side of her mattress and she on the other. The hidden thousand dollars zipped up between us.

"If we can all just get outta here, Mom and me can help you! I swear — " I spun on my heel, faced Mom. "Right, Mom?" I asked breathless-like, my face stretched into my old surefire pleading-boy pose. Only this time it — my pleading — was for real.

Here we were shut away in this basement, Rakeen coming back any second, maybe with the gun from the safe. Couldn't Mom see that this was an emergency, that we needed One on our side?

But Mom hesitated, started to shake her head.

"You say no and I'll — I'll tell Dad about you and Frannie who's-it!"

Here Mom stepped right up to me. Her pale eyes, my eyes, going paler. "You'd — tell him that — that you saw — whatever you saw?"

"Yeah, duh, I'm not *blind*, Mom. Not deaf either. I saw you two in the art room thingy, saw you and Frannie stripped down and talking dirty, talking 'bout having fucking 'breakfast in bed' . . ."

Again Mom didn't flinch. Her face looked stripped-down, her eyes and skin and lips so pale.

"I'm sorry you saw that," Mom breathed in her careful almost un-hearable whisper. "But don't use that against me this way . . ." She shook her head, her eyes dry and sad. "Oh Joezy, who *are* you?"

I was wondering that myself, wondering it about my maybe-lezbo mom too. "Look Mom, you tell on me and I'll tell on you."

"Joezy, good God, don't be ridiculous," Mom snapped at my childish words. "Here we are facing who knows what and you're talking about some foolish — Look, I can only imagine how it looked but it was just two drunk moms, just a, a game — "

"But see, that's what I thought — with her!" I shot a look to intently listening One, then back to impatiently listening Mom.

"With One," I told Mom, "I even said I wanted to play, just play. And to me, One and me were just — playing around, down here. Then it all just turned so freaking — serious." I gasped a breath. "That's the thing, Mom; it might make Dad mad to hear about you 'playing around' with that Frannie, but it wouldn't *kill* you . . ." I jerked my head at One. "I mean, it could kill One, that's what she thinks, to get sent back to Vietnam and all. With no money and all . . ."

Mom leaned close to me again, so I smelled her unshowered sweat, her panic. "What are you saying we should do — ?"

"Moany." One finally spoke behind me, raising her voice louder than I'd ever heard it. "He bring — me for — ?" One dropped to her knees on her mattress. She seized my denim jacket, unzipped the pocket. She yanked out one of the three rubber banded money wads.

Battered cash from PTA pockets, from the door tickets and the cash bar. Dirtier than stolen money ever looks in a movie.

"Joezy!" Mom marched over. "Good God, you did — last night — ?"

"Steal," One filled in for Mom like some bright-eyed star student. "He steal moany? I — I tell po-lice if, if — " She struggled to re-construct my vengeful sentence. "I — if you — tell too — "

"Nobody is telling any police anything!" My mother announced in full teacher mode. "No police would believe a word we'd say, it's all so crazy. Now let's stop all these threats — "

Mom held out her hand firmly to One. She wiggled her fingers.

One stood, clutching the money, biting her lips so her big teeth showed.

Moany, moany, I was thinking, a moaning sound in my throat where my breath was trapped. My mom planted her hands on her hips like she was about to scold One. Make things even worse.

"No, Mom," I tried to say, plead. Then I gulped the chill toilet-cleaner air of One's cellblock room. Straining to catch my breath.

Mom was spinning around, rushing back to me, and hugging me close. It had been years since I'd hyperventilated, years since Mom had pressed me to her slim body so tightly. I gripped her back and gasped for air. My head going light; my breaths wheezing louder.

"A bag — is there a bag in this damn room?" Mom barked out to One. I heard muffled shuffling sounds. Suddenly Mom was shoving a cigarette-smelling plastic bag into my face.

I held the crinkly bag over my mouth and nose, its smell different than the paper-bag and hot breath smell of years ago. Still, I drew big shuddery breaths, my eyes squeezed shut.

When I raised my face from the smoky CVS bag, blinking, Mom still stood before me. Flustered but determined. "You OK, Joezy?"

I managed a nod. Mom nodded too, smoothing her mussed hair. She took the mini CVS bag from me, stuffed it in her raincoat pocket.

"Listen, you two," Mom said to One and me. For once I was glad to hear Mom's teacher voice. "We're in trouble here. We can't think now about anything but — now. But getting out of this mess, trying to reason with this boy Rakeen . . ."

The thing was, though, *now* kept right on coming.

Outside One's door, we heard footsteps — multiple thudding sneaker-steps — down the wood basement stairs. Rakeen and all his brothers? Marching toward us like an army?

Only One sprang into action. She dropped down again to her knees. She stuffed the rubber banded money back into my jacket. Boy-steps outside thumped the carpeted floor. One quick-zipped the stolen money back inside my pocket.

So now that money was our — hers and mine and Mom's — secret.

CHAPTER ELEVEN
IN THE SAFE

MAURA

Loud footsteps sounded outside the door, but no one came in.

The three of us stood paralyzed by the shut door, hearing metal clanks: the bikes, the skateboards? Then hearing the door to what must be a backyard open, slam, open again.

A boy shouting as if he'd found something. The door slammed a final time. Footsteps thumped again: first carpet, then wood stairs.

That door: had those younger boys re-locked it? Was it possible that Rakeen didn't know those boys had just snuck down here? That the door to the outside might no longer be locked?

I held up my hands, still brightly nail-polished from last night, signaling Joezy and One to stay where they were. Not that either of them looked like they knew what else to do. One still knelt on the mattress, having zipped the money my son stole back in his pocket.

So maybe she was more trustworthy than my own son? This was my unmotherly thought as I turned my back on mutely staring Joezy. I pressed my ear to the door, remembering old fire safety instructions. *Feel the door; if it feels hot, don't open it.*

"Sounds like no one's out there." I drew a breath of the dank closed-in Lysolized air. "I'm going to go see if that back door is still locked," I announced in my falsely sure-sounding mom voice.

At the same time, another voice inside me wondered if those footsteps had been some act, some trap. If Rakeen was crouched in the rec room, waiting to jump whoever stepped out first.

On impulse, I turned to Joezy and hugged him again, less tightly now that he could breathe. He didn't cling to me like he'd done while hyperventilating minutes before, but he didn't push me away.

Oh Joezy, I thought as I held him, *I used to be your one.*

I gripped my son's tall tensed-up body and stared over his shoulder at the girl on the mattress. Now, would he really betray me for this — whatever-she-was?

Girl, I reminded myself as I let my son go. The teenage girl pushing back her bangs nervously, acne on her forehead. A girl regarding me with the same hopeful expectant look as Joezy.

Two kids, counting on me.

"Be careful Mom," Joezy mumbled as I re-faced the door.

No turning back now. No matter how scared I was of Rakeen catching me, I was more scared of becoming (the absurd news voice headline boomed in my mind) "Hostage Mom Fails to Save Son; Takes Blame for Basement Room Bloodbath."

"And Mom?" Joezy added in a clearer voice as I turned the doorknob. "They — the family — they keep a gun in the safe . . ."

"In the safe," I repeated, my brain overloaded.

"I saw it, Mom — this safe under the basement steps."

"Right." I nodded like I had a plan. I opened the door.

No one. The rec room was still lit-up, still empty. Footsteps shuffling about upstairs, but none near the kitchen, its open door to the basement. I crept across the carpeted floor, tiptoeing in my boots around the ping-pong table. I tried the knob of the door leading out.

Locked. I rattled the knob, feeling some sort of bolt lock outside the door hold it fast. Damn; Rakeen didn't miss a trick. Was he dangerous? Was I assuming that based on the panicky prejudices my ACLU member blog railed against? All those emailed rants so distant as I crept toward the basement steps. In the safe, *in the safe.*

That was where I had to keep my son, keep him and that young girl. I'd keep them safe if I could somehow get that gun out of the safe. Into my hands before it got into Rakeen's. *There it is,* I realized, blinking into the dimness under the stairs.

A big white washing machine; a small grey metal safe.

I crouched down, ready to creep up to the safe and try its lock, when — with a crack of wood that stuttered my pulse — footsteps thumped again, directly above me.

I jumped sideways; I ducked behind a large sheet of plywood leaning on the wall. I flattened myself against that cinderblock wall, holding my breath, hearing a young boy's voice pipe up defensively.

"I *did* lock it, like you said! I climbed the fence, I swear to it!"

Rakeen's deeper voice answered with an Arabic word that had the universally harsh ring of a curse. "What I *told* you was to stay upstairs, stay away from them down here," Rakeen admonished, reaching the foot of the stairs. His own voice was softly accented; the younger boy's voice held no accent, only an all-American whine.

"But why? You let me be the one on Halloween — "

This boy and Rakeen were crossing the basement.

"Halloween was a game, Rasha," Rakeen told the kid curtly. "This is — for the real."

And I heard the doorknob to the outside door I'd just tried to open rattle: Rakeen checking that it was, as the kid named Rasha had claimed, locked. For the real; what in hell did Rakeen mean?

"See?" Rasha piped up more quietly, still on Rakeen's heels as Rakeen crossed back over to the stairs. "See you *can* trust me. You gotta tell me: what're you gonna do to Pig-Boy? And his mom? Are they in there with One? We really got those piggies in, like, prison?"

Both boys had stopped near my flimsy slanted plywood shield, so close my throat pulse thumped again. So loud I half expected them to hear it and turn to me. But they kept standing where I'd been standing a moment before, facing their washer and their safe.

Rakeen swore again in Arabic, but softly. "I will tell you, show you. Then you will go up the stairs, you understand me?" Rakeen's voice held the weary pseudo-parental tone of any oldest brother.

"Here is our problem, Rasha. One: she has been telling the Pig-Boy everything, everything I have been telling Mother. Saying she is staying here 'against her will,' how this is against all America's law. All of that. You have heard me tell to Mother how much trouble we could all be in, how much safer we would all be with Uncle Izrin — "

"Yeah, yeah," Rasha cut in with his American-boy impatience. "Uncle Izrin in Paris; Auntie P. in Saigon; yada yada yada. Tell me something I *don't* know. Like what you wanna do — "

"Not 'want to,' Rasha; must do. Do you not see? One, she is a smart girl; she has told everything to this Pig-Boy; she must be telling it now to Pig-Boy's mother. There is no more keeping of this secret for us, no more keeping of One here — "

"'Less we *make* 'em keep this secret! Those piggies. They scare easy, like you say, like Halloween. We can make 'em do what we want, Rakeen! That's what you're down here for, right? For Papa's gun?"

Rakeen shot back an Arabic word, something along the lines of: Shut up. "No, not for that, for something else," Rakeen mumbled. "I will show you what; then you will go up the stairs — "

I heard movement. I dared to angle my head so I could see Rakeen crouching down as I had done: Rakeen disappearing into the cave-like space under the stairs. My pulse thudded my throat so hard, so loud in my own ears. Surely one of them would hear.

But young Rasha — ramrod straight in his new-looking jeans and Star Wars t-shirt — watched only Rakeen. I heard a metallic click, a squeak. A metal door opening.

"One's papers," Rakeen was telling his brother. "They are in here somewhere — "

"Papers?" Rasha whined, bouncing on his heels, holding himself back from lunging forward. "But the gun, it's there; you gotta take it out. You might need it with those piggies — "

"I said no, Rasha," Rakeen faintly replied. A sound of papers rustling, like he was looking through a pile. In the safe, in the safe.

Not the gun, I found myself thinking to that same beat, what Joezy called brainwaves, aimed toward Rakeen. *Not the gun; please don't take the gun. Anything but the goddamn gun.*

"Ra-keen — " the boy Rasha blurted out, pleading the opposite case, "Don't leave Papa's gun — "

A clear decisive squeak: a door starting to shut. Then a thumping whoosh. The muffled bumbling sounds of boy struggle. Rakeen shouted an Arabic curse; something heavy clanked the empty washer. Behind my plywood, I stood stiffer than that bendy board.

My fingers twitched. Should I lunge out too, jump into the fray, try to seize the gun? What would a brave competent mom do?

"Give me that," Rakeen demanded, his voice stretched tight. His cool about to crack. And his kid brother had the gun? A real gun?

I tensed my limbs, pushed my board forward slightly. So I glimpsed Rakeen's rigid back, his own arms reaching out. He must be facing the Rasha boy, who must be holding the father's gun.

Rasha's boy-voice was suddenly high-pitched, incredulous.

"But you all-ways say, Rakeen — you always say they should be pun-ished, those piggies — And now we've got two of 'em right here and you know he — He de-filed One and all — that Pig-Boy — "

He's not a Pig-Boy and you're not going to shoot him.

Those words burst out only in my head. My throat full of pulse. But I was shoving away my plywood board, my shield. It tipped with a crack against the floor. I stumbled forward into view; both boys spun 'round in the cramped space, startled, bumping each other.

Rakeen took advantage of the disruption to seize hold of Rasha's arm. I glimpsed a metal muzzle glint. A real gun; the real gun; my God, there really was a gun.

"You stay away from my son — " I cried out as Rakeen and Rasha struggled, so loud surely my son could hear. "And you stay where you are, Joezy — " I added in near shriek, jerking my head 'round.

One's room door cracked open an inch, then slammed shut.

"Stay — where — you — are — " I repeated in hyper-enunciated don't-mess-with-me mom speak. The door stayed shut.

"And you, Missus — you stay. Where you are . . ."

I jerked back around. I was standing by the fallen plywood, facing Rakeen, his glasses crooked. He was holding it now. Not pointing it; just holding it at his side. An unwieldy pistol-style gun, its handle oversized. Only a flash, but real. A gun from Hollywood, only I knew by the way Rakeen's hand tensed to support its weight it was all too real.

And loaded; why keep it in the safe if it was not loaded?

My fingers twitched wildly. To keep from raising my hands in the air like Joezy, I gripped my ribcage. I was still wearing my open raincoat over my Fairwell t-shirt and jeans. I was still the mother here, the teacher. I met Rakeen's eyes, fierce but frightened too.

Did I detect a shakiness in Rakeen's own hand, the hand that held the heavy-looking gun, pointed, for now, at the floor?

A gun, the gun, the audible pulse in my throat pumped.

I didn't trust myself to speak. But I stood planted in place, my way of saying: *Yes, I am staying where I am. No, you will have to shoot me before you'll get near my son with that goddamn gun.*

If Rakeen raised the gun, would I be brave enough to say all that, for real? Behind Rakeen, half-hidden, young Rasha fidgeted.

"Get upstairs," Rakeen said loudly and flatly, still facing me. Did he mean me? I wondered even as his wiry brother scrambled out from behind him. "You will keep them up there too —" Rakeen added. Meaning the other boys? Or those boys plus their mother?

Rasha managed one quick nod. Those long-lashed eyes, the half-scared half-bold boy face. Definitely the same boy who'd worn the fake-blood-stained Toys"R"Us Marine uniform.

Skinny harmless-looking Rasha in his Star Wars t-shirt scuttled between Rakeen and me to reach the stairs. Then he trudged up, slow, as if he hoped we'd start talking while he could still hear.

"You will shut that door behind you," Rakeen added as his final loud command. The door above us thudded, sullenly shut.

So I was left alone with the boy with the gun.

I dared one direct glance at the gun — I'd never seen a real and presumably loaded one. Not unsheathed, anyway. Only the bulky heavily encased guns on policemen's belts; guns that looked like they'd be impossible to pull out fast, in a flash.

But the gun that Rakeen held at his side — his hand tensed though his arm hung loosely — that gun looked plenty easy to pull.

I drew another deep disinfectant-tasting breath; I mustered a hoarse version of my teacher voice.

"Look, you — you don't want to — do this." I raised my voice above the ringing in my ears. "You — you point that — gun at me,

Rakeen, and there'll be, you know — con-consequences. Big consequences for you, your family. I — I'm sure you don't want — "

"This gun is not pointed at you," Rakeen cut in. He swung the gun slightly as if testing his loose arm. He had switched back to his maddening detached philosophical tone. He would make a good teacher himself: unflappable and effortlessly commanding. Numbly, I watched the slight swing of that downward-pointing gun. "This gun, it was my father's, Missus . . ."

"Your father is — very sick, isn't he?"

Rakeen didn't nod; he did the opposite of nod. He stiffened his neck and held his head extra still. Listening to me.

"I — I saw you out there by the van. You have a lot of, um, responsibility here, don't you? You're a — smart boy. So why do you keep doing such, such — stupid dangerous things? Things that could get you and your — your family in so much — serious trouble?"

Rakeen's dark alert eyes flicked up at me. The ringing in my ears sharpened. "You make a threat to my family, Missus?"

His already tense hand tightened around the oversized gun handle. He wasn't used to holding guns, I felt dazedly sure.

"You — you're the one with the gun," I pointed out, keeping my voice classroom steady despite shooting pains in my lower back. "You're telling us we can't leave, holding us here. You're the one who showed up on our doorstep talking about — 'dead Americans.' "

Rakeen's stern close-lipped mouth twitched on one side. He met my gaze as if he expected me to grin too. Like a long-ago music student who'd pulled out a folded Swiss Army knife in my class. But I'd faced him down; the knife had stayed folded.

"You may have meant that Halloween stunt as some kind of, of —joke," I pushed on, "But you frightened us, frightened our neighbors. And how — how could you put your whole family at risk? Right now, with everyone all riled up and police looking for anything suspicious. You had people calling the police about that, you know — "

"Oh I know, Missus," he cut in fast, like he had to prove some point. "People such as you, I have not a doubt. But then, you all were already afraid of us, my brothers and me. You all run across busy Mystic Avenue to avoid us. And you see, Missus, that time, Halloween, that time we — I did want for you all to call po-lice."

"But why?" I burst out, so exasperated that I actually stepped forward. Rakeen's smug expression faltered. He still didn't dare raise that gun. "Why after everything that happened in, in New York — why on earth would you want to stir up trouble with the police?"

"Stir up — a little trouble," Rakeen answered, pointing at me with his free gun-less hand. Boyishly eager to assert that he knew what he was doing. "Little, not big. We'd get in little-not-big trouble, not in Land of the Free, not on Halloween — you see?"

"But to stir up even a 'little' trouble; it's so risky and foolish."

"The fool is you," Rakeen interrupted curtly, his glasses still crooked, his pride offended. He swung the heavy-looking gun at his side as he launched into a rushed defensive explanation. "You and your neighbors: so foolishly frightened. We only dressed up, Rasha and me. Nothing not-legal. But — you see, Missus, I did want police calls. I wanted you-all to make a big fuss over a little fun." Rakeen looked at the gun he was swinging, nervously. Muzzle still pointed down. "I wanted police, even, to call my home, tell my mother. Warn her. Make her see that we, our family, we are not safe here."

"And — where do you think your family *would* be safe?" Surely this was good that I had him talking, telling me his plans. Boys loved to tell their plans. I knew that much as a teacher, a mom. Now if only Joezy and One knew enough to stay put. I side-glanced at their door: cracked open again. Damn them. I looked quickly back to Rakeen. "Do you mean — back in your home country, in Saudi — "

"Ha." Rakeen stopped swinging the gun. He glared up at me as if forbidding me to say his country's name. "We have no place there anymore, among my father's enemies." He shook his head, talking on, maybe despite himself. "You think I am stupid, Missus?"

He stopped shaking his head, looked back at the gun at his side.

"So where do you think your family should be?" I repeated boldly, to keep him talking. "I overheard your, your brother say something about relatives in Saigon or, or France?"

"France, yes," Rakeen mumbled to his gun. He shook his head again. "Not that it is of your business." Yet he added: "I tell my mother we ought to go to France, but she will not listen."

Rakeen straightened his glasses. With his lilting Arabic accent, he sounded detached and professorial as he went on, still addressing his gun. "She will not listen, so I try to make her see. How you all hate us here. That is why we do what you call foolish. We dress up for Halloween; we paint threats on our garage. And the police do call, do warn. But my mother, she still does not listen."

Rakeen looked up at me, blinking as if awakening. As if half-expecting to see his own stubborn mother standing before him.

"OK, I — I get it." I took a firm motherly step closer. Close enough so if Rakeen raised that damn gun I'd stand a chance of lunging at him, knocking it from his hand.

"OK, so you, you tried to make just enough trouble to make your mom want to leave, to fly you all to France. OK, I get that. But do you get that this," I nodded toward the motionless gun. "This could be real trouble, big trouble? This could land you in jail?"

A hysterical edge was creeping into my voice, I'd raised it so high above the ringing only I could hear. Yet Rakeen wasn't blinking, was listening. I almost had him, I sensed.

"You don't want — this." I jerked another stiff nod at the gun. "Y-you don't want to hold us, me and my son, hostage — "

"Oh but Missus, I used to think I did want . . ." Rakeen stopped himself, half-raising the gun, speculatively. Halfway pointing it at my knees. I backed up one step. My pulse was throbbing so hard and my ears ringing so loud I didn't think I could speak again.

Only, if he moved one more inch, scream.

"But now that I have got it, got you here, you and your Pig-Boy son," Rakeen lowered the gun. "It is not, you are not, worth it."

He shifted the gun to his other hand. To his right hand, I noticed somehow through my ear-ringing and pulse-pounding. Rakeen flexed the freed fingers of his left hand. With his right hand, surely his shooting hand, he curled his finger into the trigger.

This time his arm, his right arm, did not hang loosely. He tensed his whole arm, maybe ready to really lift that gun.

Everything went quiet inside me.

"You all are so easy to frighten. This gun — " Rakeen merely wagged it at his side. "This was my father's gun. He has carried it into battle. My father has medals from his battles, and scars. He is a good man, good Muslim man. Not like — " Rakeen jerked his head around, facing One's door. The cracked-open door slammed shut.

JOEZY

I spun 'round to One. Away from that door I hadn't meant to slam. "A *gun*, I saw it, kinda glimpsed it. A real fucking gun."

One nodded solemnly, her whole face so serious and knowing.

"Holy crap, he's gonna shoot my mom? We gotta do something." I reached again for the doorknob; One stepped up fast beside me.

She planted both hands flat on the door, holding it shut. I knew I was stronger. But she shook her head in that freaking babysitter way. Calmer than me, because she knew Rakeen wouldn't blow her head off? "No-no. She say, you mama say, stay here."

"Stay here? When that psycho's holding a gun on my mom?"

One shook her head harder, still holding the damn door. I could hardly think: my insides so churned up, that gun so real.

"You talk to him!" I grabbed One's bony wrist, hard. Her bone felt small, like I could snap it with a squeeze. My stupid stomach fizzed. "Listen, One, he'd freaking listen to you!"

She lost her hold on the door, wrenched her wrist from my grasp. She faced me with wide shocked eyes: like I was gonna throw her out there alone with Rakeen and Mom and the gun.

For a second, I saw my pale panicked face in her widened eyes. "I mean we; I take you out there. And we talk to Rakeen."

"We? Rakeen? He no hurt, no hurt me, never-no."

"*No* hurt!" I banged the door with my fist. I had to stop myself from grabbing One's wrist again, twisting it. "No hurt? He's hurting my mom, just holding that gun out there! He's *crazy* One! He *hit* me! He came to our house dressed like a freaking terrorist!"

My voice rose squeaky high. And One held up her hands to stop me from grabbing her wrist again or worse.

"You," One shouted. "You terror me! You terror me!"

I wanted to clamp my hand over her mouth. But One's big white teeth gleamed on me. Like if I tried, she'd bite me.

"OK, OK," I told her, keeping my hands clenched, forcing myself to slow down. Only way I'd get her to help me disarm her psycho-boyfriend. "OK, I get it that y-you hate me. But is he your, your . . ." I swept my hand 'round; found myself gesturing right at her mattress.

She drew a sharp breath. "He no, he want, but he no."

"What, what?" I demanded. Christ, which was worse for Mom and me; if he was or wasn't screwing One? "You're saying he's not, like, having sex with you? But he's, like, telling you he wants to?"

"He no tells! No tell me — I just — I can, me — *tell.*"

"You can tell he wants to, he likes you — OK, OK: then let's get out there and you tell him to stop, just freaking *stop* with the gun!"

"He no hurt!" One grabbed hold of my shoulders. How could she be so sure of that fucking lunatic? "Rakeen no hurt no one. He — want help me. He buy for me — cigarettes!"

The smoky CVS bag; that small-sized bag he'd slipped to her in the parking lot. I was breathing so hard I'd need that bag again soon.

"Rakeen — he al-way say. Some-day, he — he try help me."

"What day? How about freaking today?" I pulled back from her hold. "How about we go out there and *make* him help you?"

One looked from me to the closed door in front of us. "You no know. They, Jiluwi family, they have, have, with my un-cle."

"A deal?" I prompted, clenching my hands harder. Was this why she wouldn't help us? "What Rakeen said, some deal, with your uncle, your mom's brother, some bad deal?"

One nodded, teary-eyed now. "Can no-tell, no-tell."

"What, it's drugs, right? Drug-dealing or whatever?" Those midnight deliveries, I was thinking fast, that Dad saw at their garage.

"No-no. Not like you say." She shook her head stubbornly.

"Fine, OK, you keep your secret! Whatever! But you gotta, we gotta get out there with my mom. You gotta go with me *now.*"

And I reached out, grabbed hold of One's arm again. But she jerked her arm back, jerked her foot forward. She kicked me away — kicked my fricking shin, so hard I yelped.

"What the *fuck?*" I gaped at One. My pained leg tensed, wanting to kick her right back. That girl was staring me down so fiercely, I felt sure she'd freaking kill me if I tried to touch her again.

So I turned my back on One. I grabbed the doorknob and thrust open the door my own fucking self.

MAURA

"Get *back*," I screamed at Joezy: one shock-faced look at him, standing fully exposed in the open doorway.

"Back in," Rakeen behind me echoed sternly. And before he could raise his gun at my son, I spun around to Rakeen as fast as I'd just spun to Joezy. The door slammed, thank God, sharp as a gunshot with Joezy safe behind it? I lunged toward Rakeen and his still-lowered gun.

"Drop that thing," I rasped, the ringing in my ears reaching a piercing peak. I seized Rakeen's elbow, jarring his arm. He almost lost hold of the gun, but he pulled away roughly, shaking off my hand, catching his balance. Keeping his gun grip. Backing away fast from me.

"You," Rakeen gasped, sounding startled and indignant, "You are not my mother!" He rolled his eyes dramatically toward the ceiling.

"Your mo-ther?" I panted, dry-mouthed with panic and hope.

"No, you see, she, she would have grabbed the gun . . ." Rakeen shook his head hard. And he shook his downward-aimed gun lightly, trying to recover his cool. He narrowed his eyes at me as if not to let any respect creep in. I'd actually gotten him to back away. Now, if I could just keep him talking. I waited, unblinking, like when a shelter boy would hesitate to dictate his lyrics. Then it would all spill out.

"How can such weak squealing piggies run the world? This Pig-Boy of yours," Rakeen screwed up his face in contempt, nodding toward the shut door. "You still do not know what he has done. Your son, taking that girl, taking One and, excuse me Missus, but you must know, stuffing his manhood in One's mouth."

I felt my own face screw up, my brain whirring. Yes; Joezy had said, with her mouth, yes; Rakeen must indeed have seen it all.

"And you think we are the dirty ones, the dirty Arabs, when it is not we, Missus, who defile young girls."

"Yes, yes!" I held up one hand like a shaky cop stopping traffic. "Y-your religion, it—it condemns violence, right? Everyone thinks the opposite, since September. But, but the Muslims, the real Muslims."

"*You*? You tell *me* about 'real Muslims'? I will tell you this about my religion," Rakeen hefted the gun as if judging its weight. "It is not just talk, not like your so-called 'religions' here. It is not just empty talk in pretty churches! It is action."

And he turned. He turned his back on me. Now was my chance to jump him, I thought, the ringing clear as a siren in my ears. My spine tensed. But Rakeen ducked his head, edged under the stairs toward the open safe. I craned my neck to see.

What action? What "real Muslim" action he was talking about?

Rakeen reached into the safe, resting the gun there. Then he lifted an envelope. He swung the metal safe door shut with a loud satisfying clank. *In the safe*, I told my numbed self, slumping. The ringing in my ears at last beginning to retreat. The gun is in the safe.

Rakeen stepped out from under the steps, holding only the envelope, muttering. "Father was the soldier; he is the brave one . . ."

"But your father's so sick now," I ventured carefully. Under his manly deadpan, I sensed Rakeen waiting like my son for a mother to tell him what to do. "You're the—the man of your house now."

Is this approach too corny? I wondered. But Rakeen was nodding and I pushed on. "You—you're right to put that gun away. Right, too, that your family could be in trouble. Believe me, big legal trouble for, for holding that girl here," I nodded at One's abashedly shut door.

Rakeen waved the envelope he held, impatiently. "I have told my mother this, Missus. But she thinks she is fulfilling a promise to One's dead mother, keeping One off dirty dangerous American streets, keeping her safe. That is how she sees it." Rakeen rolled his eyes again at the ceiling, helplessly, "My mother . . ."

"She's up there now?" I asked the flaky plaster ceiling, wondering if her silent presence had protected us all. Rakeen nodded, sighed.

"My mother, she sleeps. Most of the day."

"And takes care of your father at night?" I dared to guess. Another resigned nod from Rakeen. "So it's up to you?" I reached out to touch his shoulder. He stiffened all over; his forbidding stare stopped me.

Wasn't I stupidly violating a rule about touching Muslim men? Was I going to lose all the advantage I'd painstakingly gained? My hand dropped. Behind his glasses, Rakeen glared at me yet again.

"Look, Rakeen. I know you don't like us. But my son and I both know about One now. Even if you try to, to blackmail us with some silly photo, One isn't going to just sit still here. She wants out; she knows more now, knows what trouble your family could be in."

Rakeen nodded. Weary, wary. Behind those grown-up glasses, I sensed a teenage boy relieved to have an adult laying down his options.

I kept talking, dry-mouthed but gaining steam. "Your family could be arrested; at best, deported. You need to . . ." I stopped myself from saying *let us all go.* I knew enough about boys to know it had to be, to seem like his own decision. "Need to do something."

Rakeen looked at the worn envelope in his hand. I looked at it too, glimpsing the name "Le Ti One" and the word "Immigration." Rakeen folded the envelope decisively so only its blank side showed.

My own spent heartbeat rose. Had I actually talked him down? Would he let her go, let us go? Would it really all be over?

"You're doing the right thing," I told him impulsively, too soon.

Rakeen snapped at me, his eyes on the envelope he held, "You have no idea, Missus, what it is I am doing, will do."

"I — I didn't mean," I sputtered, a sinking in my chest. It wasn't over. The gun was in the safe but we, Joezy and me, weren't safe.

"This will cost you, Missus." Rakeen shouldered by me, striding over to One's door. He shoved it open. Coming up behind him, I saw Joezy and One both stumbling backwards, like they'd been crowded up next to the door. It was One who stepped forward, facing Rakeen.

"What?" One's voice came out soft, sure, aimed only at him. Maybe he and she were somehow together? One gazed up at him through her bangs. "What do?" she asked Rakeen.

I wondered before he answered if she meant what should I do to them? Or: What are you going to do to us?

CHAPTER TWELVE
LAND OF THE FREE

JOEZY

We'd heard only basement-muffled bits of what Mom had said to Rakeen after I'd opened that door. Seeing Mom face me all fucking furious; only halfway glimpsing behind her Rakeen and a dull grey flash of what must've been his gun. How the hell had Mom gotten him to put it away? He had put it away, hadn't he? That fucking gun.

After I'd shut us back in, after we'd shut up our own shouting, we'd stood side by side just panting and listening, my shin throbbing.

Now Rakeen stood planted yet again in One's doorway, still wearing his Clark Kent glasses and his blank smug face. Like my kick-ass mom hadn't just talked him out of killing-or-whatever us.

"I will tell you." Rakeen answered One's quiet question loudly, addressing us all, like he was our ruler or something.

Jump him, I tried telling Mom in brainwaves. She stood behind Rakeen with her arms folded, her raincoat rumpled. Her face all drained of color except for her freckles and her gleaming green eyes.

God, had Mom somehow fought Rakeen out there, under the steps, while I'd been grabbing One, threatening One? Shouldn't I have run forward despite her command, tackled Rakeen myself like I'd always thought the 9/11 plane passengers should've done?

"I will tell you what we are going to do," Prince Rakeen told us all from the doorway. No big-bulge gun visible in his sweat jacket.

He glanced at me, the boy who'd cowered safe behind the door. Kicked by a girl, my shin so sore. Rakeen and me thinking I was a worthless boy and my mom the only one worth fearing. Anyhow, he turned on his heel. He faced Mom fast like she might jump him.

"You Missus: you will come in here too, if you please."

Tell him you do not please, I told Mom in raging brainwave. But she stepped quietly by Rakeen, into the room again, letting him run the show. She met my widened stare with her own. Her whole tensed-up Mom-face told me silently: *Hush.*

She stepped beside me so we stood shoulder to shoulder, her arm brushing mine. *God Mom,* I thought. And, in the same brain-breath, *Thank-God.* My shaky-brave mother was still here, beside me.

"All right then." Mom nodded at Rakeen. Maybe they, in the conversation One and I had strained to overhear, reached some sort of agreement. Thank God, I thought again, reaching for Mom. I took hold, squeezing her slim warm familiar hand. She squeezed back so hard it hurt. A firm-fingered Mom squeeze that told me: *I love you; now shut up.*

Rakeen cleared his throat. I clenched my teeth to keep from yelling, *Outta the way! You let us go, you mother-fucking A-rab bastard! You leave my mother alone!*

"You will give me, Missus, the one thousand dollars your son has promised. And you will, none of you will, say a word about One."

No, I brainwaved through clenched teeth to both Mom and One. The two of them stood listening to Rakeen like he wasn't the freaking control-freak holding us hostage.

No — don't fucking trust him. But Mom was nodding; Mom was saying in the firm teacher voice I began hating again: "And you will give me that camera, that photo of my son?"

In ambiguous answer, Rakeen patted the pocket of his sweat jacket. The mini-camera in there. Maybe less than an hour ago, I'd zipped the stolen PTA money in my own pocket.

I'd forced One to stare at that pocket. How mean that seemed now, as smug-faced Rakeen patted his own pocket.

"The photo, yes, of your son forcing himself upon One," Rakeen pronounced coolly. "Listen to me, Missus. If there is any word to the police about my family and One, our arrangement, then there will be word to the police about your son and One. We would not need the photo to make our claim if we have One."

And did he have One? I shifted my stare to the black-haired back of her head. One's head did not nod yes, did not shake no.

"What about that 'arrangement'?" I cut in. "What about those late-night deliveries to your garage, huh?"

Finally I had his fucking attention. Rakeen rounded on me. "That is not of your business!" He lunged toward me and shoved me. I swayed on my sore shin, flailing my arms.

Mom grabbed my shoulders, holding me back. One was taking hold of Rakeen's tensed arm too, though he seemed not to notice.

"You speak to your police about any of this," Rakeen told me in a strained held-back voice, "One may speak to them too."

He shook loose One's hold; he pushed the folded envelope into her hand. "Your visa, One. I believe that this document is in fact use-able, I cannot say for sure, but this is what my mother says."

One gave a loud girlish gasp, looking down at the envelope.

"So most likely you — you do not need to fear the police deporting you," Rakeen told One in a low-voiced rush.

Mom squeezed my shoulder. Maybe Rakeen's family's whole hold on this girl had been cut off with those words.

"But — but," One was stammering, "But Un-cle?"

"*If,*" Rakeen announced, shooting his fucking princely look over at us, "If Pig-Boy should go to police about those boxes, those deliveries — then you, One, you would go too. And you would not need any photograph to tell them how this Pig-Boy, he forced . . ."

"Force?" One cut in, her soft voice confused. Mom kept tight hold of me. "How, me-force?"

"How he *made* you." Rakeen reached in his pocket and pulled out the soap-sized cardboard camera. "How he paid you with his dollars and then made you do, what you did to him."

Rakeen shook that camera. But of course, I was thinking, straining against Mom's grasp, if One were to claim force, it would be better if she did not have whatever photo he supposedly took. Because that maybe-nonexistent photo would not depict any force.

Not any force that showed, anyway. Not like minutes ago, here.

One began nodding, haltingly. Taking, in-fucking-credibly, Rakeen's side. "Yes-yes. He, that time last week, yes. He make me."

I shook my head. Like she picked up on my brainwaves, One turned around to face me. Me standing there unsteady on my kicked shin.

She clasped the envelope in both hands. "I know you no mean."
I know you are not mean? Or: *I know you did not mean to?*

"But. You must-no. No tell any-one about boxes in garage."

"But don't you see," I tried making my voice deeper, like Rakeen's. "All this shit, what this family's pulling, it's all wrong, One. All dangerous to you."

"No," One cut me off. "No like that; you no know." And One re-faced Rakeen. Saying loud enough for us all: "Yes. He make me."

At this, my mother made a small pained sound in her throat, a choked-back sob. I felt like crying too, but for a different dumb reason. Now that Rakeen had given One that envelope himself, he'd taken from me my chance to be the one to save One.

Save this girl who'd just said she might report me to the police.

"No one is going to believe that," Mom was pronouncing, not too convincingly. "And no one is calling any police. Not if you let us go, Rakeen, and give us that damned camera. Then we'll give you your money and, and . . ."

"And One too," I cut in. "You let One go too," I told Prince Rakeen, like my words carried any weight. He eyed me through his glasses the way he'd done on Halloween.

"That is for me and for One to decide," he murmured. "After you go . . ." You intruders, he seemed to mean. You Americans.

One kept her head bowed, pulling a folded paper from the envelope and studying it as if none of us were there. Rakeen raised his hands and rested them on either side of the doorframe, reminding us all that he was still blocking our doorway out.

"Now," he went on, addressing at least this to me. "You claim to me that you did bring the money, all the one thousand dollars?"

"I *did* bring it," I cut in, like it was something to be proud of.

I turned and stepped up to One's mattress, and then I knelt like she had done. My shin ached. My hands shakier than hers, I unzipped the denim pocket she had zipped.

I pulled them out one by one: my three clumsily rubber-banded wads of money. Dirty crumpled-up money. Handed to me by Fair-well parents, paying to get into the auction.

Then there was the cash-bar take; I'd been handed that money by Alison's drunk mom at the end of the evening, when my own way-drunker PTA-Treasurer mom could not be found.

As I laid the wads out on the mattress, I noticed how the rubber bands I'd stupidly used had cut into the bills, leaving mini-tears. God, what if some of the dollars were ruined?

Rakeen seemed to have no such worry. He stepped briskly over to the mattress. He bent, swept up the three wads of money.

"Oh Joezy," my mom exhaled, stepping over to the mattress. She looked down at me with bright disappointed eyes. "You did, then—you really did take all that money, that 9/11 money." I think that, even with all this, Mom still believed her own son wasn't capable of this. He, I, was.

Bills were riffling. Rakeen stood hunched in the doorway, his glasses sliding on his nose, counting through the wads. Beside him, One practically stood on tiptoe to watch.

I pulled myself up from the mattress to face Mom, to try to feel tall again. But I felt small. "C'mon Mom, you can, you know, pay it all back . . ."

Mom shook her head at me, her eyes dried up, "You will, Joezy; you'll earn all the money I pay back. If," She shot a glance at Rakeen counting away, "if we get out of here."

Rakeen stopped counting. He nodded as if satisfied by the amount. He straightened the wads of bills, struggling to hold it all.

"Don't forget," I rallied my nerve to tell him from across One's room, "You said that money was for you *and* One."

Here, proving she was not totally unaware of me, One nodded.

Did she realize we'd made Rakeen recognize the big-deal trouble he and his family could be in, over her? Plus trouble over who-knew-what illegal garage deliveries? Why couldn't One see that Mom and me weren't the bad guys? I took a small shaky step toward One.

Now that Rakeen realized this gig was up, wasn't it in his best interest to give One her so-called visa and some money? And—my heart lightened, even though it wasn't me who'd do it—set her free?

Rakeen squatted on his haunches, laying the three neatened-up wads of money on the carpeted floor, between him and One. Then he pushed his glasses up, stood and faced us.

Mom stepped over beside me; she held out one hand, palm up. "The camera," she prompted.

Rakeen, like a reluctant magician, slipped the camera once more from his pocket. Mom reached out and grasped it. She took a quick step back like she was going to do a drop-kick. And she did drop the camera. Then, with her boot heel, she stomped on it.

The plastic body beneath the cardboard broke with a crack. Mom bent fast, snatched the camera back up. She dug into the crack with her nail-polished fingers, straining to open it.

"Lemme, Mom." I pulled the half-broken camera from her hands, dying to do something, break something myself, even if it was just a crummy drugstore camera. Just a fuzzy never-to-be-seen shot of what I'd done with — done to — One.

Pig-Boy. I dug my own fingers into the camera crack. *Dumb-fuck Pig-Boy,* I thought, cutting my fingertips from gripping so hard. How could I have gotten Mom and me trapped here? How could I have grabbed One's wrist, demanded *she* stand up to Rakeen?

The camera cracked in my hands, broke in two. I let one plastic halve drop; I thumbed out the spool of film. I squeezed its tube in my fist 'til it cracked. Why didn't I lunge out that door myself, fight back? I yanked the film. It spiraled and twisted, reeking of chemicals.

I let the whole mess drop at my own feet. The chemical smell made me feel light-headed. "Make sure — that One gets some money," I managed to say, breathless in this closed room.

Closed-up, closing in. Rakeen now crouched beside One.

"What I have always intended," he told her and me. "One will get your money yes." Rakeen shoved the biggest money wad toward One. She reached for it clumsily, still clutching her visa envelope too.

"Money, ha; my family has plenty of it. Enough of it. Not that they've given me any of my own, yet." Rakeen pulled himself up in one athletic movement, his glasses bouncing. The other two money wads still rested at his feet. Would he take some himself? He brushed off his pants as if brushing off the dirtiness of my money.

"We do not need Pig-Boy's money. On our own, we may make our own escape. So if anyone should attempt to go piggy-squeal to police after all, they, those police, they may find no one here."

"I no-tell," One cut in quietly. "I tell no-thing, no of it." She gazed up through her angled bangs at him, Rakeen. How tall he must have looked from where she squatted.

Really he's no taller than me, I stupidly wanted to point out. *Really he wouldn't be setting you free if it wasn't for me.*

"But," One added in her quietest voice, "But Uncle? If po-lice?"

"I can make you no promises there, One," Rakeen told her quickly, quietly too. "You have not talked of it, explained it all, have you, to . . . ?" He shot a glance at Mom and me.

"No-no," One told only him, solemnly. Why was this Uncle such a secret?

"My family will not talk of it either," Rakeen assured her in his hurried hushed tone. "And we may not, I am hoping, be here long."

"Because me? M-maybe I should not?" One quavered, shaking her head. "For Uncle, his children many; m-maybe if I should stay . . ."

"Do not be foolish," Rakeen told her brusquely, kicking a second rubber-banded wad of money her way. "Already you have decided?"

One did not reply. But she stuffed her visa envelope into her sweatpants pocket. Then, her head bowed as if she felt ashamed, she scooped up the two money clumps, pressed them against her chest.

Her breasts in that black bra; One in that bra in my arms, only an hour ago. Kissing me back. But had she really been hugging, like she was hugging for real, now, my money? Who could blame her for hugging it, this girl with nothing else to hold onto?

Keeping hold of both money wads, One wobbled up to her feet. She stood before Rakeen, her head barely reaching his shoulder. She looked down at her armful of cash then back up at Rakeen, like that bastard alone was responsible.

"I sank you," One told him in a softer more heartfelt voice than she'd used with me, to say the same thing. She inched toward Rakeen. She stood on tiptoe, planted a light quick kiss on his cheek.

Rakeen pulled away, shifting his face from surprised and maybe-pleased back to deadpan.

"I have told you I have a — a girlfriend from Mosque," Rakeen murmured to One in a low intent voice. "But this is not the truth."

One nodded slowly, her back to me. I could feel (though I couldn't see) her round face flushing. Rakeen folded his arms, holding his elbows real tight, staring real hard at her. Maybe if he had lied to her about a girlfriend, it was really true. Maybe he hadn't touched One: Rakeen, who'd bought her cigarettes. Maybe One had sensed he'd morph into her own Superman if she just did something, and I was that something, to make him so mad he'd take action.

"We have sheltered you well here," Rakeen informed One, raising his voice again. "My mother, she has been right about that, at least. You were safe here; as she had promised your mother. Now you will see how you will fare on these American streets." Rakeen nodded toward Mom and me, his lips curving contemptuously. "This 'land of free,' where no one, you remember this, One, no one ever does anything for free."

Casually, showing me up one last time, Rakeen bent and lifted the final wad of money. He handed it to One, wedging it atop the other two wads she clutched. So she had to lower her head further, pin that last wad in place with her chin.

I couldn't see if she was smiling, if she was still gazing up with gratitude at this boy-man who'd helped hold her hostage. If only I'd given her all that money myself, before Rakeen even came down; if only I'd done something bold and brave instead of just letting my mother take over. Letting her let Rakeen do what he wanted.

I was breathing heavily again, wheezing again, when I heard the first clank. I turned on my bruised leg. A heavy clank-clank-clank: someone dragging something metal down the basement stairs.

Was I the only freaking one who heard or noticed? One was busy kneeling and pulling a cloth string bag from her box of clothes. She stuffed her money wads inside. Rakeen still stood in the damn doorway with his arms folded like an invisibly armed guard.

And Mom was saying in her fake-calm teacher tone: "Well then; now that everything's settled . . ."

But it fucking wasn't. Behind Rakeen's shoulder, I glimpsed the brother from Halloween. Rasha, with his big eyes even bigger.

"Wait now, Pigs," Rasha commanded with his boy voice. And he squeezed by his startled brother in the doorway. Rasha Jiluwi burst into our room, clattering. Because Rasha dragged at his side a heavy-sounding real-looking gleaming, clanking sword. *What kind of game's he playing now?* I thought. Then this skinny kid in the Star Wars shirt gripped with both hands, by its carved rusted handle, this big mother-fucking sword. Real-metal heft. The blade was the one part that shone, scary sharp.

"You can't just let 'em go," Rasha whined to Rakeen, who was steadying himself in the doorway. Caught off balance, like me.

"And you cannot tell me what to do," Rakeen began sternly, starting to step toward his wild-eyed sword-wielding brother.

But Rasha turned his back on Rakeen. He braced the sword-handle on his flat belly. He yanked the sword up. The blade made screechy swipey sounds as Rasha waved it back and forth, slicing air.

We all shrank back, all looking at him like: *what the fuck?*

"Yeah!" he shouted, spinning round with that big fucking blade stuck straight out. Mom jumped sideways just as Rakeen jumped forward.

So they collided, Mom and Rakeen, Mom suddenly on her hands and knees at his feet. Blocking him. Meanwhile, Rasha swayed in place and faced me. I backed up, wobbling on my sore shin, cornered.

Rasha spread his legs and bent his knees, warrior stance. He still gripped the sword handle with both white-knuckled hands. He waved that whole two-foot-long screechy-sharp blade, swiping it at me.

"No-no Rasha," One called out, her voice small. Everything

sounded small except for the wheeze of my breaths. The keen whipping slash of that blade against air. I stiffened into a crouch. My skin felt electrified, my limbs super-tensed for a fight.

First real fucking fight of my life.

"*No*," Rakeen commanded from behind my fallen-over Mom. Mom, still on her hands and knees, was gaping at Rasha, her face open-mouthed blank. I knew she couldn't fight this fight for me.

God, Mom, I thought like a prayer.

"Stop *now*," Rakeen started to step forward, glaring so hard at Rasha that he bumped against my paralyzed mom. As if that was my fault, Rakeen fixed on me.

Through the blade Rasha was waving, above Rasha's messy-haired boy head, I met Rakeen's angry incredulous stare. Through his glasses, Rakeen and I locked eyes. Rakeen thinking in brain-waves, like me, like those 9/11 plane passengers should've: *Jump him.*

Or maybe, from Rakeen: *I'll jump him.*

But see, I was already in the air.

MAURA

My son screamed. All I knew for sure was my son was screaming.

I tried to pull myself up off the floor, but Rakeen knocked me down again. Rakeen was pushing past me. He was scrambling over me to jump the brother with the sword.

And I fell again, this time flat on my face, my nose smashed against scratchy dirty carpet. Then I was up on my knees and Joezy was screaming and One was yelling at him to stop.

But nothing stopped. All three boys were fighting, tangled up and tumbling on the floor in the dim cramped crazy room. I could barely tell who was who, or who'd taken hold of that insane sharp-bladed sword.

I only knew it was my son, first, who was stabbed, was screaming.

"Give me," Rakeen commanded in a harsh throaty voice. Some-how he rose between the two struggling boys. The younger brother yelped like he'd been stabbed too. Joezy shrieked louder.

Rakeen shoved the boys apart. He'd seized the handle of the unwieldy sword. He swung it away, letting the sword drop with a spectacular clack and muffled thud onto the mattress. The brother was on his knees, clutching his shoulder.

My son lay on his side on the floor, not screaming.

There was blood. That was the second thing I knew for sure. My son screaming, now not. And blood. A flash and smell of unmistakable meaty red. Joezy flopped over on his back, hoarsely wheezing. His leg was somehow slashed, blood soaking from his knee, darkly, into his jeans. At least a leg wound, maybe more.

And that high-pitched tightening wheeze in his throat. I crawled over to him, hunched over him, ready to — what? Give mouth-to-mouth? Had his windpipe been slashed?

"Where? Where you hurt?" Rakeen demanded of his brother. Rakeen had hold of the younger boy, the two of them upright now in the middle of the room. I could feel them standing there; I hated them for standing when my son was flat on his back.

"Bag, give bag," a voice beside me demanded. The girl One was bending too, her elbow bumping me. She jammed her hand roughly into my raincoat pocket. What the fuck was she doing: robbing me as my son laid bleeding and wheezing?

"*Stop* that," I jerked away from her furiously.

But One had already pulled it from my pocket: the crumpled plastic bag. The CVS bag we'd used when Joezy was — yes, that's what she was doing now; no blood at his throat — just hyperventilating.

I snatched that crackly bag from One. This at least I knew how, my hands knew how, to do. I stretched the opening of the smoke-scented bag, holding it over Joezy's gaping mouth and nose so my red-faced boy could breath.

"Mama, Mama!" a young child cried out from the doorway.

"9-1-1!" I was calling louder and clearer, the numbers in my mouth before I could think what they meant. Everything ripped open now like the bleeding gash in my son's leg.

Fumblingly, Joezy reached up, helping to hold the bag to his mouth. A good sign! My free hand, the hand not holding the bag, groped and pressed against Joezy's gash. Wanting to somehow force it together. But my palm sunk into sticky dampness and my son bucked his back in pain. I pulled my bloodied hand away.

"9-1-1; someone call 9-1-1!" I was saying, maybe screaming.

Then I gasped for breath too. I hunched over Joezy, helping him hold that bag to his mouth, clenching my sickening slippery fist.

Someone had listened. I heard through my own and my son's wheezy breaths a distant angelic chime.

A cell-phone; a cell-phone switched on, thank-God. Then Rakeen's voice, urgent and tense but still commanding, clear. Explaining to us all what the hell had just happened.

"22 Mystic Avenue, an emergency, a stabbing—no, no, an accident—two boys. They, ah, were playing with a sword. A sword, yes, Army issue, it—Yes, one with wounds in the leg and one with a shoulder wound and you must hurry: there is much blood."

Then Rakeen was listening and saying "yes, we will" to whatever the voice on the cell was saying. I wiped my bloody hand on my raincoat. One behind me murmured to the other boy. What I heard clearest was the youngest boy in the doorway crying for his mother.

"Mama, Mama," the kid called out, not scared now but relieved. More footsteps, softer faster footsteps.

A woman's voice, deep and sure as a man's.

Another mother: asking in another language, but one I understood, what on earth had happened to her son. I glanced sideways and saw the mother from Whole Foods: her striking lined face, the dark mole above her mouth, the lush grey-streaked hair.

Outside the doorway, she was kneeling in a loose silky robe beside the chubby earnestly upset young boy in glasses. She was holding him close like I longed to hold Joezy.

I turned back to my son, no time or place for "Hellos." I was too afraid. Afraid to let go of the magic bag that Joezy was now holding and breathing steadily into. What if he started hyperventilating again, stopped breathing altogether? What if by hugging him, moving him in any way before the EMTs arrived, I made his wounds worse?

"Rasha, ah *Rasha!*" the other mother exclaimed, full-throated.

Then she hurried in with her heavy tread, her purplish black robe flowing. She crouched with a grunt of effort and anguish beside her other son. The sword clattered and clacked; she'd swept it aside.

Rasha was kneeling now on the mattress. One, crouched on his other side, pressed a wadded-up sheet to his bleeding shoulder. None of us were looking long at each other, only at the two boys.

The other mother asked something in lightning-fast Arabic. Rakeen answered in the same language, suddenly close to Joezy and me. Blinking in confusion, I looked up from Joezy's flushed contorted face, his squeezed-shut eyes.

Across from me, Rakeen crouched now too and pressed a wadded pillowcase to Joezy's heavily bleeding knee.

I swallowed, tasting blood, my throat dried and my tongue thick in my mouth. I wanted to ask Rakeen if the 9-1-1 operators had told him to press a cloth to the wound, but I didn't speak Arabic.

Then I remembered through the ringing in my ears that of course Rakeen spoke perfect English.

But Joezy wheezed again and I readjusted the breathing bag. A distant siren had begun screaming, reaching the pitch of the shrill ringing inside me, closer and closer.

"No po-lice?" One asked in a far-away voice.

I wanted to slap her for thinking of anything but these boys. Getting them, getting Joezy patched up.

Help us, I wanted to croak in my own scream as the sirens shrieked to a halt in the driveway outside. Red light pulsed through One's narrow underground window. *Thank God, thank God.*

"Get the front door, let them in," Rakeen commanded as I wished I could have done. He whipped his head around, looking for someone who could follow his command. Rasha's mother and One were tending to Rasha; the chubby brother with glasses was still standing wide-eyed in Star Wars pajamas in One's open doorway.

"Izrin," Rakeen barked to that befuddled boy. "Go upstairs; let them in, those doctors. They will not hurt us; let them in."

Izrin turned heel and thumped up the basement steps. I wanted to kiss that little boy, to muffle his maniac brother.

"No, they *will* hurt us," Rasha piped up from the mattress, his voice only a little strained. His wound the lesser. "You al-ways said they hurt us, Rakeen — these, these — *Pigs!*"

"I said; I *said?*" Rakeen muttered, shaking his head, still pressing the pillowcase to Joezy's leg. "But you know I never meant you to, to — you *know* what we did on Halloween, it was a game and . . ." Rakeen looked up at his brother, his stare stern but his authoritative voice almost cracking. "Rasha, Rasha, what have you done here? What have you done with our father's sword?"

The mother beside Rasha chimed in; again in Arabic. She was bowing her head, her skin creased at the chin and neck. Her lavish hair, uncovered today, fell on one shoulder, its dense black streaked with grey.

For one flash, I pictured Frannie and the dramatic white streak in her own black hair. Then Dan with his steady dark-brown eyes and beard; Dan, who'd know how to stay calm in a crisis. Both Frannie and Dan seemed impossibly distant, part of another life.

I was still trapped in this cinderblock cell that I feared we'd never escape, not even as big booted footsteps thundered above us.

Louder and louder on the basement steps, those wood steps no doubt shaking. Joezy pushed weakly at my wrist, trying to speak. I pulled back the plastic bag, relieved to see Joezy's face whole and pink-flushed and open-eyed, gazing dazedly up at me like his baby self used to gaze after nursing.

"Dad . . ." Joezy mumbled, sounding as dry-mouthed as me.

"Dad's in New York," I managed to tell him as the thudding men reached the basement floor. "But I'll — I'll call him; soon as . . ."

Soon as we get you fixed up; soon as I can use a damn phone; soon as we can get out, will we ever get out of here?

"He'll be back, we'll get Dad right back here," I babbled on to Joezy. I was starting to stand, hearing big men in the doorway.

"Don' go," Joezy grabbed my hand. He gripped with his sticky bloodied thumb and fingers my index finger. The way he used to grip that same finger when he was a baby and he'd nurse so hard at my breast, holding onto my finger as if for dear life.

Hoarse hulking men-voices filled the room. "Arrival at 22 Mystic Avenue," one voice announced.

Remember the time they put us on the stretcher together? I wanted to ask Joezy, but the EMT man was repeating the address into a loud crackly radio. Joezy nodded like he'd heard my question anyway. Then he shut his eyes.

"Step aside please, Ma'am. Don't move the boy."

"But he, he wants me here," I protested in the weak voice that was the only voice I had left. Joezy still gripped my finger. Big brown man-hands were taking hold of my shoulders, Joezy's grip slipping. I was raised to my feet.

"I'm here, I'm here," I told Joezy. The two men directed their questions toward tall and solemn Rakeen, who stood now too, holding the bloodied pillowcase. Joezy's blood, I told myself with a lurch in my gut. A horribly wet reddish-brown stain. A raw-meat smell and taste in this dank air that we had to keep breathing.

"These two boys, Sir, yes, playing about with that, that sword; a — a military relic of my father's," Rakeen somehow smoothly lied to these men. And I couldn't waste my own breath cutting in with the truth. I wasn't even sure I knew the truth.

What in hell had happened here, this past hour or more?

The two big-booted big-voiced EMTs were crowding the room with their belted radios crackling panicky static and a fresh smell of rain on their coats and some sort of metal-railed stretcher parked just outside the basement room's door.

The closest EMT to me was a bald bullet-headed man with a fleshy dark brown face and a supernaturally calm voice.

"Stat 3, stat 3," he chanted placidly into his radio.

Was three a high number, low? Good or bad? Could this man possibly sound so blasé if my bleeding son were in real danger?

"He may hyperventilate," I told the EMT, tugging the damp rubber sleeve of his orange raincoat. I was still wearing my own cloth raincoat, blood-stained now. It was suddenly sweaty warm in this overcrowded room. And Joezy's breaths were wheezing.

"We need us some oxygen in here," the calm-voiced man announced to the man in the doorway. That second EMT was fussing with the stretcher, positioning it.

"'Scuse us Ma'am; Ma'ams." The first EMT addressed both of

us mothers together. Under his radio static, I heard the second man repeat, "Stat 3, stat 3; transporting now; two teenage males."

The bullet-headed EMT tugged out plastic tubing from a black bag; he positioned a plastic oxygen mask on my son. Then everyone was moving together, shoving me and the other mother against each other.

Mrs. Jiluwi smelled of sweet herbal bath oils. Her silk robe brushed my wrist, her skin beneath warm and soft, the plush slack skin of a woman only a few years older than me.

She kept her queenly profile turned facing me, keeping her eyes on her sons. Rasha was hobbling but upright, led along by Rakeen.

As we all climbed the quaking basement steps, the Jiluwi mother talked steadily to Rakeen in Arabic. Rakeen was answering in kind, telling her God-knew-what to explain Joezy and me.

At the top of the steps, I pushed around them all and hurried ahead to keep up with my son's stretcher. I followed the EMTs through the kitchen and tiled front hall, out into cold wet air that I gulped hungrily. Halfway down the path, I glanced once behind me.

Bringing up the rear of our little group, following the Jiluwi trio, One slipped out the front door too. Maybe only I noticed her, hesitating on the stoop. She was pulling a man-sized sweat jacket over her pajama top. Then she bent, her hair hiding her face, and she re-lifted her bulging string bag, our money. She too was gulping the fresh freezing air, her mouth half open with a first taste of freedom.

Yet she was hesitating, her eyes on Rakeen's back like she wouldn't or couldn't leave that boy. I turned away from One like everyone else. The driveway was pulsing with the ambulance's spinning silenced red and white lights. Inside me, the ringing in my ears was silenced too. Joezy at least, at last, was safe.

EMTs were loading Joezy's stretcher into the ambulance's open rear doors. His curly hair was disappearing. I staggered in my rush to cross the overgrown damp-grassed lawn, reach the driveway.

Rakeen and his mother were walking behind me. As I reached the ambulance, panting, I glimpsed one shelf-like bed and three built-in seats. The not-bald EMT was maneuvering Joezy onto the bed.

"Only got room for two passengers besides these boys," the bald EMT announced to Rakeen, his mother, and me. There were no questions asked. Automatically, the EMT motioned for Mrs. Jiluwi and me to board the ambulance. "Ma'ams? In here."

Regally, Rasha's mother stepped forward, as if accustomed to always going first. She took hold of the not-bald EMT's extended hand and let the young man help her up into the ambulance, as if she were accustomed to that, too. A woman who'd always had servants.

Icy drizzle was blowing into my face. The red and white lights blinked in code. I bowed my head and started to step forward, but Rakeen stopped me, gripping my arm lightly, familiarly. He bent close and spoke low-voiced into my ear; his tone matter-of-fact, as if what he was saying was in both our interests.

"Do not tell them what really happened, or why," he told me as icy raindrops pelted both our faces. "They will blame Rasha, blame my family. Just say it was a foolish fight, sword-play gone wrong . . ."

Or else you'll do what? I might have asked back. And I might have pointed out that One, his last threat, was possibly right now escaping. But even though he'd held us hostage, Rakeen had jumped his own brother. He had pressed a pillowcase to Joezy's wound. He'd put his gun back in the safe. He'd called 9-1-1.

"I'll tell them that it was, yes, a foolish fight."

Rakeen nodded, fingering the beard bristle on his chin. Looking unsure, behind his glasses, whether to trust me or not.

"Rakeen?" His mother called out from the open ambulance. She sat straight-backed in one of the seats, Rasha strapped in beside her. The seat closest to Joezy's bed awaited me. Mrs. Jiluwi still did not deign to look directly at me. But she issued an Arabic command to her oldest son, one that contained the word "One."

Had she too noticed One and her packed string bag? Or not?

"Yes, I will keep an eye upon One," Rakeen told his mother in English, nodding like he'd just nodded at me.

I wondered, as I stepped up into the ambulance, whether either of Rakeen's nods could be trusted.

Then my back was to Rakeen. I was crouched over, squeezing myself into my seat beside the narrow built-in bed that Joezy lay on with his eyes shut and the oxygen mask strapped over his mouth and nose. Only his curly unbrushed hair looked familiar, unmarred.

I reached down and smoothed back his rain-dampened bangs. Then I leaned closer beside him, my knee bumping Rasha's mom's knee. She was squeezed beside her own son, who sat slumped in his seat opposite my Joezy. His seatbelt strained to hold him in place.

Still, Rasha's mother did not look at me. Somehow in the house, she had grabbed a headscarf, and she was knotting it under her chin. Her mouth frowned beneath her large dark mole. She wore no make-up but her lips bore a purplish trace of longtime lipstick.

The bullet-bald EMT slammed the ambulance doors, sealing us with him inside the compact medicine-and-death-scented space.

"Gotta get their vitals," he mumbled, kneeling beside upright Rasha, pulling a blood pressure kit out of his bottomless bag.

I bent forward to gaze around stony-faced Mrs. Jiluwi and see Rasha. He slouched sullenly, ignoring the EMT, staring out the window, his hands clenched like he wanted to punch a hole in it.

"Wha' hap-pen," Joezy croaked to me, muffled by his bubbled plastic mask. "In th', in th' fight . . ."

"The fight?" The ambulance engine revved. I leaned down and whispered in Joezy's ear, hoping Rasha wouldn't overhear and contradict me. "What happened in the fight? Well you, you jumped right in there, Joezy. You, you fought for that sword and, and . . ." *And Rakeen was the one who got the sword*, I could have added.

But Joezy was listening so hard, eyes widened like when I used to read him to sleep, sometimes improvising happier endings so he'd shut his eyes peacefully. "And you fought hard; you were very brave."

"I was brave?" Joezy nodded sleepily, his eyes above the plastic oxygen mask drifting shut. I held out my index finger, poked his limp hand. My painted fingernail crusted with his blood.

He took loose hold. He was breathing steadily behind his mask. His face relaxed like he might suck his thumb. With a reverse lurch, the ambulance began backing away. I glanced down at Joezy's leg, the makeshift bandage that the EMT was readjusting.

And I noticed a slick glint: a torn scrap of exposed camera film attached under the Velcro of Joezy's half-undone sneaker. I wanted to tug that film scrap loose, toss it out. But I couldn't reach it. Couldn't erase what that film showed, even if no one ever saw it.

The siren above us yelped; the ambulance backed fast down the driveway. The other mother glanced over at me at last, double-knotting her headscarf. Her lined face looked calm and commanding, down to her dramatic mole and subtle queen's scowl.

Her un-made-up eyes were almond-shaped and deeply black like Rakeen's. She met my own bewildered gaze head on.

She's a mom too, I reminded myself. Surely we both just wanted to keep our kids safe. The ambulance hit Mystic Avenue, picking up speed.

In the bump and rumble, I nodded at Mrs. Jiluwi as if we'd agreed to something, mother to mother. Then we each turned back to our own wounded young son.

CHAPTER THIRTEEN

BAD NEWS ON THE DOORSTEP

JOEZY

By Thanksgiving, I was a paperboy on crutches.

I'd been set to start my paper route only days after what Mom and I called "that crazy day," when my knee tendon had been severed.

I was the one to insist we somehow go ahead with the route. With my first paychecks, I planned to pay my mom back $30 of my debt to her, and to leave our Maid Pros a double tip to make up for what I stole. That, at least, was something I could do.

Since I could barely walk, much less ride my bike — I only rode it in my dreams, nightly, escaping the basement room. Dad drove me on my route. He was on leave and I kinda felt I was too.

"I got 'em all," Dad told me at dawn as I limped on my crutches into our open garage. Behind me Dad hauled the unfolded inky-smelling *Boston Globes* we'd picked up in Arlington Center.

"I know," I muttered through the pang of pain in my knee. I halted, leaning my crutches on Dad's long-unused workbench.

Of course, I'd been hired for this neighborhood paper route back when I was a normal bike-riding boy. And I'd told the paper people (no one dared contradict me, not yet) that my leg injury would soon heal. That until then, my dad or mom could keep driving me.

For now, for me, Dad wasn't traveling. He'd finagled a short-term leave from out-of-town business. So he was the one driving me slowly round our neighborhood each day at dawn, even on this chill Thanksgiving morning.

Dad and I folded papers side by side, our elbows brushing.

BIN LADEN HIDING IN TORA BORA MOUNTAINS and
BLOODY BATTLE IN AFGHANISTAN and HUB's 9/11 FAM-
ILIES DEMAND FURTHER INVESTIGATION and LOGAN
AIRPORT HANDLES HOLIDAY BOMB THREATS and SUB-
DUED THANKSGIVING FOR NATION IN MOURNING.

"Bad news on the doorstep," Dad sang under his breath to the
"American Pie" tune, one of the songs most often played by the
'70s and '80s station I allowed him to switch on during our drives.

I gave a brief laugh, my breath showing in our cold open
garage. Then I noticed that Dad sucked in his own breath instead
of singing the next verse, which made me mad enough that I sang
it myself, loudly and flatly: "I couldn't take one more step."

Dad gave a gruff, game, "Ha."

But I could tell, as we folded on, our breaths frosty, that Dad
wondered too: if I'd ever again take one normal step.

Officially, the doctor and the physical therapist I met three times
a week said "no problem," of course I, unlike the permanently
slouched wheelchair teens I held doors for in the waiting room,
would walk normally again, and soon, barring complications.

Before One, I'd have cheerfully believed that my slashed tendon
only needed time to heal, that complications wouldn't strike me;
that it was OK for the doctor to say if there was not significant
improvement in three months, we'd see if laser surgery is indicated.

"Because knee injuries," the oldest grimmest doctor told us, "are
damn tricky."

Trick-or-treat, I thought in my bulky down jacket as I tied bright
green plastic bags, wrapping each snowy-day paper like a present.
Picturing, unwillingly, Rakeen and Rasha at our Halloween doorstep, only one month ago.

The beginning of this saga; and maybe today, if I could carry
off my secret plan, would mark an end. At least for One and me.

"Hey Dad?" I knotted the last bag, trying to sound casual. "I
told Mom we'd stop by Whole Foods after our route, to pick up,
y'know, that kind of cranberry nut bread she likes . . ."

"Oh?" Dad asked absently, stuffing the wrapped papers into one
stretchy sack. "She didn't mention that to me."

"Well she did to me; so we gotta get that bread, OK?"

Dad started to reply, maybe to snap at my impatient tone. Instead he nodded, slinging the sack on his back like a Jewish Santa.

"OK, whatever," Dad told me. Sounding more like me these days, now that he was spending more time with me. I hobbled behind him into the scattered snowflakes, the barely begun day.

We settled the jumbo sack into the back seat, where I would sit, tossing each paper with my still-strong arm and Frisbee flair.

Dad loaded in my crutches and closed the garage door, his longish curly hair blowing over his bald spot. "A yarmulke will cover that," he'd taken to joking. His whole born-again Jew shtick.

Poor bewildered Dad didn't know everything that had happened on Mom's and my crazy day — not by a long shot — but he knew enough to know something big was up. Something that could've crippled his son. He hadn't managed to get back from New York 'til the day after I was injured. The day Dad insisted on marching over to the Jiluwi family's house himself, and found that house deserted.

"The family had apparently fled in the night," the police officer told Dad. Possibly, the cop speculated to Dad, this was due to "numerous minor complaints" filed against the family's boys. As well as, Dad told us the cop had added, some possibly more serious charges involving illegal drug deliveries to their home; unknown drugs shipped from Asia at low cost and sold here at below the high All-American price. Not to mention the assault charge Dad might've leveled. That cop and Dad didn't know, no one but Mom and me knew about Le Ti One being held as slave labor. And only I knew where One was now, or at least where she seemed to work.

And I knew too, thought I knew, what her uncle had been up to.

"See," I told the balding back of Dad's head as we pulled away from our driveway, "Mom's favorite bread, they only make it at Bread and Circus, I mean, Whole Foods. And they open at 7AM today."

Bread and Circus was the name of the store franchise back when I was a kid. Mom still sometimes called it "Bread and

Circus," like I was still a kid, or maybe she wished that I was. And that she was still younger, happier. Or I guessed she was happier back then. Maybe it was just that I didn't know her secrets then.

"Well let's pick up a loaf, by all means," Dad agreed. He pulled onto Mystic Avenue, turning left so we could do long twisty Ridge Road first. We eased by the abandoned Jiluwi house, not much different-looking than it had looked with the family inside. Only no more messages in Arabic painted on the garage door.

I never did find out what those messages had said.

"It bother you, seeing that house every day?" Dad was fiddling with his radio dial. Songs swelling up then dying down.

"Sure," I answered, as brusquely as him. The old him, real him.

"Y'know," Dad switched off the radio, turning onto Ridge. "I still don't understand what-all happened that day, why the hell you'd get yourself into a fight like that."

"I can't figure it out either," I answered Dad, rolling down my window to make my first throw. "But I'm working on it."

And there was one person who could help me, if I could confront her today. Tell her the information the police (but I couldn't mention them) had told Dad. Make her see that with certifiably illegal drug-whatever going down, she'd been in real danger.

That I had helped her. So she'd feel for me—what? I snapped back my arm as Dad slowed before the first sleeping split-level home. Number 1, Ridge Road. Our Volvo shuddered almost to a stop. I hurled the bad news, hard. The paper thumped the brick stoop, a freaking bulls-eye. And Dad sped up abruptly, my getaway driver.

MAURA

I woke early to stuff our bird. A ten-pounder, though there would be, this year, only us. I popped two slices of stale white bread in the toaster. "Stale bread works best," my mother always told me.

This year, for the first time, I actually followed her advice, buying not fresh springy whole wheat bread for our stuffing but two-week-old Wonder. "I'm using your recipe this time," I'd assured Mom by phone, the same call that I'd told her, in a voice unconvincingly casual enough for her to ask if anything was wrong, that I wanted this Thanksgiving to be just us. Just me and Dan and Joezy.

But I'd invited my parents up for Hanukkah in a few weeks. Dan and I sharing a laugh, as in days of old, over my mom stiffly asking what they'd be expected to do. "Nothing," I'd told Mom, glad to give her something to worry about besides her looming six-month cancer check. "Just be there; that's the most important thing parents do, right?" Long-distance Mom had, for once, agreed with me.

Maybe she somehow sensed how hard I was trying, in my newly contrite and stripped-down life, to concentrate on just that. Being there for them. My husband; our son.

Joezy was my boy again: needing me in a way I'd thought I wanted.

Dry brown slices of toast popped up. I lifted the hot bland bread. I chopped it into tiny same-size squares, breathing its comforting white-bread scent.

"White lies," I'd told Joezy we were telling his father when we repeated the simplified tale of Joezy and his ill-advised sword-fight. No mention of One, of the stolen thousand dollars, of the two of us trapped in that basement room. Held — if you wanted to be what my mom would call melodramatic — hostage.

Ping. More Wonderbread popped up from the toaster. My bowl of bread-squares was nearly full; my fatty beef sausage (the kind I'd scorned in previous years) sizzled in its pan. "Better enjoy it now," I'd joked to a grudgingly smiling Joezy, "before Dan makes us go Kosher."

I breathed the mingled greasy yeasty smells as I chopped more little bread squares, adding up all those little white lies I'd told.

At the hospital in the ER, Mrs. Jiluwi had gravely shaken her head, claiming not to speak English. Though I doubted that, judging from her canny attentive gaze as I told several distracted ER personnel, then one suspicious but sleepy-eyed social worker, the story of how my son Joezy had gotten in a spontaneous pretend sword fight with Rasha. A foolish fight that simply and stupidly got out of hand. Nothing more, nothing real.

Then there was the matter of the one thousand dollars I'd

withdrawn from Dan's and my joint checking account to cover for the silent auction dollars Joezy had stolen.

I'd pseudo-confessed to Dan that I'd taken out that money to pay for some initial sessions with the therapist I claimed I suddenly needed. That part at least felt true, that need. Dan told me he'd sensed something off in me for some time. He offered to fund my therapy sessions through his company's insurance.

So I found a therapist via professionally neurotic Sheila Jester. So far, the most useful advice he'd given me, after I'd ranted on about how guilty I felt over neglecting my son and taking for granted my lucky life and letting post-9/11 prejudices overwhelm me in that basement and not truly working on my marriage and still, even after everything, wanting to kiss Frannie again, was to list to myself, daily, three concrete things which make me feel thankful.

What I ought to list right now, I told myself, *when I'm done listing my lies*. I spooned sausage into the bread mix, stirring aggressively. And I added on a few last little white lies.

Because when Dan finally escaped from New York and arrived home to find Joezy bandaged and woozy from painkillers, I concocted a more elaborate white-lie version of what had happened: Joezy on ill-advised impulse confronting those Terrorist Trick-or-Treater boys; Rasha somehow pulling out his father's sword.

In my version, the older boy Rakeen breaks up the fight, as in real life, and then phones not only 9-1-1 but me also. A fact I tried to use to convince Dan not to contact the police himself, press charges.

Not that there was anyone to press charges against. The Arlington police officers Dan defiantly rallied about twenty-four hours after the sword-fight incident confirmed 22 Mystic Avenue to be deserted, only the sparse rented furniture left behind.

I'd still been awake on midnight of our crazy day, waiting for word from Dan about his New York train. So I had glimpsed, as I'd paced out onto our frosty front yard to peer down toward Mystic Avenue, a giant shadowy U-Haul truck parked by the open lit-up garage of 22 Mystic Avenue. Go, I'd thought. Then I'd trudged back inside my own house to await my husband's call.

"You broke your promise," drugged-up Joezy had slurred from

his bed the next day, when I'd told him Dan couldn't be stopped, that he'd phoned the police to report the sword-fight.

I insisted to Joezy that the police wouldn't find One or the Jiluwis, just as Rakeen had promised. That if, as the police had implied to Dan, the Jiluwis really were involved in illegal drug deliveries, it was best that they disappear. But Joezy gave me a disappointed dilated stare.

He sat propped in bed with his sketchpad, inking visions of One. I'd told him I hoped One escaped that crazy day. And I braced for Joezy to make good on his threat to tell Dan about Frannie and me.

"OK, so that's thing number one," I announced to the headless trussed-up turkey, it's gaping and emptied gut.

I plunged my bare washed hands into the bread and sausage mix, gripping a crumbly grease-soaked handful. Yes, I was thankful my son had not turned against me, that I knew of, and told my secret.

But Joezy was watching me now; this was clear. He needed me, as he hadn't in years. How selfish I'd been to wish he needed me more. "Be careful what you wish for," Mom would say.

Amidst caring for Joezy and lying to Dan, I'd barely had time to think about Frannie. But I did. I missed her. I confided in her in my head. Still, I'd avoided talking to her beyond a few hurried words in the school hall as I carried Joezy's backpack for him. She'd sent me several emails in the week that Joezy was out of school, unable to walk. *Hey, Mara: whatonearth HAPPENED? & i don't just mean between us, in the art room. i mean: a SWORD FIGHT? what'll our kids think of next to drive us crazy?*

But I didn't answer; I couldn't concoct a suitably wry reply. Though I was tempted to tell Frannie, and only Frannie, the truth. She'd be the one who'd listen, who'd understand how freaky it all had been. How my son and I had virtually been held hostage in a basement room; how Joezy had virtually stolen one thousand dollars from the 9/11 fundraiser; how I could barely sleep without waking from gun dreams in a breathless sweat, convinced for a few panting panicky late-night minutes that the dark around me was dank basement dark, that there was no way out.

Then I'd grope beside me and press one trembling hand to Dan's solid snoring chest. *This is the way out,* I'd tell myself. Something I wouldn't tell Frannie, because she'd see it as false comfort. As cowardly. The only way out of this fear, I'd tell myself at night.

Stay together, stay a family. Damn well make it work. Right?

But when I finally emailed Frannie back, I felt not relieved but — what? Resigned, trapped. I told her I couldn't explain all that had happened to me since the silent auction. Or why I'd decided, much as I'd savored her kisses, much as I wanted to enjoy more than that with her, I couldn't go any further. I had to stay where I was, now.

Before I could revise the email, as stiffly worded as the thank-you notes my mom had taught me to write, before I could delete it and start over, I'd pressed SEND NOW.

That had been days ago. Early on this Thanksgiving morning, as Dan and Joezy had begun shuffling around at 5:30AM, I'd emailed Frannie again, saying cryptically that I just wanted to wish her happy Thanksgiving and to make sure she'd gotten my previous message. I just want to get closure on this Frannie thing, I had told my new nodding therapist in our most recent session.

"Are you sure that's all you want?" he'd asked flatly.

"I'm not expecting to find 'all I want,'" I'd snapped back in the tone of a fed-up mom. Not anymore I'm not.

I'm thankful to be alive, I kept reminding myself. *And to have Joezy alive. And not to be under a cancer-watch like my mom.* I was the ultimate (a new term for a post-9/11 block of voters) security mom. Moms who list security as their number-one concern.

"So what'll be thank-you number two?" I asked the goose-bumped turkey. I skewered its thin yet tough skin with metal pins, to hold in all the stuffing. I tightened the greasy strings that tied its legs. No, its drumsticks. And I pictured Frannie's sure hands tightening the knots the day we hung our silent auction banner.

I washed off my hands then set aside the little plastic bags of turkey innards for gravy. And I found myself thinking (the kind of dark unwanted thought that flashed in my mind these days, at unguarded moments) about the African tribal practice of, what was it called? Cutting off a young girl's clitoris?

As a way of preventing not only sexual pleasure in general but maybe lesbian attractions in particular? I turned my back on the turkey innards, trying to cut short my next whiny wondering. Would I be pursuing my first full-fledged lesbian affair now, if Dan had answered me differently about the affair I'd imagined he'd had?

Don't be Miss Melodrama, I told myself as sternly as my mom used to do. Don't wish for what you really didn't want, couldn't handle. I hoisted up the ten-pound bird on his metal pan. The oven light was blinking; its door was open. I shuffle-stepped over; bent into the heat, thrust the bird inside. Then I slammed the oven shut.

I would've, yes, told Dan the truth, at least about Frannie. I was ready (or thought I was ready) to tell Dan all about Frannie and me. With my new-found basement-hostage boldness, I'd vowed to finally confront him about Philly, and then spill my own secret. We'd just driven Joezy to the doctor's together. While Joezy's knee was being x-rayed yet again, I, sensing this was our last chance for a while to talk alone, asked Dan to come out to the car.

We turned on the Volvo's heater; we sat in the frosty Symmes Medical Center parking lot. My pulse was thumping so hard I could barely form the question I'd decided to ask Dan at last, expecting that his own expected confession might open the flood-gates between us.

If he admitted the one-night-stand infidelity I suspected, that might make it possible, even easy, for me to offer my own confession about falling in love with Frannie. For us to discuss — this part I hadn't dared to imagine in detail — what might come next.

"Philadelphia," I began in our heated humming car, taken aback when Dan seemed only mildly uneasy. He sipped his bad Health Center coffee like medicine he was forcing himself to swallow.

I described the phone call I'd gotten only months before, though it seemed longer, from the wife of his colleague, Bob. How she'd implied that he and her husband had, well, had what in Philly?

"OK, OK," Dan, muttered into his Styrofoam cup, his muddy coffee. His hand holding the cup stayed steady. "We — I — came close, I admit it, Babe. Look, Bob was ten sheets to the wind; we both were that whole trip, seems like, starting on the flight out. Remember, Babe, it was a couple weeks after 9/11; the drinks were really flying on that flight, I'll tell ya. Then Bob and me got stranded at the airport bar. And these two women come over to our booth."

They laughed; they drank; one of the women squeezed up beside Dan. He was tempted, he admitted. But by the end of the night, Dan finished, meeting my eyes so I sensed he really wasn't lying, Dan turned down Bob's drunken offer to cab it to a hotel together, the four of them. Bob left with both women, all of them shitfaced.

"And I sat in that bar, Babe, drinking black coffee and thinking about how close I came, how screwy and kinda pointless things had been feeling to me since September, but before that too. Vowing to myself to go to Synagogue when I got home, if I got home . . ."

"Of course you were going to get home," I told Dan roughly, touching his solid shoulder, trying to feel relieved like a good wife. Trying to hide my real and muddled mix of emotions. What could I do? He hadn't given me the opening I'd dreaded and awaited.

So I told Dan that I'd been distracted and depressed lately too, neglecting Joezy. I paused to give Dan a chance to ask me what had distracted me, exactly. But he was slurping the last of his coffee, checking his watch. He was right; we needed to get back inside.

Then I told him, in our last moments alone in our humming car, that I'd decided he was right about Joezy and the Bar Mitzvah. Yes, I agreed as Dan and I headed back toward the Medical Center, arm in arm, we'd make Joezy get Bar Mitzvah'd whether he liked it or not.

After I'd slammed the turkey in the oven, I splashed water over my flushed face at the sink. *Hot flash?* I wondered. Mother had early menopause. Maybe I'd been experiencing hot flashes for months. Could it be? Maybe if Joezy ever did tell Dan about me and Frannie, I could blame pre-menopausal madness. Plus post-9/11-what-am-I-doing-with-my-life panic?

Not that I'd have accepted any such lame mid-life crisis excuse from Dan. Not that any of that crap explained or excused anything, really. Now that I'd experienced real panic, now that I'd faced down a wanna-be teenage terrorist holding a gun, shouldn't I be able to get things into what my all-too-predictable therapist calls "perspective"?

I shut off the kitchen faucet but didn't reach for a paper towel. In the faint early-morning chill of our not yet heated-up house, I stood leaning over the sink. I let my face drip-dry. Like tears, only not. Appropriate, I thought, for an affair that never happened, never would.

I knew Joezy was watching now, was capable of threatening me with any secrets he might discover. I knew too, when he'd called out in his pain for Dan, that Joezy needed his dad. Needed Dan and me together. And maybe Dan, whatever his own temptations, on the road — understood that simple fact too.

His New York trip — his homeward-bound train stopped and evacuated for another bomb threat — had shaken him up. Dan had promised me in his new November attentiveness that he'd at last apply for a management position in the Boston office.

Too boring, he'd protested before. But after the last few weeks, boring didn't, shouldn't seem so bad.

I pushed away from the sink, finger-combed my hair. I still wore my slept-in exercise sweats. Dan had mumbled to me last week, the last time we'd had hurried early-morning sex — over too soon and leaving me wanting more — which was good in a way, right? He'd mumbled that he wanted to buy me, this coming Christmas-Hanukah, something new to sleep in.

He was trying. What more could a forty-plus-year-old pre-menopausal housewife realistically ask of her husband of twenty-plus years? Yes, Dan the Man was damn well trying. That should be my thing two.

I am thankful for him trying, I told myself firmly enough to make it, at least for this November-dawn moment, true.

I started to pad out of the kitchen, upstairs to shower and change from my funky sweats into the burnt-orange sweater and black wool slacks Dan liked. As I stepped from the kitchen, the phone rang.

My heart froze. God; what would make a phone ring at 6:30 AM other than bad news? Had Dan and Joezy crashed on the icy streets?

I seized the kitchen extension receiver in my still-damp hand.

"Yes?" I asked breathlessly instead of hello, braced for the worst of news. But not for Frannie's voice.

"Mara? I — I'm sorry to be calling so early, but you sent your email before six and you mentioned that Joezy and — and Dan would be out delivering papers. So I — well, I took a chance because you've been avoiding me at school and I — I wanted to say this in person, or as close to in person as — you'll let us get."

"Oh?" I asked dumbly. I had never heard Frannie sound so uncertain, her low voice tense. Was Frannie's heart pounding too? Had she somehow been missing me too? Not that I deserved to be missed. But was she nevertheless going to beg me to reconsider?

"See, I'm up early too, we have my sister coming for dinner — Veronika's still asleep. Look, I get your message — your non-message. Whatever it was that made you cut me off. I'm sorry you feel you can't give this, give us, a try. I mean a real, serious try."

"I'd want to," I cut in with what-the-hell honesty, "if things were different, but they aren't. And I can't keep concentrating on what I want, not right now."

"OK, yeah. And I can't wait around for you to be ready to go for that, what you want . . ." Frannie sighed, more impatient than wistful. "I mean, Maura or Mara or whoever you are — I'm not your own personal midlife crisis. The only time I ever hear from you lately is when I read your postings in the ACLU-Boston chat-room."

"At least someone's reading those," I muttered, irrationally stung by her tone, protective of my late-night anti-torture email outbursts. Those counterbalances to my sleepy murmurs of agreement when Dan voiced his increasingly neo-conservative views during the late news shows we'd begun, in these last strange suspended weeks, to watch together. "Look, I, I'm sorry, Frannie. You're right, I, I haven't been thinking enough about you, here."

"More about me thinking about you," Frannie filled in, but levelly, not unkindly. And I had to do an inner double take, like when Joezy read my mind.

"Except when we were, you know, then I was thinking of you, Frannie."

"Wouldn't call that thinking, Mara. You do too much thinking, you know?"

"I know. But I am, you know, sorry."

"Me, too." For a second, I thought Frannie sounded choked up. But she went on matter-of-factly. "Anyhow, Mara, my sister's got someone she wants me to meet. I just — I know you're going to deny this. But I just hope someday you figure out what you really do want."

"I don't," I answered as matter-of-factly. Thinking of Jesse Jackson's wife facing tabloid reporters, asking them not to investigate rumors of her husband's infidelities. Because she had children to raise, she said. She didn't have time for all that.

"I mean," I was saying to Frannie more haltingly than Mrs. Jesse Jackson. "If I'm not getting it, everything I want from my marriage, it's not necessarily my husband's fault. It's not Dan's fault if I've got feelings for women. I downplayed that to him, back when I could've done everything differently. But this is now. Plus, I think I was probably wrong too about Dan on his trips, Dan running around on me."

"And those are reasons to stay 'marred,' Mara?"

"I've heard worse." I sighed impatiently too. "Look, the bottom line is: Joezy is all the reason I need to want to, make it work, my marriage."

"Make it, right," Frannie muttered. But she added, with the reasonableness that made me think we could have worked, "Well, Veronika's my bottom-line too. I hear you on that . . ."

"And I hear her, hear Veronika," I said, detecting delicate laughter in the background.

Then Frannie added in the low cello voice I still loved: "How is

Joezy anyway? Everyone's talking about this fight he had. What on earth is going on with him?"

"I can't say."

"You can't say because you don't know or you can't say to me?"

"Both," I answered. We both, at our separate ends, laughed.

"Look," Frannie finished briskly, Veronika's laugh going rowdy, "I got to go, Mara."

Mara. Who else but Frannie would call me that, would find that name and my past so fascinating, if only briefly?

"See," Frannie added in her brightest mock-housewife voice, with its sharper new edge, "We've gotta put our bird in the oven."

"Mine's already in," I told Frannie with a half-real half-not laugh. Then I was the one to hang up. Just as well, I thought, letting go of the receiver. But standing still, heavily. *I ought to make that my third thank-you,* I told myself. Ought to be glad it was officially over. I stepped stiffly from the kitchen, warming up from the oven, into the chillier living room.

But no. I paused by the living room window, gazing out into the grey wash of slush. No; my daily thank-yous were only for me. And I damn well had to mean each one or they didn't (my rule, not the therapist's) count.

No, of course I was not thankful to cut things off with Frannie. Not that we'd ever had anything real. And if she had been calling to try in earnest to win me over, would I have been strong enough to resist? Bold enough to not resist? Had my near-death experience made me wiser or just more scared? Or both.

Get over yourself, the new harsher Frannie voice in my head said. *Quit brooding and do something useful. Search out some more specialists for Joezy's knee. Visit your mother before Hanukkah; go to the dreaded oncologist appointment with her. Get moving again on that Songs for Shelters project. Get off your pampered ass. Find a way to raise those funds you need,* Frannie's voice went on firmly.

A voice I got to keep, maybe, even if the real Frannie was gone. I remembered the glint of pity and contempt in her eyes when I'd said fear was my ruling emotion. Was it still, after what I'd been through? Hadn't I at least learned I wasn't quite the coward I'd feared to be?

Like a reproach, something thumped outside the front door. I sidestepped from the window, my pulse thumping too. I flung open the door in time to wave to my son as Dan drove him further up Riverview Road. We were the middle road of his territory. So they were entering the last leg of their morning rounds.

Joezy's hand from the Volvo passenger window waved back. His aim had gotten better after only a week, I noticed. I bent into the chill to lift the soggy plastic-bagged Globe he'd thrown so expertly onto our front stoop. I'd objected at first, but going ahead with his planned paper route was good for him. Giving him something to focus on rather than the uncertain state of his leg, his knee.

A familiar medical dread settled in my chest. Our Volvo crested the top of Riverview Road, another well-aimed paper slung out at the top. I glanced at the paper I held, its smell of cold wet newsprint, and its plastic-wrapped headline: BIN LADEN, then something unreadable.

Other moms at Fairwell already worried, post-9/11, that if military retaliation of some kind might drag on for years then our sons might be drafted. God: maybe if Joezy really was stuck with a seriously bad knee, it could turn out to be, in one sense, good.

Shaking off the wrapped paper, trying to shake off my morbid thoughts, I stepped back inside and I shut the door on the cold, the half-rain half-hail. I dropped the Globe with a wet thump on the little rug by our door, the paper still in its droplet-dotted wrapper.

Not yet, I told myself. I didn't have to worry about Joezy being drafted and I didn't have to read today's bad news. *Not yet*.

CHAPTER FOURTEEN
GIRL HELD IN HOME

JOEZY

"No Dad, I wanna go in myself," I told him in the Whole Foods parking lot. "I can do it; I'm not a freaking baby, y'know."

In short, I played the cripple card, my strongest hand. When I wanted Dad or anyone off my back, I exaggerated my real limp, the way I did crossing the slushy Whole Foods lot, Dad left behind in the Volvo watching me. Acting like I'd be A-OK. Because he wanted to "encourage Joezy's continued independence" (as Joezy's new physical therapist would put it) by acting like gimpy crutched-up Joezy could walk into a freaking supermarket alone.

OPEN THANKSGIVING was soap-printed on the Whole Foods sliding doors. The THANKS and GIVING split to let me in.

One, One; was it really her? Would I actually get to see my One—a new freed One, maybe a grateful One—alone, assuming my hunch was right and she'd be one worker eager to sign up for the Thanksgiving shift that the all-American workers would want out of.

One, One. I hobbled under the looming metal WHOLE FOODS/WHOLE KIDS globe, past the gleaming leaves of freshly hosed-down produce and the pale splotches of limp untasted meatless turkey samples arrayed on cracked wheat crackers. One. One. I dragged my bad leg into the sweet doughy air of the Bakery corner. I'd glimpsed One working behind the counter in the barely visible kitchen area a few days before while I was shopping with Mom, lagging behind her. The first time I'd seen One since that crazy November day, which felt way longer than two weeks ago.

I had frozen behind Mom, watching the skinnier-than-ever girl with pinned-back bangs and a round-cheeked profile lift from an unseen oven a rack of rolls. Staggering slightly with the weight of the rack, she slipped out of view, her spine straight despite her burden.

I'd ducked away too, following Mom on my crutches, wondering, Is that really Le Ti One, hard at work only miles away from the house, the deserted house, where she'd been held?

I hesitated now behind a wire rack of the French bread loaves Mom used to let me hold and gnaw on in the cart. My empty stomach gurgled. The early-morning Thanksgiving store was nearly empty except for a few sheepish last-minute moms scurrying around.

And super-sheepish me, standing suspiciously still.

I seized a cranberry nut loaf, gripped the knot of its plastic bag in one fist. Awkwardly, because I was holding onto my crutch at the same time. I hobbled forward, my knee clicking in its weird new old man way. Then I hesitated by the counter, wobbling back and forth. My knee ached like it did whenever I walked too freaking far.

My hair felt chilly damp from snowy rain more frozen than the drizzle two weeks before. The day that keeps replaying in the back of my mind by day, the front of my mind by night.

Swordfight nightmares where my whole leg — plus sometimes my penis too — gets chopped off or almost chopped off. My lower leg swings from my shattered broken-hinged knee. 'Til I wake in sweaty short-breathed panic; 'til I scurry down the hall to peek in my parent's bedroom, make sure the two of them are still lying there, side by side.

Mommy and Daddy, I told myself now, mocking myself, eyeing what Dad would call a hippie-dippie couple. They were pushing their corkscrew-haired baby (a toddler with girlish curls but a bull-dog boy's face) in a cart piled with leafy produce.

He or she — the kid — held a jumbo-sized carrot. He or she whipped its feathery green stalk, and then pointed the carrot straight at me.

"Carrot, see the carrot," the kid's mom crooned.

"Gun, see-da-gun," the kid answered back, clear as day.

The mom shot a long-suffering fellow-soldier look at the dad. He gave a stagey shrug and an easy-going ex-hippie grin.

I grinned weakly back. But I couldn't help thinking as I turned again to the unmanned counter, that maybe these healthy mom and dad faces were a holiday show. A big disguise.

Like my mom's Miss-PTA act when really she was lusting after Frannie who's-it. And my dad's Mr. Good Dad act lately, which I did appreciate. But once the holidays were past, would Mom be driving my paper route and Dad be back on the road? Though maybe he'd check in more often. Maybe he'd worry — the worry part was real in both Mom and Dad — about his son who might not walk right again.

Not that Mom or Dad or any doctor said any such thing to me. But I felt it, from inside: something fucking vital in my leg got severed, that day. Maybe — a dreadlocked bakery counter lady materialized and took my money — maybe One would get that. Get how bad it all was.

If I ever fucking find Le Ti One again. I craned my neck to see past the counter into the kitchen behind; no workers visible.

Lingering at the counter, fussing with my crutches, I unsnapped my down jacket pocket so I could reach it easier and quicker if I got a chance to give it to her: my folded pen and ink super-heroine picture of One. I'd been working on it during the dreary damn afternoons I'd spent in my bedroom, supposedly resting my leg.

My knee clicked as I began sidling away from the bakery counter. I clutched the knotted end of that bread bag. Maybe I'd bag the whole idea of seeking out One. Of finding out if she was OK: working here and maybe at last grateful to me. Maybe even open to being more than grateful. Especially if I told her what was really going down in that fucking drug-running house where they'd told her she was so safe.

Some safe, I thought with scorn, about to slip safely away. But I froze at the counter's end, at my first glimpse of One. A skinny green-aproned worker bustling in back of the Whole Foods kitchen area. Her black ponytail twisted into a braid. I stood dumb, leaning on the counter. I shook my head when the counter lady asked if I wanted anything else.

I wanted nothing more than to see One again, speak to her.

"No," I told the nosy apron-wearing lady. "I'm just waiting for someone."

MAURA

It never made the papers. Every week when I unfolded my Arlington Advocate I'd imagined the headlines: GIRL HELD IN HOME; LOCAL MOM AND SON AID HOSTAGE-HOLDING SAUDI FAMILY. Or was it the girl we'd aided, or wanted to aid? That's what Joezy still wanted to believe.

After I left the Thanksgiving *Globe* behind downstairs, unopened and unread; after I made our bed and tidied our bedroom and laid out my festive clothes, I did my yoga. I bent and stretched into my easiest poses, trying to clear my head of anti-Thanksgiving thoughts.

I sat twisted into Lotus Position on the bedroom rug, opening my thighs wide. Then opening my mouth wide too in my prescribed Silent Lion Roar. I froze my roar, straining my aging face muscles.

I should be, and I was, most of me, thankful that Dan hadn't confessed to cheating like so many men his age cheating on women my age. Would I really have been foolish or rash enough to commit adultery of my own if he'd confessed? To wreck my whole longtime marriage? I released my roar, rolling back and raising my hips so my legs stuck up straight. My bare feet arched ballerina-style, pointing, straining like a quavery arrow toward our high bedroom ceiling and slanted skylight. An arrow ready to be shot, yet held back. Cold snowy light outside filtered through the tinted skylight glass into our heated bedroom with a softened gray glow.

It had been ridiculous of me to feel, so often lately, trapped. "Trapped" was the wrong word, of course; "trapped" was a word for a girl being held in a home. Not a word for a middle-aged mom doing yoga alone in her house, her own all-too-comfortable home.

In the bathroom, recently Maid Pro cleaned, I pulled off my sweats. Then I dug out, on impulse, the delicate copper necklace that I'd hidden in my bathroom drawer. Standing naked and chilled before the full-length mirror, which was usually fogged with flattering steam when I posed before it, I hooked on the necklace. And I faced my otherwise unclad forty-four-year-old body head-on, nothing blurring it, me.

A pale freckled mom, slim still. My face bony as ever, my fine skin showing its lines. Worse, the flesh on my hips and upper arms was slightly slackening; my once-pert breasts sagged. Frannie's copper necklace picked up the copper of my hair, still my best feature. If I hadn't had that hair and this body, would I be here, in this neat well-appointed bathroom?

I leaned forward and touched the hard unyielding glass, flattening my hands, framing my reflected face, close-up. My un-made-up face, real face. The smile lines around my mouth and the frown lines between my almost invisible eyebrows showed plainly. I met my palest green gaze, bloodshot from lack of sleep. Naked middle-aged me. Hadn't I been stripped down in a different, deeper sense that crazy day in One's basement room?

The day I was brave enough to face down the basically sane Rakeen, but not his manic brother Rasha. No, when Rasha burst in with his sword, what did I do? Freeze on my knees. Freeze on my knees on the floor as Rakeen lunged forward to grab that sword. Of course, if I'd bravely foolishly lunged myself, I might have only gotten in the way, like poor Joezy.

I'd told Joezy he'd saved the day but really it had been Rakeen. I shouldn't have told Joezy that particular white lie, I thought as I pushed away from the mirror. That particular lie. He and I both needed to look at things the way they were.

Maybe, my brainwave connection with him told me, maybe Joezy was better at that than me. Maybe I was believing Dan about Philadelphia too easily; sticking with him because it was easiest. I hugged my bare cold-skinned body, picturing in a flash Frannie. Maybe I was telling myself I could tamp down my feelings for Frannie, for women, but I couldn't really, couldn't just make all that go away.

But no. I released myself, impatient with myself. With, Dan would say, my over-thinking everything. Frannie accused me of that too, in her gentler way.

I turned from myself, my body.

I cranked on HOT and climbed in the tub, pulling shut the plastic curtain printed in cheery colors with a map of the world. After our ordeal, I'd tracked down on this transparent map — to remind myself where it was — Vietnam. A snaky little sliver; a world away.

Was that girl One sent back there? Because of us, what we'd so blunderingly done? Or did she escape to God-knows-what here on the streets of Boston? Was either fate worse, in the end, than what we'd saved her from?

I soaped my hands, ran them up and down my body, trying to smooth out my lines and slack skin, smooth out my thoughts as well. But my hand, my fingers, lingered between my legs. I was squeezing shut my eyes, picturing that dark art room closet. Fingering myself, telling myself clearly: this might be the closest you ever come. To coming with a woman.

But I moved my hand back up my body, cutting short a full-fledged fantasy. *Pumpkin pie*, I told myself. As I rubbed and soaped my skin, I pictured how I'd grip my mother's rolling pin today. How I'd force the springy flesh-colored piecrust dough to lie flat.

If only I could control my real flesh that way. I lathered my breasts, my almost invisible breast-biopsy scar. My nipples. And I imagined again, unstoppably, Frannie's hands on my body. The maybe-transforming touch I wouldn't know, now. I let the soap slip from my hands. I hugged myself in the hot soothing stream.

I held my face up to the stream and took advantage of this perfect chance, an empty house and a loud shower, to cry.

I cried lightly with longing for the illicit thrills I might've shared with Frannie. Then cried harder for how pathetically much I kept missing the way Frannie gazed at me, the way she listened when I talked. Dan listened, really listened, only when we talked about Joezy.

If only we'd both listened more, more attentively, to Joezy

himself. I crouched down in the tub, hugging my knees. Could we have, I have, spared him what happened? I sobbed with shame that I'd frozen on my knees in One's basement room, that I'd almost lost my son there. That my teenage son needed me so badly now, again. Just what I'd thought I wanted.

Then I stayed crouched in the still-warm shower and cried on over Joezy, over all of it, let it all out. A good cry. A pleasure, in its way. So my final Thanksgiving thank-you wound up two-sided. I was thankful to be alone so I could cry and thankful too that my husband and son would be coming back soon so I could, so I had to, stop.

J O E Z Y

Then finally, fucking suddenly: One. She stepped into the open archway leading to the bakery kitchen. She held an empty tray. Seeing me, her body halted. Her face went instantly distant, like she was thousands of miles away, back in freaking Vietnam or something.

She tilted the tray like a shield. She started shuffling sideways though she'd been stepping forward before.

"One?" I blurted. Then I bolted toward her, maneuvering my crutches around the counter edge. Maybe my crutches made her hesitate in the archway. Still holding that tray at a slant, between us.

"That you, One?" I asked stupidly, though I knew it was. I swung my body toward her, my bread loaf bumping my thigh, my crutches click-clicking the bakery kitchen tile. I managed to stop in front of One, breathless, losing hold of my wrapped loaf.

It fell, soft and soundless, onto the tile floor. Everything felt soundless all around us, though water was running hard behind One in a metal sink. Clutching her empty tray, One shook her head.

No-no. Like, *No, I'm not One.* Or (to anyone watching) *No, I don't speak English.*

Only one other worker was visible in the small kitchen area, a man rinsing pans at the metal sink, his broad back to us.

"I just wanted to see if you're OK." I tried to stand in place steadily on my crutches, my knee throbbing extra hard.

"O-K?" One repeated stiffly, glancing behind her shoulder at the oblivious broad-backed pan-washer, then back at me.

"I mean," I pushed on, "You must be OK; you're working here and all. So it looks like your visa was legal after all."

At mention of her visa, One's eyes flared. She shook her head no-no again, as if at a dense student. "Not-know, not-yet. Rakeen's friend." She glanced back again at the stocky man. "He manag-er. He get me in, get me temp for hol-i-day. Only hol-i-days. But he say there problem be, may-be. With visa, not work visa."

"Because you're — not old enough for a worker visa?"

"No can say," One shook her head. Her bangs were pinned back; acne on her forehead showed. More acne than before, her eyes more tired, puffy lidded. She looked skinnier too, or maybe I'd just never seen her in clothes that fit, before. Long sleeves; tattoo hidden.

She inched closer in her green apron. I braced myself for a hug or a slap in the face. Instead, One bent and lifted the loaf. She held it out to me, dangling in its bag.

Then she watched me take hold, awkwardly grip both bag and crutch in one hand. I cleared my throat, managed automatic words.

"Jeez, if there's anything I can do to, like, help with that. To help you stay here, help with your whole visa thing."

One shook her head No-no. Like she'd had her fill of my help.

"Go way," she told me plainly. Her wary acne-dotted face and tensed-up body were so different from the joyous strong super-heroine in the ink drawing I'd planned to give her.

I told her, lamely: "Well, um. Anyway. Happy Thanksgiving."

"Thanks-give?" One asked back. "That you want?"

"No, not thanks from you," I told her, though that was what I wanted. Kind of. Even just a little bit of thanks. After all, One wouldn't be working in the Land of the Free, if not for me blundering into her life. Right? The guy at the sink shut off the water. He strode into an Employee Only bathroom, shut its door.

I kept standing there before One, wavering on my crutches. Remembering how she'd stared like this when I'd grabbed her wrist so hard, too hard. Then she'd kicked me, hard too.

"No, I don't want, not thanks, but still . . ." I dared to look down at my trashed knee. "I did try. To get you, outta that house. And then too, if I hadn't jumped that crazy Rasha . . ."

I still couldn't remember clearly what happened after I'd jumped Rasha. Mom had said I'd been brave, but I didn't quite buy that. From the skeptical screwed-up look on One's face, she didn't either.

"Rasha?" One shook her head decisively, babysitter firm. "Rasha and Rakeen, they not-hurt. Never-not hurt me."

"But they *could've* hurt us, could've hurt me or Mom or any of us," I insisted, squeezing the plastic knot of the loaf bag. Holding onto my vague version of the story. "Rasha was swinging that freaking sword and then me and Rakeen both jumped him and, and . . ."

"*Rakeen* got hold the sword. *He* stop fight." Her babysitter tone again, like I was some dumb kid. And I guess I was, believing my Mom when she'd said how brave I'd been. "Rakeen, he got hold: Rasha-sword."

"Rakeen, right," I mumbled, lowering my eyes again.

I'd jumped Rasha when maybe I should've just let Rakeen. So it had looked, to One, like Rakeen breaking up a fight between two troublemaking boys, not like I'd trashed my knee to rescue her.

"Anyhow. I — I am glad you got out, One. That's a good thing, right?" When she didn't answer, I added on impulse, playing my last card, "I mean, my family, we heard a . . ." I left out that Dad heard it from the police. "A rumor that there really was some kinda drug-running-or-whatever going on with the Jiluwis, those midnight deliveries."

"Shish," One hissed, looking behind her as if someone might overhear. "I — I go break," she called toward the shut bathroom.

Startling me, she turned on her heel, headed across the kitchen. Was this it? The last time I'd talk to her? I tossed my bread on a metal table. My heart pumped with dumb determination; no, One couldn't just walk out on me. No, One could at least realize that there really was dangerous stuff going down at that house, that I really had helped her. Right?

Anyhow, I fucking followed her.

Faster than I'd ever done, I heaved myself on my crutches through the small kitchen area with its oversized sink and oven. Still not looking back, One grabbed a shabby sweat jacket from a metal rack and shouldered open a side door marked EXIT. She started to step into the cold morning air, onto a sheltered concrete step.

But I stuck my crutch in the swinging-shut door.

It jammed, leaving a crack open between us. One turned her full face on me, anxious and angry, her mouth sealed shut. Then, with that babysitter frown of disapproval, she stepped back. She let me shoulder the heavy door and hobble onto the stoop, into a bracing chill.

The door shut with a thunk. I panted hard, my breath visible. Not looking at me, One dug into her jacket pocket, lit up.

"So, you knew there was a real drug-thing going on?" I pressed.

"You go to po-lice?" she asked on smoky exhale.

"No," I lied, sort of lied, since Dad did. "No, I just wanna know." I couldn't keep my voice from hitting that American boy whine. And I couldn't stop from leaning closer to her on my crutches, insistently.

"You *push*," she burst out, like she thought I might try for a kiss. She was shaking her head, spewing smoke. "You much too push."

And she pushed back. She shoved my rigid arm so my crutch lurched. I lurched too, lost my balance on the icy stoop. But One quickly gripped my arm. I steadied myself, with her sure-handed help. Her same strong touch. She sighed a fed-up sigh of smoke.

She took a step back from me. She shook her head.

"Drug, yes, Uncle. I know, yes-yes, that his deal. He let me go work for Jiluwi family, in America, like Mama wanted. Uncle work shipping, Saigon Hospital. He get deals, special deals. He let me work Jiluwis if Jiluwis let him ship boxes to house." One lowered her eyes. "But not-bad drug. Was *good*-drug-thing."

"Good?" I managed to ask skeptically, still breathless from my near-fall. One shook her head like I was such a boy, so dumb.

"For drug Jiluwi father need, others too. So Uncle. Make moany, need moany. Now is hard on Uncle, on Uncle children . . ."

"What, the Jiluwis were, like, letting him send his drugs to their garage? Drugs from the Saigon hospital: medical drugs? With American drugs way high-priced, I bet he made out on that deal. But what about you? Your Uncle letting you be the Jiluwi's slave?"

"No more slave," One mumbled, drawing a hungry drag of smoke. Shivering in her thin jacket. I wanted to wrap my arms around her. But I knew from the stiff stubborn way she stood she'd pull away.

"So you *were* working for them, the Jiluwis, for nothing?"

"No-thing *me*." One waved her cigarette. "But Uncle. Drug too ex-pense, here. Too ex-pense for Viet im-grants here who Uncle know of. Up in Lowell, in 'Lit-tle Saigon.' So Uncle special de-liver."

Insulin, not heroin, I thought. I faced the endlessly grey morning sky. Nothing black or white; all mottled grey. Selling drugs cheap to immigrants — was that what One was claiming? Was that a lie? If not, was that bad or good? My knee throbbed. What would I do without my own freaking painkillers, my all-American insurance?

"Lowell men pick up, late night. Sell here, Little Saigon, low price. People need; Jiluwis too. And Uncle need moany. For feed kids. Some-day, he say but he no-ever *do*, he buy back me."

"*Buy* you back?" I faced her but she was stubbing out her half-smoked cigarette. "Someday he might buy back his own niece?"

She looked up fast, spoke fast too: "You never no moany. You no know what like. For Uncle, many kids. You no know . . ."

"I know I 'no know,'" I shot back, just as fast. Though I hadn't known how fucking much I didn't know, not 'til I'd crashed into One, her life. "But I *do* know it's, like, wrong to buy someone."

One met my gaze levelly. "You should see."

You should know, I knew she meant.

"I do see," I muttered to that hopelessly grey sky. I sighed a cloud, leaned against the cold concrete wall. A wall like that between me and Le Ti One, for good, because of me and my fuck-ing *moany*. The money I'd wanted to give her for fucking.

"But still, you — you had to get outta there, One. For yourself."

One beside me nodded again, slow again, her eyes on her smashed smoky cigarette butt. "For me-sell. Yes. This I learn here."

"Yeah, it's the American way all right," I tried half-joking, but she kept nodding, seriously. "Everyone out for what they can get . . ." Including me, I didn't need to add.

"So what made you, made you decide you should," I resorted to Americanese, "Go for it?"

"Because you," One answered, finally looking up. "You in garage, in house. . . . It sign for me. Chance for me. I take. Because you."

I nodded, meeting her bright ever-wary gaze. Glad I'd done something fucking right, if only by chance. By the accident of biking by, of being born in the land of free. *Or land of cold*, I thought as One shivered. She turned to the door. I fumbled my crutches.

I wanted to grab hold of One, press her shivery thin body to mine. My arms kinda quivered, wanting that so bad, like my legs quiver lately, wanting so bad to ride my bike. But instead I swung myself forward on my crutches, back into the door she held open.

I was getting used to not getting what I wanted these days.

I panted and faced One just inside the Whole Foods kitchen. Maybe this was how Rakeen had felt. Wanting so bad to grab her but holding back. I tried to make my face manly blank like Rakeen's as One shut the door. But I winced, the door bumping my knee.

"You OK?" One turned to me, her face flushed with cold and maybe more. Her voice sounded like she might even give a shit.

"I'm OK, I'm good." I started to back away but my crutches slipped and my knee buckled. I had to stop, wincing again, wobbling.

"You no OK?" One let me meet her knowing, darkly bright eyes. Fixed wholly on me, just for one moment in the Whole Foods kitchen.

I nodded down at my knee. "Nope," I told Le Ti One.

Unlike anyone else in my life, everyone these days, she did not instantly contradict me.

"My knee, see, it's trashed. It might never work right. The doctors don't say that, but I — I feel it. How bad it is, my leg."

One nodded, all at once solemn, her seen-it-all eyes locking mine. Sharing with me, for that second, one bit of her own sadness. Behind her, pots clattered. Loud water in the sink shut off.

I fingered the snap of my pocket. One glanced behind her again at the stocky guy, manager of this bakery kitchen, and Rakeen's friend. One seemed scared he'd come over to us, maybe scared this friend of Rakeen's, who'd somehow gotten underage One in as a holiday temp worker, with no work visa, might turn on her.

I left my pocket snapped, deciding my dumb hopeful folded-up cartoon didn't fit. One as Super Girl, bursting into so-called freedom.

I'd gotten the idea from the end scene of *Pretty Woman*, which Joo brought over among other vintage videos from his Dad's collection. Joo was the only one to visit me the days I was out. Maybe he was the one I'd eventually talk to, about One.

Joo and I had rolled our eyes when Richard Gere told Julia Roberts at the end that she'd rescued him. When really he was still the guy with the big bucks, the guy who'd bought her for the night. So wasn't it a lie to tell her she was some superhero herself?

Still, it had worked in the movie to win her back. It had echoed in my mind when I'd inked Super Girl One. But I should've known it wouldn't work in real life. I lowered my hand from my puffy pocket. One actually touched me, but only to nudge my shoulder. To motion me toward the archway.

I dragged myself a few steps away on my crutches. "You ever hear from Rakeen?" I turned to ask her, a dopey jealous pang inside my chest, where she couldn't see. Her chilled face flushing deeper.

"He write to me. To here." One pointed to the Whole Foods floor. "Rakeen walk me here, that-day, find his friend," She nodded sideways toward the man at the sink, who'd turned now. Black-haired and black-browed like Rakeen, but with a thick-necked surly American-guy face. Maybe from a fellow Saudi family, maybe not.

Either way, he was watching One and me suspiciously.

"Rakeen-letter, from France, it French. We find-out, after he go. Find both French speak. It one language he, Rakeen-me, speak . . ."

A new bond besides cigarettes, I thought as Rakeen's buddy approached. They'd found they both spoke French, One and Rakeen. I could see by the glint in One's eyes, by the half-smile on her soft pale lips, that yes: she had wanted Rakeen the way I'd wanted her to want me. She must want Rakeen still, now more than ever.

She handed me my bread. I gripped the bag in one hand, straining to hold my crutches too. I drew a breath but halted like I didn't, in fact, speak her language. Her eyes far-off, still in France. In the end, it had been Rakeen who gave her the money, saved her like I'd wanted to do. Her fucking hero.

"'Scuse me," Rakeen's manager-buddy broke in, his voice unfriendly and unaccented.

One jumped at this voice. Like she was a servant still, she hurried over to a metal cart of rolls, turning away from me without a glance. Her hair hung down her back in a tight braid.

She left me standing on crutches, facing Rakeen's stand-in thug.

"Can I help you?" he asked me, reciting with a sarcastic edge the line all clerks here asked. "You finding what you need?"

"Not exactly," I mumbled. Then I hobbled on into the store, without a backward glance to One. Not that she likely noticed.

She doesn't speak my language, I told myself as I swung on my crutches, tap-tap, across Whole Foods. The bread bumped my thigh, but softly.

To the see-saw rhythm of my crutches, my thoughts zagged up and down. Yes, One had it hard out here alone. But no, it wasn't better to be trapped in that house. Yes, her Uncle needed money and Vietnamese immigrants needed cheap medical drugs. But no, it wasn't right to send those risky shipments, to sell your own niece. Yes, Rakeen had been braver that day than me, but No, he'd been wrong too, way wrong, helping his deluded family hold One.

Right? Hadn't that been wrong? My crutches seesawed.

One and Rakeen spoke the same language, all right. Not just French but the grey language of —what? Tough lives, not-OK places? A language I didn't speak when I first crashed One's life. But I'm learning, I thought grimly. I dragged my bad leg past checkout.

The hippie-dippie couple was blocking the main Exit, their toddler in meltdown. Sobbing so his-or-her curls bounced wildly.

On impulse, I halted my crutches. I set down the bread I kept losing hold of, and unsnapped my pocket. I unfolded it and dangled it right in front of the startled kid, who straightened in his cart seat.

My ink cartoon of One in black super-girl cape and leotard, flying off into the sky above what only I recognized as 22 Mystic Avenue.

"Wan' dat!" The curly-haired toddler — a boy, up close — snatched the picture.

"You want it? It's yours," I told him grandly. He gazed up at me with still-wet eyes. At least I was a big deal to someone.

"Wow, what do you say?" the Mom prompted the kid as my mom had to prompt me for too many years. "What do you say, Noah?"

"Zank-Ooo," Noah managed from behind the white paper he gripped wetly.

"Isn't this a nice boy?" his over-enthused mom persisted, beaming at me, like my own mom, years ago.

"Don't answer that, kid," I told little Noah, my voice strained from throbbing knee pain. "It's a trick question."

Back at the car, after I'd hauled my sorry-ass self across the sloppy slushy mess of parking lot, dropping the plastic-wrapped bread in two separate puddles — I collapsed into the passenger seat. In our warm vibrating Volvo, Dad sat hunched beside me in the driver's seat, smoothing his curly beard and leaning into NPR.

"—*Further military options the White House appears to be considering . . . ,*" a disapproving British newscaster was intoning.

"What took so long in there?" Dad turned in his seat to ask me. I nodded down at my bum knee, my cold damp hair smelling doggy.

Dad patted my good knee. "Any way I can help?"

I shrugged roughly, though I didn't move my knee, letting Dad rest his warm-palmed hand there. Holding me in place.

"—*said the President would not rule out further intervention . . .*"

Dad switched off NPR with his free hand. "One good thing that might come of all this," he told me gruffly in a man-to-man tone he used when expressing the so-called "neocon" views that drove Mom so crazy. "We'll get in there and straighten out the whole screwy Arab world, hopefully before you get much older, son."

I shrugged again. But I wanted to say something, give Dad something; he was trying so hard, lately.

"Hey Dad, if, y'know, you still want me to go down to the synagogue-or-whatever and talk to the Rabbi-or-whoever about the whole Bar Mitzvah thing and all. Well, maybe."

Dad patted my good knee again, meeting my gaze, man to man. He hadn't brought up Bar Mitzvahs these past weeks and I was grateful for that. I felt grateful now that Dad kept his voice low-key, despite the giveaway gleam in his dark for-once-focused eyes.

"That'd mean a lot. To me, maybe to you too, son."

His "son" still held a sit-com ring to me, like he was trying too hard. But at least he was trying. I nodded, fiddled with my seatbelt.

"Anyhow, we'd better head back." Dad patted my good knee once more, firmly, and gripped the wheel. But I liked it just him and me. I didn't want to go home yet to Mom and her watchful hovering.

"Hey," I cut in as Dad revved the engine, "How about we post some of these thingies first?"

I lifted a manila envelope wedged between our seats. The circular *Globe* flyers we'd kept putting off posting. The envelope was jammed full and stamped: GLOBE NEW-CUSTOMER INVITATIONS: TO BE POSTED AT ADDRESSES LISTED, NOV. 20–DEC. 10.

"Not on Thanksgiving morning, Joezy." Dad lurched into reverse, began backing up.

But I tugged out the list of addresses; I fixed on one, the paper shaky in my hand. "Hey, 22 Mystic Avenue made the list! Must be there's a new family moving in there already."

"22 Mystic Avenue?" Dad tightened his grip on the wheel, slowing in the Whole Foods lot. "You can sure skip that one. Hell, you don't want to go back there . . ."

"But I *do*" I insisted, my voice suddenly pleading, the cripple card, yet again. Because suddenly this was the one fucking thing I knew I wanted. "It'll be, like, good for me to see the house again, to see the Jiluwi family really is long gone; C'mon Dad,

I'll just hang the thingy on the freaking doorknob. Where's your sense of adventure?"

"Fine Joezy, if you want to . . ." Dad swung onto Mystic in his old decisive style. "We'll just drive up to the house; you can decide if you really want to get out. If you really think that'll help you."

I nodded hard, acting more decisive than I felt. "Maybe a new family there can make me stop, y'know, re-living it all the time, how dumb I was, thinking I could help out anyone, fighting that kid."

We passed warmly lit houses with wispy chimneys. We were approaching 22 Mystic Avenue from the opposite direction of what I was used to, the traffic light this Thanksgiving morning.

"Help out *who*? I still don't understand the whole goddamn thing, Joezy," Dad grumbled as he'd done before. "How in hell that foolish fight got started."

I shrugged again, trying out a coolly philosophical Rakeen tone. "How does any foolish fight get started?"

Dad at the wheel heaved a black-coffee sigh. "I still wish we'd taken more action right after that screwy Halloween stunt."

"C'mon, Dad. Like Mom says, we did what we could."

Dad sighed again, reaching reflexively for the radio knob. Then he stopped himself, in case I wanted to speak again. I had more to say, but only to myself.

I did what I could, I thought to the dull rhythm of my throbbing knee. Even One herself said she might not have been freed from that house if I hadn't happened into her life, the Jiluwi's garage.

I did what I could: how many fucking ways that was true. I found myself listing them as the Mystic Avenue numbers ran down toward 22.

I did what I could get away with, with One.

Then, in the fight with Rasha, I did what I could too, but that didn't turn out to be fucking much. And today: I did what I could, said what I could, but I couldn't make One want me like I wanted.

Dad slowed our Volvo. I felt glad at least that I'd given away my happy-ending cartoon of One. Kid stuff. At least I was strong enough — unlike Mom, clinging to her idea of me as a good boy, of herself as a good happy-enough wife — to see things like they are.

Dad was turning into the 22 Mystic Avenue driveway, super-slow.

If I ever do draw One again, I vowed to myself, *I'll draw her real.* Her hair and bangs pulled back tightly so she can work and work, just to stay alive. Her anxious acne showing. Her blackest eyes taking me in warily, with a no-nonsense babysitter frown. Her big teeth bared like they'd been in the basement. Like she'd fucking bite me if I clamped my hand over that mouth, her mouth.

Yes, I'd draw a badass One, staring down the likes of me. Like I'd better not try taking advantage of her, ever again. She did what she could, too, to get free.

"You sure you want to get out?" Dad asked me above the rumbly motor. He'd parked us by the closed garage. That garage door scrubbed clean; no traces of must-be-Arab lettering that spelled out who-knew-what. Clean of all traces of them, the Jiluwis.

"Hey, I gotta earn my pay, right?" Stifling a grunt of effort, I pushed open the door. I heaved myself up into the cold, hanging onto the car door for balance. Dad poked my crutches at me one by one. I managed to grip the circular *Globe* flyer and my crutch handle in one hand. Positioning the crutches, I faced the house.

All the windows were shaded, as usual. The icy rain had let up, as if to let me do this one freaking final thing. Hobbling awkwardly, my crutches scraping stone, I hauled myself up the overgrown walk to the front door. The luckily low concrete stoop.

I'd entered this house several different ways, but never from the front. It's just a house, I reminded myself. *Tap-tap*: first one crutch, then the other, and I swung myself onto the stoop.

Just like Rakeen and Rasha had planted themselves on our stoop.

The paint on the door was faded; the scrolly brass knocker looked polished and grand. Yet the mailbox bolted beside the door was ordinary, a black metal box like you'd buy at a hardware store.

Maybe the same hardware store where the Jiluwis had bought the plain metal safe that housed their gun. At least, I reminded myself as I fumbled with the circular flyer, Rasha hadn't come at us with that gun. No, I had stupidly opened that door and Mom had shouted me back inside One's room. Somehow she'd faced Rakeen, made Rakeen put the gun back in the safe. Braver than me, that day. Brave for me.

I oughta thank her for that, I thought, *sometime today.*

Then, with shaky chill-fingered hands, I hung the stiff paper *Globe* flyer on the mailbox, its heading visible. LET THE GLOBE BRING THE WORLD TO YOU.

Hadn't this house done that for me, to me? I leaned on my good leg and straightened the lightweight flyer. Hadn't it brought a whole different world to me, whether I liked it or not?

A fresh gust of rain wet my face and the flyer. I did what I could, all right; now I'll do what I can to make up for it. Anyhow, that's what I vowed as I repositioned my crutches. And lurched away from that door, that flimsy flyer. How long would the flyer last in this wet wind? How long would my noble sounding vow last? Who knew?

Tap-tap. I swung myself off the stoop. Then I made my way back up the weedy stone walk, seesawing slowly on my crutches like someone much older. But I didn't fucking fall.

Keeping my head bowed, feeling my curly hair grow damper and denser, I lurched toward Dad. Our big rumbling car. I chanted to myself in the light but icy November rain, in loves-me, loves-me-not rhythm.

I did what I could; I'll do what I can; I did what I could.

ACKNOWLEDGMENTS

Parts of this novel appeared in *roger* magazine and in the anthology *Men Undressed: Women Writers and the Male Sexual Experience* (OV Press/Dzanc Books).

My thanks to my first reader and forever husband John Hodgkinson, to my stand-up agent John Talbot, to Al Davis and Suzzanne Kelley and everyone at New Rivers Press, to the Providence Area Writers' Group, to my parents and family; to my literary soul sisters, especially Gail Donovan, Lise Haines, Ann Harleman, Suzanne Strempek Shea, and Jessica Treadway.

AUTHOR BIOGRAPHY

Elizabeth Searle is the author of four books of fiction and two works of theater. Her previous books are: *Celebrities in Disgrace*, a novella that New York Times Book Review called "a miniature masterpiece"; *A Four-Sided Bed*, a novel nominated for an American Library Association Book Award; and *My Body to You*, a story collection that won the Iowa Short Fiction Prize. *Celebrities in Disgrace* was produced as a short film in 2010 by Bravo Sierra, with script co-written by Searle. Searle's theater works have been featured in stories on *Good Morning America*, CBS, CNN, NPR, the AP, and more. Her most recent theater work, *Tonya & Nancy: The Rock Opera* (new production in 2011), reviewed as "brilliant and touching," has drawn worldwide media attention.